Wakefield Press

Uncanny Angles

Sean Williams is a multi-award-winning, *New York Times* bestselling author for readers of all ages. His work includes series, novels, short stories and poems that have been translated into multiple languages for readers around the world. He lives in Adelaide and teaches creative writing at Flinders University.

Uncanny
Angles

SEAN WILLIAMS

**Wakefield
Press**

Wakefield Press
16 Rose Street
Mile End
South Australia 5031
www.wakefieldpress.com.au

First published 2022

Edited by Julia Beaven, Wakefield Press, and Darren Nash
Text designed and typeset by Jesse Pollard, Wakefield Press

ISBN 978 1 74305 892 3

 A catalogue record for this
book is available from the
National Library of Australia

 Wakefield Press thanks
Coriole Vineyards for
continued support

Contents

For Ruth

Introduction

My writing life commenced in 1989, the day I finished my first short story. There had been a few novels before then, but they existed to prove that I *could* finish them, not that I *should*. Only by adopting the short form did I really begin to gain a sense of what kind of writer I might be, and what I might have to say. For several years I embraced brevity, experimenting quickly and boldly – and if all went awry, no one needed to know. There are a lot of stories in my bottom drawer.

In 2000, after a thrilling run that included awards and other accolades, I decided it was time to stop writing short stories. The very serious and sincere reason for this was because I had achieved my original goal of writing novels for a living and would be busy doing that for the foreseeable future.

The problem, though, with short stories is that it's always tempting to squeeze just one more in, particularly when a friend commissions you to do so for their anthology, or because you need a break from the monolithic task of meeting a book deadline. Compared to their more overwhelming cousins, short stories can be less work and more fun, yet no less satisfying. They are enigmatic windows through which a much larger world can be glimpsed; haunting, memorable and seductive.

So here we are with a collection of stories that shouldn't exist.

They are testament to ideas that didn't stop building, characters that just wouldn't give up, and fates that couldn't be avoided. Their implacability is, I hope, part of their appeal. And maybe their variety too.

This collection presents work across and between several tent poles of my writing career (those in the speculative genres, mainly) plus some actually set in the real world, or reasonable facsimiles of the same. The one thing they have in common, apart from their determination to exist, is a desire to take something familiar and twist it to reveal a different face. Be it a dragon, a guitar, a boy's club, or one's true and only love, my intention is always to leave the reader seeing these things differently. From a new and uncanny angle.

How to Read This Book

You can read *Uncanny Angles* from cover to cover and experience it perfectly well. Alternatively, you can follow tips at the end of each story as to which one you might enjoy reading next, like a choose-your-own-adventure book. Or you can follow your own path. The decision is yours.

At the beginning of each story is a behind-the-scenes sketch outlining its origin or personal significance (except for one instance, where the sketch is at the end – you'll know why after you've read it).

Why? To squeeze something new around the strictures, from the interstices, in defiance of the oft-misapplied maxim 'write what you know'.

Nothing takes flight without something solid to push against. And flying looks easy until you take that leap of faith into the arms of gravity and try to soar. (Something I reckon everyone should try at least once in their life.)

Familiar places, new eyes.

That, for me, pretty much sums up the essence of this book.

Notes on *The Second Coming of the Martians*

Writing in the fantastic arts might seem incredibly freeing. After all (most people think) an author in this field can make up anything they like, and it counts! In my experience, however, rarely does fantastic fiction work like that.

For starters, all stories need to be grounded in the real for them to have any chance of capturing an audience. (Not for nothing is the heart of a tale called a 'plot', as in a scheme to steal a reader's time.) This realness can take the form of a place that exists in the world as we know it. Or it could equally be part of a world created by another author: a framework that exists beyond the boundaries of the new story to which other readers have gifted a sense of concreteness. Pre-existing worlds include media properties like *Star Wars* and *Doctor Who*. They also include *Jane Eyre*, the Bible, and the works of Agatha Christie.

The first story in this collection exploits both methods of grounding in reality: Antarctica, a place I was extremely fortunate to visit on an Australian Antarctic Arts Fellowship in 2017; and H.G. Wells' *War of the Worlds*, which I've loved ever since I heard Jeff Wayne's musical adaptation in the 1970s.

The Second Coming of the Martians

This is already the vastest war in history. It is war not of nations, but of mankind. It is a war to exorcise a world-madness and end an age.

H.G. Wells, *The War That Will End War*

The storm had a rage disorder unlike anything in Joel's experience, and he'd recently interviewed a man convicted of bludgeoning nine people to death. One moment the screaming wind retreated to the point where he could stand, if leaning at a heavy list; the next he was battered flat, clinging to ice for dear life.

Pressing on seemed increasingly pointless. Better to dig in and wait for the blizzard to pass. He slid his heavy pack with its grisly burden off his shoulders and un-stowed a collapsible shovel, but the ice beneath him had been scoured free of loose snow and what remained was as hard as rock. He needed to find the lee of something and burrow into its 'blizz tail', as the expeditioners in Mawson station called the snow dunes that remained when the fury of the storm had passed.

Crawling, skidding occasionally, barely able to see even his fingertips, he blundered in a blind zigzag in search of shelter.

For the first time, he felt fear.

He had been warned that Antarctica was a fool's errand, and a dangerous one at that, but he had refused to listen. Nature didn't kill investigative reporters: war zones or ex-spouses did. Now, as his limbs grew heavy under him and treacherous sleep beckoned, he wondered if he should have paid more heed. Death was a high price for chasing a phantom that might not even exist.

'Fuck you,' he shouted into the storm. 'I didn't come all this way for nothing!'

An answer was the last thing he expected, and indeed he received none.

Only later, in the grey nimbus between life and death, when all strength had fled and his breath froze into a hard crust on his lips, did a dark figure step out of the storm with a ponderous tread and scoop him up in chill limbs that curved unnaturally around him.

Joel stirred, moaning weakly. Through ice-dusted eyelashes he glimpsed the distinctive shape of his rescuer, and came immediately to full consciousness. The fire of discovery – of being proven *right* – banished all thought of dying.

'You!'

Sleep, whispered an alien voice in his mind. *Forget.*

'Wait . . . I have . . . to ask . . .' He shook his head, fighting incipient torpor with all his will.

No. The answer was as firm as the footfalls beneath him.

'One question!' Wriggling in the embrace of the tentacles that held him tight, he reached for his pack. 'I bring . . . payment!'

You have nothing I desire.

'That's not true. Blood . . . *human* blood . . . You've never tasted it. I know, because of the stories they tell about you.

The ghost of the ice. Rescuing the lost and injured and bringing them back to the station. Never seen. Never . . . *feeding*. Haven't you ever wondered what you missed out on?'

For a long moment, all Joel could hear was the wailing of the wind and the walking machine's steady, three-beat plod. Did the latter falter, just for a moment?

'You must be draining seals and fish,' he pressed on. 'Maybe the odd bird. Sterilising the plasma somehow. By boiling it? That can't be satisfying. What I have is clean. Pure.'

Yours?

The question shocked him, unexpectedly. He was tempted to lie, in case such an intimacy would tip the scales in his favour. Who knew what this strange lonely being at the end of the world might crave most?

Truth, however, was ever the best mask for deceit.

'Three volunteers from the station,' he said. 'I paid them well.'

The walking machine let out a hiss and came to a swaying halt. The wind squalled around them like a ferment of banshees.

What is your question?

Joel swallowed, his throat suddenly thick. If his suspicions proved correct, the reply he received would cast the previous century in an entirely new light – and make him a celebrity into the bargain.

'Who are the real Martians?'

I do not understand.

'I think you do, but I'll clarify so there's no ambiguity between us. The architects of the Great War . . . the ones who sent the cylinders to Earth in 1894 . . . sowing the Red Weed and killing millions . . . Who were they? I know it wasn't you lot, so spare me that fable, please. You were shock troops, not tacticians. The bullet in the gun, and someone else pulled the trigger. You are going to tell me who that was. You, the last ... the sole, perhaps ... survivor of the original invasion. Who heard the original orders. You alone will remember who gave them.'

How do you know I will tell you?

'Because you're hiding out here, helping the ones you once wanted to kill. Out of guilt, right? So consider this an unburdening. A shriving. An expiation. I'll throw that in for free, along with the blood.' Joel suppressed a rising tide of triumph: he wasn't there yet. 'Do we have a deal?'

The creature considered for a minute that felt like an eternity, warring, no doubt, between habitual secrecy and the need to let go of the past. In Joel's experience, need trumped habit every time. He risked everything on the assumption that this held true for every species.

Very well. I will answer your question.

Breath whooshed out of his lungs. 'Thank you.'

The blood first.

'Of course. It's in my pack. Put me down and I'll get it for you.'

Not here.

The massive walking machine lurched into life, turning about and heading back the way they had come, presumably away from Mawson research station and the warmth of human safety. Joel felt his heart pounding in his throat. Adrenalin made him feel unnaturally alert. At last, he would discover the truth that no one else in a century had even suspected.

He, and he alone, would know the true face of humanity's enemy!

◆ ◆ ◆

The alien walked for half an hour to a patch of wind-ravaged ice that seemed to Joel's eyes little different to any they had crossed. Parallel ripples of sastrugi stretched to the edge of visibility, casting feathered lines of snow from their summits. The storm had eased from full-throated rage to mild fury: it no longer hurt Joel's eyes to open them to their fullest extent. He could clearly make out the domed summit of the walking machine above him, rocking with every swing of its three many-jointed legs.

There *was* a faint hitch in its gait, the cause of which became immediately apparent when they arrived and the machine crouched, relaxed its tentacles, and allowed Joel to tumble free.

Joel tested his extremities for frostbite or other injuries, observing as he did so that the walking machine had also endured much hardship in its sojourn in Antarctica. There was evidence of repair in every strut and joint. Materials from another machine had been employed to replace that which had been damaged beyond repair, creating a patchwork effect down one side. The hood where the pilot sat opened with a drawn-out groan that spoke of poorly lubricated bearings.

Lithe feeding tubes – *they* worked just fine – snaked from beneath the hood.

Joel kept a close eye on them as he opened his pack and produced the first of three carefully labelled blood bags, each containing a litre of precious fluid.

He hefted the bag in one hand, proffered it. 'Female, Eurasian, forty-three. A meteorologist with a very pleasing singing voice.'

The thin tubes lifted the bag out of his hands and, with a sucking noise, drained the liquid contents. Crimson threads snaked up to where the alien sat at the controls of the machine, a metre above him. Beneath a broad, leathery-brown scalp, two immense eyes regarded him impassively as the creature drank.

Joel had met so-called Martians before and marvelled at the frond around their mouths that operated as hands and the giant ear on their backs. But none was like this one, this relic of a war older than his great-grandparents. He felt an atavistic thrill that wasn't anticipation or dread or fear, but contained a little of each. Was this what the first proto-human to subdue a sabre-toothed tiger had felt? Facing down the monster, finally!

'How does it taste?'

Sweet.

'I'll give you the next in a moment. After you have to give me something in return.'

The cylinder . . . landed off-course, it told him. *Our intention was not to attack this continent, for it was uninhabited at the time. I, the only survivor, tried to contact the masters and my fellows here on Earth, but no one was listening for me here, at first. My call went unnoticed, and then . . . my fellows fell silent.*

'The masters . . .' Joel said, unable to keep a certain smugness from his tone. 'Is that what you called them? They didn't anticipate the bacteria that wiped you out, poor fools – like you wiped out the feedstock you brought with you. We found the drained bodies of your passengers in the cylinders after you were defeated. You ate them just like you ate us, and then the bacteria ate you.'

Yes. Here, I was safe from the pathogens, provided I was careful.

'Home sweet home,' he said, with a shiver. Antarctica, the coldest and driest place on Earth, where it never rained, was often described as the most like Mars in nature. 'Where is your species originally from?'

We evolved in the oceans of Mars, then migrated below the surface when our water retreated.

'So you *are* Martians after all! I thought you might be slaves from another planet.'

There is a hierarchy of species on my home world.

'Yes, I see,' Joel said. 'It might have been the same here, once, before we wiped out the Neanderthals and the hobbits. That was my clue, you know. You were selfish enough to prey on an intelligent race, and yet you threw yourself carelessly into battle. Who does this? Someone taking orders, that's who, from someone else – the masters – to whom you were as disposable as your feedstock.'

This is true. You reason well.

'Tell me more about them.'

Where my species harvest blood, they harvest thought. Except . . . 'thought' is not entirely correct. Your mind lacks the concept. Perhaps this analogy will make it clear. Blood contains nutrients necessary for the survival of the body; those nutrients can be stolen by predators if they evolve a means of removing the blood from the body. Imagine, if you can, that your mind is sustained by your thoughts in a fashion similar to body and blood. One creates the other, but without the other, the one could not exist.

'I think I get it. The masters are psychic vampires.'

I do not mean thoughts such as the means by which I

communicate with you: your lips and ears contain blood, but the spoken word travels through quite a different medium. Perhaps 'cognition' is a better word . . . or 'consciousness'.

'So they eat your thoughts or whatever you call them and you eat the blood of the feedstock. What do *they* eat, or does the hierarchy – the food chain – stop there?'

They prey upon another specialised species. Mars is an ancient world that changes slowly, unlike yours. Equilibrium, once established, is only reluctantly abandoned.

'Hence the Great Invasion, I suppose. There are lots of theories about what led you – sorry, the masters – to attack us, but they've all felt incomplete to me, because they don't explain the enormous *need* behind this vast effort to conquer another world. You don't do that on a whim. You do it because you have to.'

All equilibria fail, in time.

'But that's no reason to just lie down and die, no. Things went wrong with the hierarchy on Mars, so the masters sought to build a new one on Earth. They sent you and the feedstock to soften us up. They obviously planned to follow, but then the bacteria got the better of you. You fell foul of our own food chain.'

Yes.

'And then . . . nothing. No second invasion. Why not? That's always been the flaw in my reasoning, or so people have been eager to point out. Was it a revolution? Did your kind turn on the masters for sending you to your deaths? Are you now top of the food chain? Or was there someone above *them*, who shut their efforts down?'

Neither.

'So why *did* a super species of Martian with the technological ability and will to invade Earth give up at the first hurdle?'

Perhaps they did not.

'Bullshit. I'm sure we would have noticed a second attack.'

Perhaps you were looking in the wrong place.

Joel had slumped into a relatively sheltered nook and wrapped his arms around his knees, forming the closest thing to a sphere the human body was able to achieve. Now, he sat upright and studied the Martian closely. It was still in the hood of the walking machine, still inscrutable, but he sensed something new in its mental tone.

'What are you trying to tell me?' he asked. 'That there *was* a second attack, and it happened here, far from civilisation? In Antarctica?'

He looked around, struck by the thought that *this* nook might be the hollow under a fighting-machine's knee-joint, or that *that* sastrugi might be the side of a cylinder.

Nothing so . . . prosaic, the Martian told him.

Joel returned his attention to the enormous eyes, watching him closely. Did he see amusement in their alien depths?

Or hunger?

He fished in his pack for the second bag.

'Perhaps this will help you find the concepts you need to explain.'

♦ ♦ ♦

While the creature drank of a male Islander electrician, the youngest of the three who had agreed to donate their blood, Joel took a moment to assemble what he had learned so far. Mars had once possessed a highly stratified and threatened ecosystem. Seeking to avoid the consequences of environmental collapse, the apex predators of that ecosystem had cast their eyes toward Earth, where a veritable bounty of 'thought', 'cognition' or 'consciousness' awaited. Not to mention blood for their shock troops. It was a perfect plan, with just one, tiny, unforeseen flaw: the bacteria, the pathogens.

This picture felt more authentic to him than many of the alternatives. It was clearly, however, not yet complete.

'I refuse to believe that the others like you who live here now are some kind of fifth column,' he said when the lines of blood snaking up the feeding tubes ceased. 'If bacterial species were on the retreat I would wonder, but they're getting stronger, more virulent if anything . . .'

Indeed. The ecosystem of Earth is one of constant internecine conflict. To survive here, Martians must assimilate, becoming no longer entirely Martian. Such was far from the masters' desire after their defeat in the Great Invasion.

'Go on.'

Consider this war of worlds, the striving for dominance, less between two populations than between two entire philosophies of life. For Martians to win Earth, the entire natural order must be overturned. Humans have made their own attempt at doing that by subduing the very same pathogens that mercilessly attacked us: however, as you observe, the pathogens merely and mindlessly evolved new means of assault. The masters, therefore, accepted the impossibility of owning Earth, and chose instead to harvest its bounty from afar. Consider: the sustenance they craved was not material, and their ability to connect with us, their shock troops, was not affected by distance—

'My god!' Joel exclaimed. 'They attacked us telepathically?'

In a manner of speaking. Once the masters understood the futility of subjugating humanity using their instruments, they embarked on a plan to subdue your ranks using your own. Hierarchy is not unknown here, after all. The masters exercised their superior minds in order to create puppets who altered your development, thereby creating a new herd species for the masters' sole benefit.

'Speak sense, will you? They did no such thing.'

They very nearly succeeded.

'What are you talking about? There's no evidence of any such attack, no proof—'

The proof is littered all through the middle of your twentieth century. Mass education, migrations, baby booms – mechanisms intended to increase the fecundity of Earth's thought. Communism, Fascism, Capitalism – the means to facilitate its harvest. There is no part of your recent history that was not influenced by the masters of Mars.

'Impossible!'

Even as he protested, however, Joel felt his certainty undermined. He had come looking for answers, and he had found nothing to offend his reason until now. What had this forlorn creature to gain by lying to him? Unless it was itself mistaken . . .

But was it? The picture it painted, of human puppet-tyrants and the bloated masses under their control, had no obvious flaws, except that it had previously been invisible to him. The masters must have acted swiftly and in secret while humanity yet lacked the means of reaching Mars. They must, indeed, have put this new plan into effect soon after the Great Invasion itself, the very time all the social upheavals listed began in earnest. The story had a plausible edge to it, however much he wanted to deny its veracity.

'How can you know this? You've been tucked down here all this time, alone . . . No, I understand! The masters could still talk to you, once they heard your calls. I expect you knew everything they were doing.'

Yes.

'So what went wrong this time? How did we win a war we didn't even know we were fighting?'

You did not win. Do not imagine that the human puppets turned on their new masters. If we could not, they could not.

'But—'

No, the war was won for you, as it was the first time. Just as we foot soldiers of the first invasion were attacked by pathogens hidden in humanity's veins, pathogens that reproduce within and feed off their unwitting hosts, so too were the masters attacked by fragments of thought that live in your minds; tiny, conceptual viruses too small to see from afar that infect all your kind. It was these allies, deadly to the purely rational, that defeated the masters.

Joel was frowning, picturing at first creatures like demons from ancient myth, hebephrenic possessors of the vulnerable . . . perhaps influenced by this prolix confrontation with a creature from beyond his everyday world.

Then, however, as the twenty-first century's more modern perspective on the mind re-asserted itself, he began to understand.

'Memes,' he said. 'You're talking about memes! Ideas that spread from mind to mind like diseases. Adversative and . . . what's the word? Proselytic!'

There is a better noun. Its ancient root, in one of your dead languages, is 'to bind'.

'Religion?'

Yes.

Joel gaped more in shock than disbelief. 'The masters caught God . . .'

They caught irrationality, tribalism, sacrifice, and genocide – concepts against which they had no defences. The result was carnage. Within two of your generations, the masters were decimated, and have trembled on the brink of extinction ever since.

'Hence, we missed them while exploring Mars. This is incredible! I don't know what part of this story is the most appalling: that it happened to us, or that we had no idea what happened to them . . .'

It was unavoidable.

'If they had reached out in peace, or at least for help—'

Interspecies collaboration is something neither of our species has learned. Survival is predicated on adversarial behaviours that require one or the other to dominate.

'That makes us out to be the villains of the piece, but we did nothing deliberately to harm the masters.'

Would you not have, if you had the means?

'I . . . can't say. We were never given the chance to prove ourselves!'

You have, many times. As you yourself observed, there were once many hominid species on this world. How long did it take yours to wipe out the Neanderthals and the others?

Joel felt small pains prickle across his cheeks as blood rushed into his chilled skin.

'That was then,' he said. 'This is now.'

So it is. Tell me, what you will do with the knowledge I have given you? Will you take it back to your people in order to prove your theory dominant? Will they use this knowledge to reveal my kind to be a lesser species than the one you now consider your true enemy? Will this reduced status allow you to discriminate with greater impunity against those of us seeking peaceful asylum on Earth? Will that spell the end of all attempts at assimilation between my people and yours?

'I don't know.'

I do. The only alternative to the dominance of one species over another is for both to change. That process must be allowed to continue. I cannot let you interrupt it.

Instantly alarmed, Joel leaped to his feet. 'We had a deal!'

You have not completed your side of the bargain.

'Here, then!' He tossed the third bag, the one containing the sedative powerful enough to knock out a legion of Martians, so it landed at the walking machine's feet. 'Take it. It's yours.'

I have had my fill.

'Drink it. You've earned it. Then—'

What? Let you go? Without knowing in which direction the base lies, you cannot survive.

'I'll take my chances!'

His legs were stiff from crouching on the ice, and he went from standing to running in a series of wild jerks. The wind snatched him up and bundled him along, whipping the walking machine from his sight, and hopefully he from its. The alien's implied threat was undoubtable: Joel knew too much to be allowed to live, so his only hope, however slight, was first to get away from it, and then to worry about how to reach the base.

The walking machine boomed heavily behind him. He scrambled up the side of a sastrugi and flung himself over the top. Slipping without control down the other side, he realised that in his haste to escape he had left his pack behind.

Damned fool! Perhaps he could lead the Martian away, then double back to collect it. Without it, he had no chance.

He hit the bottom of the slope and braced himself to stand.

Then came the piercing crack and the thin ice bridge giving way beneath him. With a weightless cry, he fell.

◆ ◆ ◆

The crevasse wasn't as deep as some, but it was deep enough. Joel regained consciousness with one arm twisted painfully beneath him. Unable to feel anything below his waist, he could only grunt uselessly in pain and despair when he tried to move. All around him was blueish ice and fallen snow. Far above, dimly visible in the Antarctic light, grey clouds scudded rapidly across the jagged hole he had left in the ice. Blearily, he supposed that they would be the last things he'd ever see.

A rounded silhouette blocked the view, and he groaned.

'What, have you come to gloat?'

Be still.

With great care, using legs and tentacles equally, the walking machine positioned itself across the crevasse and began to descend. Cold flakes of ice dusted Joel's face, and once a fist-sized lump thudded against his one uninjured limb. In mere moments, it seemed, he was eye to eye with the Martian once more, the two of them cramped together in the tight confines of his tomb.

This region is densely mazed with such cracks as these, the alien told him. *They form a natural barrier to discovery.*

'And to escape, I suppose,' he said. The bitter words made him cough, which caused him to show more pain than he cared to. 'Ah, god. Soon there'll be one more skeleton for your collection.'

I have no desire for you to die.

'No? Changed your mind, have you?'

That was never my resolve. I stated that I could not let you be an interruption, not that I would kill you. Judge me by your preconceptions rather than my actions, if you will. The blame for this outcome is not mine.

A distant prospect of salvation occurred to him. 'Right, you don't kill people. You save people. What kind of atonement would it be if you let me die?'

I cannot save you now, the alien said with heavy finality. *You are too badly injured. All I can offer is the entire truth, for you do not yet know all.*

'Forget our deal,' he spat in wretched disappointment. 'I was going to betray you anyway. The last blood bag was poisoned.'

I know.

'Read my mind, I suppose.'

I did not. Hidden I might be, here, but I was the masters' conduit for their second assault on Earth. I know more about your kind than I once cared to.

'Conduit . . .? Oh, I see. The psychic vampires needed a beachhead when the rest of you died. That was you, the last survivor. You were still useful to them.'

Yes. Until I was set free by the poison in your minds.

'So, if not atonement, then what? Gratitude?'

I explained it to you earlier: the only alternative to the dominance of one species over another . . .

'Is that both must change. And the masters have changed . . .

lost their power, their place in the hierarchy. But how?' A series of wracking coughs took Joel's voice from him for more than a minute. When regained, it was almost too weak to be heard. 'A new meme. The ghost of the ice . . . obviously a Martian. Makes you look good, not the enemy, even to the most close-minded . . . I did think so . . . Easily fooled, at least . . . Turns out I was . . .'

There is no deception. I have no need to lie.

'No. I'll be dead soon enough.' He suppressed a sudden urge to weep. Antarctica had been the end of him, after all, but for a moment he had held the truth in his hands, he alone of every human on Earth.

Hadn't he?

'There's something . . . you haven't told me.'

The identity of the masters.

'Yes.' He said no more, accepting the Martian's ability to understand him without words.

You already know them. You have seen their face . . . in the face of Mars itself.

Joel winced, feeling his body's last efforts shivering down into the numbness of his lower limbs. *The face of Mars?* That meant nothing to him. Why did the creature have to be elliptical now, when the remainder of his life could be measured in mere breaths? Better if the Martian came out and just said what it meant, rather than confuse him with the suggestion that some mystery lay hidden behind the perfectly obvious.

What everyone knew about Mars was the way it shone in the sky, a symbol of war, and strife . . . and blood.

Joel might have laughed then, had he the breath, for understanding came to him in a flash of delicious irony. The heights of the Martian hierarchy? The creatures that had twice assaulted Earth from the depths of space, and might have won had not fortune ruled against them?

The face of Mars was red.

The red of its *weed*.

The last true Martian on Earth saw him smile as he died, clutching his good hand close to his chest, as if to take the knowledge with him, where it could do no harm.

Jump to . . .

another science fiction story,
'The Missing Metatarsals' (p. 165)

another riff on an old idea,
'Ungentle Fire' (p. 51)

something completely different,
'Death and the Hobbyist' (p. 303)

The Seventh Letter

The stroke hit him like a thunderbolt in front of every member of the board. The world vanished as if a shutter had been drawn. Later, he remembered the feel of his left hand at his temple, where a knife seemed to enter his brain and twist, before all consciousness was snuffed out. He didn't remember the blow that left a deep, purple bruise above his left eye, where his head struck the table so hard it would've knocked him out cold if he hadn't been already.

Then . . . shadows, shapes, distant conversations. He wasn't truly aware for some time. Forever, it seemed to him, when he could think at all. He was a puzzle in its box, with all the pieces tumbled and unlikely to fall into place on their own.

When he returned to himself, he was flat on his back in a well-lit white room, loomed over by an ashen-haired woman with protuberant ears.

'What happened?' he croaked.

The woman looked pleased but not unsurprised. 'Welcome back, Mr Jameson. How are you < . . . >?'

He blinked. 'How am I what?'

'< . . . >, I said. Is there any pain? Can you move? I'm Doctor Harrod. We put you on < . . . > within an hour of your stroke and the scans seem mostly clear now. The devil, however, is always in the details. Can you feel it when I do this?' The doctor lifted his hand and manipulated the joints.

He pulled it back. 'Yes, I can feel it, but—'

'What?'

He didn't want to say it. He knew what a stroke was. Everyone in their fifties knew. If his mind was broken, would it be better or worse to see the cracks?

'Talk to me, < . . . >. If you describe your symptoms fully, there's a chance we can see to them.'

'What did you just call me?'

The doctor lost some of her bedside cheer. 'Your name, Mr Jameson. I used your first name. Don't you remember what that is?'

He shook his head, and the full force of his mortality struck him in that moment.

'Excuse me, Mr Jameson, just for a second. I will be back.'

Unlike me, he feared, as the doctor swept out of the room. Unlike me.

A battery of tests consumed the next few hours. He wasn't entirely well, despite the full recovery of his physical functions. He could sit, point, eat, and excrete to the satisfaction of the therapists summoned to examine him. The problem was more subtle than that. He had trouble with some instructions, particularly those specific to one side of his body – a problem of comprehension, not volition. If he couldn't understand what was asked of him, how could he comply?

Some part his brain, then, was definitely impaired, even if its exact nature proved stubbornly elusive. Some words were simply absent, excised from his brain with a semantic scalpel. There seemed to be no pattern to the excision. Nouns, verbs, adjectives, and adverbs were victims, but not all nouns, verbs, adjectives, and adverbs.

His wife came to visit, flamboyant in sombre tones. She

too called him by a name he could not understand, and looked appropriately dismayed when he could not say hers.

'Oh, pumpkin. What's happened to you? Do they think you'll recover? The board is anxious. They can't keep the < . . .> on hold forever.'

He suppressed a flash of irritation. Who cared about the board when his life had been shattered?

'Please don't call me pumpkin,' he said, aware of a nurse by the door. His circumstances embarrassed him sufficiently as it was.

'Well, what am I to call you, then? You've already made it clear you won't hear your name, and you won't use mine either.'

'It's not that I won't. I can't. They don't sound like any words I've heard before.' He searched for an appropriate metaphor in his oddly truncated vocabulary. 'There are times when we're not in the same country. I'm here and you're in Paris. You speak French and I speak—' He couldn't finish the sentence. The name he needed wasn't in his mind any more, escaped like so many other words. There had to be a way to talk about such matters, but all too frequently he found himself road-blocked.

The expression on his wife's face was one he would come to know well in the days ahead.

More tests. Flash cards and electrodes taped to his scalp. Extended, self-conscious conversations with psychiatrists and speech therapists. Occasional incarcerations in claustrophobic tubes in which every neuron of his brain was untied and examined. The lesion proved difficult to isolate, and without isolation a cure would be impossible. He endured it all, keenly aware that with every day his case became odder, strayed further and further beyond the medical norm. Sometimes it was difficult to tolerate, the awareness that the puzzle he represented was more important than who he was. His condition was to be defeated, not cured.

In the end, an intern achieved what all the experts had not. Sam was affable, warm-natured, and had taken to him despite the difference in their years. He came frequently to chat. The topic of Jameson's condition could not be avoided, but Sam seemed interested in a personal capacity, as well as professional.

It was Sam, the intern, who had proposed that he, the patient, use his middle name, Lee, in place of his first. That worked. Lee Jameson was acceptable to his inconveniently broken mind.

'I had an idea, Lee,' Sam said on another occasion. 'You can turn left but not < . . .>. You can run but you've never been < . . .>. You can say Lee but not < . . .>. Has anyone asked you about the alphabet?'

Lee shook his head. 'What about it?'

'How many letters there are, for instance.'

'Twenty-six. Everyone knows that.'

'Tell me them, then.'

He felt like a child but did as instructed. 'A B C D E F H I J K L M N O P Q R S T U V W X Y Z.'

'That's twenty-five.'

'Nonsense. Don't mess with me, Sam.'

'I'm not. You missed a letter.'

'I'm sure I didn't.'

'Try once more.'

'A B C D E F H I J—'

'Stop there, Lee. What comes between F and H?'

'There's no letter between F and H.'

'Then that's your problem.' Sam beamed. 'You've lost < . . .>.'

Lee shook his head. The letter Sam uttered made bore no relation to any in his lexicon. It didn't exist. It didn't exist to *him*.

More tests followed. Sam's theory was upheld. Odd as it seemed, one letter of twenty-six had utterly vanished from Lee's life. Any word spelt with that letter was therefore incomprehensible to him, whether written or said aloud. The extraordinary plasticity of the brain enabled him to fold his speech around that absent letter so effectively that its absence was invisible to him, but the consequences remained dire. His name, which contained that letter, had vanished into the blind sport, as had his wife's. Whole sections of the dictionary and the phone book now meant zero to him. Some suburbs seemed like lands more distant than Denmark. Entire tenses were denied him.

The only consolation he could see was that he hadn't lost one of the vowels – E would have been very difficult to live without – or a common consonant like S. How could he have coped without plurals?

'So you can say Jameson but not < . . .>, and Jesus but not < . . .>?'

'Yes.'

His wife looked at him in a way that revealed she didn't quite believe him. Her scepticism hurt less than he could have expected. They still hadn't decided what he should call her, now her name was off-limits. That worried him. Now that his condition had been defined and declared no immediate threat to his life, he was free to return home.

Perhaps the condition would be named after him, he speculated.

His last name, he hoped, not his first.

◆ ◆ ◆

After Sam had finished his shift and the shadows were thickest in the ward, Lee dressed in the clothes his wife had provided for him to wear home the next day. She had booked a car from him, under his new name. The clothes didn't quite fit. He had become thin in hospital, older. His hair stood up in a wild, ivory wave when he looked in the mirror. The bruise above his eye temple had turned yellow. He pulled at his cheeks and blew himself a kiss that looked more final than he had intended.

Somewhere behind that skull was a tiny scar, one that had thus far utterly eluded the finest of science's searches and could remain undiscovered for years, perhaps forever if he was unlucky. He would wait all that time for his name to be returned, for the lexicon to be restored. Wouldn't it be better to accept who he was now and move on?

Move on to what? He could be a carpenter, or a teacher. No, not a teacher. He was a card short of a full deck. His pupils would matriculate with a one-letter deficit, innocent inheritors of his own fundamental flaw. His choices were limited to ones he could pronounce and therefore think of, such as carpenter, mechanic, postman, scientist.

It would be unwise, too, he decided, to pick a field in which communication was essential, such as politics or the priesthood. How could he be a priest when he couldn't even say the word most people used for 'deity'? He lay awake in search of the absent letter and the hole in his head that it had fallen into. That was an entirely different sort of existential mystery, one he was already tired of.

He tore his stare from the mirror and put a hand on the doorknob. At that moment it turned. The door opened to reveal a tall man in the corridor outside. His cheeks were hollow. The hat he wore was broad and old-fashioned, his suit conservative and uncreased.

'Mr Jameson?'

Lee stepped backwards, filled with an unaccountable shame at his planned escape. It was his life; he could do with it whatever he wanted, even run off into a new one if required.

'I'm sorry to startle you at this late hour.' The hat came off with a practised sweep. The man's shoulders were stooped, as of one ill-accustomed to his superior stature, but his manner was confident. 'I came the moment I learned of your condition from Doctor Harrod. Here.' A business card issued forth from an inside pocket, proffered with an economical motion of one hand. 'My name is Simon Le Hunte.'

The card said: *Treasurer, Royal Society for the Semantically Impaired.*

'My condolences,' Le Hunte offered with his hat held to his chest. 'May I talk with you for a moment?

'I – yes, of course. Come in.' Lee retreated to the bed, concerned that a sudden pins-and-needles sensation in his extremities heralded a new neuronal assault.

'I want you to know, first and foremost, that you are not alone.' Le Hunte stood at the end of the bed, his hat now at his side. 'Neither is the injury you have suffered completely unknown to science, even if it is often misdia— Ah, that is, often overlooked in the normal rounds of medical treatment.'

He understood then that Le Hunte's word-choice was carefully considerate, so Lee could understand every word. The rest came naturally.

'Which letter have you lost?' he asked his visitor.

'Alas, I cannot tell you. I can only refer to it as the seventeenth letter.' A quick count revealed that to be Q.

'We are fortunate, you and I,' said Le Hunte. 'With a more inconvenient overlap, we could barely converse. That's why I am often chosen to introduce the Society to new recruits. I am pleased to be about that service today.' He executed a small bow.

A joke occurred to Lee then, but he could not put it in words. In his mind's eye he saw an assembly of the Semantically Impaired, all with different letters lost and forever stuck in the attempt of conversation. It could be impossible for them to communicate except by Morse code or numbers, or even semaphore. But he could not find the words to describe such an assembly. He had attended many such as chair of the board of his company, but could not name them now because those words were lost.

Words lost like those of the man before him and who knew how many others? Words that had never returned.

For the first time he wept, not just for himself, but for his wife whose name would remain forever unspoken by his lips – and for people without the letter L who could not speak of love, those denied M and the word 'mother', and others whose incapacities he could barely conceive of. Even Le Hunte would never toast the Queen, which had never before seemed an important part of life. To be denied any aspect of speech and perception was unbearable. Inhumane.

Le Hunte made no move to physically reassure him, but he did speak. 'It's perfect alri— I mean to say, you shouldn't feel ashamed. We've all felt this way at some point. It is not easy to be as we are, alike and yet profoundly unlike. It's not amnesia; it's not aphasia. It's entirely too difficult to explain to those without our particular lack. And to lose your name ...' Le Hunte's expression became mordantly sympathetic. 'I would have you know that you're not alone in that circumstance, either. There are others on our books in the same straits.'

'Is that supposed to cheer me up?'

'Perhaps not. But there is a chance of recovery, if that is what you need. Science has made terrific advances in recent years. Doctors cannot yet repair the lesions that cost us our letters, but there is talk of prostheses – artificial letters, if you like – rather than ones that have been reversed or distorted as offered to us in the past. I was born with this condition and remember all too well the awkward spectacles and lenses forced upon me. Now, there is none of that. Society has learned of our condition, however slowly, and makes adjustments. For instance, there exist translations of classic novels that permit even the most unfortunately impaired to read as others do. There is hope, you see, Mr Jameson. There is always hope.'

'Really?'

'Yes. And – well, I don't wish to be harsh, but people survive far worse disabilities. We are fortunate, you and I. There is much we can still say – and limitations, some believe, only make us more creative. For every common word denied, an old one is revived. Shakespeare and Chaucer would be pleased, I think, with some of our more inventive members.'

Lee reached into a pocket for a handkerchief and blew his nose rather messily. 'Has anyone else lost my letter?'

'The seventh? Not anyone I have met.'

'I'm unique, then.'

'You are what?'

'Oh, sorry. I'm one of a kind.'

'I see. Yes. That's certainly true. Is that a comfort to you?'

He wanted to say, no, not really, but that wasn't entirely true. He did feel somewhat better for the joint awareness that someone else had his condition too, that he wasn't just another in the herd.

'Well,' said Le Hunte, hat atop his head once more, 'you have my card. Call me any time. We meet weekly. Please join us. You are most welcome.'

Lee stood to shake Le Hunte's hand. 'Thank you. I really am terribly . . .' He floundered, at a momentary loss for the correct word.

'Appreciative?'

'Yes.'

For the first time, Le Hunte smiled. 'I believed you would be. Farewell, Mr Jameson,' he said with a wave. '*Au revoir*. See you anon. Until next time!'

When the sound of his visitor's footsteps in the corridor outside had faded to silence, Lee took off his street clothes and returned to bed. Prostrate in the darkness, with his hands behind his head, he considered all that Le Hunte had said. How peculiar that his condition could be so common that a Royal Society existed to assist its sufferers – and odder still that all across the world were dotted people whose alphabets deviated from everyone else's! Did such exist in China, Russia, Israel? He supposed they must. He hoped they had the equivalent of a Royal Society to cater to their needs too, to help them find a new path in their oddly contracted but expanded worlds.

No more did he feel the need to run away. There could be no escape from his condition, even if it was one that he would find difficult to explain to people. He had no visible symptoms. He could, with a little practice, function. Yet he had lost his name, which in every society had a symbolic and undeniable effect on his sense of self. He was Lee Jameson now, and who that was remained to be seen. His old self certainly wouldn't have resolved to tell his wife that 'pumpkin' would be fine, provided he could call her that in return. And he wouldn't have spoken to the duty nurse to put in a recommendation for Sam the intern. He had been too busy with the board and his other responsibilities.

Lee Jameson had new responsibilities, new demands. His relationship with the world had been turned upside down by a purloined letter. Never before had he suspected how complicated words could be. They were for much more than mere description. What one can't find the words for, he decided, cannot exist in one's experience – and what is the world, after all, other than the sum of one's experience?

Reassured that he had found a level of comprehension sufficient to survive the days and weeks ahead, he let his eyes drift shut and sleep take him away.

And his dreams, like those of the blind who dream in colour, were full of mergers, board meetings and gun-fighting guinea pigs riding stagecoaches of pure gold.

Jump to . . .

another short and quirky story
'Team Sharon' (p. 255)

more 'realism-adjacent' textures
'Impossible Music' (p. 129)

something completely different
'The N-Body Solution' (p. 267)

Notes on *The Seventh Letter*

Despite their apparent similarity, the words 'lipogram' and 'liposuction' share different Proto-Indo-European roots. One comes from 'to leave', the other from 'to stick'. The seemingly profound ability for language to bring opposites together is a mirage, I know, but I do find it fascinating.

A 'lipogram' is a story written using every letter of the alphabet bar one. A love of creative constraint led me to this form of writing, but some years passed before I could find a concept that fitted. Not until I was reading about aphasia, a language disorder often caused by strokes, did these two real things come together to create something that felt new to me.

In this story, the letter G is the one I chose 'to leave'. Why G and not E (the more usual) or some other letter? I can't remember now. While the creative process may have been meticulously planned with respect to the conception of the story, this relatively small detail and others could well have been applied at random and accepted as canon when they appeared to work.

You could draw a parallel between creativity and evolution here, if you wanted – including the evolution of language – but that would probably be a stretch.

One thing I can be sure of: this story marked a shift to shorter forms in my writing practice. The connection to liposuction is therefore rather apt.

Notes on *Go*

I've been obsessed with matter transmitters (teleporters, transporters, d-mat, etc.) from a very early age: blame *Doctor Who* or *The Fly*, or any number of science fiction staples for that. 'Beam me up, Scotty' is possibly the best-known science fictional phrase in history, despite that exact phrase never appearing in *Star Trek*.

Matter transmitters are deceptively simple in concept. When someone or something dematerialises from one place and reappears in another via technological means, matter has been transmitted – and the ability do such a thing has enormous ramifications. Imagine what we can already do with our fledgling powers of scanning, copying, printing and broadcasting. Now magnify that to include people . . .

Unlocking this ability would be an incredible engineering feat that would herald an age of possibilities unlike anything humanity has ever seen. It will change the world, and us with it.

It's not hard to capture the magnitude of my personal obsession with this idea. My first ever short story was a d-mat story, and since then I've written four novels specifically about the device, a dozen more that include it, and about four dozen other stories featuring it as well. I even have a PhD in its long literary history, from 1877 (Edward Page Mitchell's groundbreaking story 'The Man Without a Body') through to the twenty-first century.

I see more possibilities in this single trope than in any other in science fiction, so perhaps it's no surprise that half the stories in this book include it, usually in combination with another genre or story idea.

This very short story, written consciously in the style of an 'urban myth', joins 'The Fly' and every other story of that ilk in imagining the monstrous intersection of new technology and the idiot human, where anything that *can* go wrong undoubtedly will.

For more information about matter transmitters, and more stories set in this universe, see twinmakerbooks.com.

Go

My grandfather has this story from when he was young – ten, fifteen, I don't know. Back then you had to carry a card to use a 'matter transmitter': that's what they used to call d-mat, before d-mat was d-mat. The transmitting booth recognised a chip in the card, and if you had one on you, you could go wherever you wanted. Apparently it was hard to get the cards. Only important people were supposed to use them because the booths were so expensive.

Anyway, there was this kid whose mother worked for OneEarth, and she of course had a card. One day she didn't take the booth to work. She actually walked, and she left her card behind, so her son lifted it. He was just a kid, like Grandpa. I think they went to school together. The kid had never been through d-mat before and he wanted to give it a go.

Grandpa always wants to describe what it was like to use d-mat for the first time. Imagine, he says, that all your life you've walked everywhere, or ridden a bike, or driven an automobile, whatever. It takes forever. Then suddenly you can get into a box, type an address, push the Go button (that's what they had back then) and the machines get to work. The lights flash, you blink, the doors open, and suddenly you're somewhere else. Like magic, which is exactly how it seemed to the kid.

He's amazed, so he does it again. And again. And again. And again.

They say d-mat works perfectly. They say mistakes can't happen, not anymore. But this kid, he pushed the Go button so many times he broke the system, or something went wrong that had nothing to do with him. Either way, d-mat stopped sending him perfectly and started saving the mistakes because it doesn't know any better. The kid begins to get blurry around the edges, like something that's been copied too many times. He begins to change.

The kid doesn't notice, though. He just keeps jumping.

Grandpa says that when they finally stopped him, when the techs shorted out the last booth he was in and physically broke down the door, what they found inside wasn't even human. There were so many errors that the kid had become a lump of meat with a single, twisted limb and enough brain cells in its tiny head to perform just one task, over and over. The booths had preserved that much, because that was what mattered to them. That was where it had all started.

Even as it died, the thing the kid had become was still trying to push the button: *Go, Go, Go.*

Jump to . . .

another urban myth experiment
'The Legend Trap' (p. 85)

something else involving d-mat
'The Missing Metatarsals' (p. 165)

a philosophical paradox
'The N-Body Solution' (p. 267)

Notes on *The Lives of Riley*

After many years of being too chicken to write romance, I'm now a sucker for a love story, and you'll find plenty of them in this collection. None that aren't woven with other storytelling strands, though, because it seems I can't write anything in a straight line anymore. Love stories with monsters, love stories with matter transmitters, love stories with . . . well, lest I devolve into listing them all, let's just agree there are lots of them.

This story sits firmly in the 'love stories with matter transmitters' category, where I always seem to end up in dialogue with notions of the self. Part of this is the fault of the matter transmitter itself: I believe quite strongly that any serious use of this technology will inevitably confront assumptions underlying contemporary definitions of identity. Once you can be taken apart and put together, how do you know you're still *you*?

In the case of this story, could it be better to skip over that existential hurdle and see where it leads us? To a 'ménage à many', of course. But then what?

Whether we're talking self-love or the love of others, romances are supposed to conclude with happy-ever-afters. That's a feature of this mode I'm struggling with, so fair warning.

The Lives of Riley

The sirens are growing louder. Riley doesn't know how the peacekeepers found out – he was so careful, so sure he'd covered every trace of his existence, *all of it* – but that's less important now than getting away. He cannot afford to make any more mistakes.

The night seems dark and empty as he leaves the warehouse through the back door, the sound of his hurried footsteps multiplied by more than echoes. Riley doesn't need to conduct a headcount; he instinctively senses the presence of his other selves, knows they are nearby and in their proper number. There are sixteen. That's as far as he managed to get before this unexpected setback.

Riley is responsible. He is the one who came up with the plan and wrote the hack that turned his private d-mat booth into a personal duplicator. It was he who dreamed of being one but many, inerasable, safe from every danger.

That dream is still alive. If he can reach the reserve facility in Brooklyn, he can pick up where he left off. But if the peacekeepers catch him they will erase him and the others without hesitation or remorse.

He owes it to his other selves to keep them alive, every one.

◆ ◆ ◆

Riley has rehearsed this moment many times, in reality and in his mind, the better to be ready for any eventuality. He knows the escape route as well as he knows the contours of his own face. As the sirens grow louder he tells himself to breathe steadily and think clearly. There is no need to panic. If he is quick and sure, he will get out with all his selves intact.

But how did the PKs know? What gave him away?

The recent days were unexceptional, spent training in twos and threes, or sleeping, or on the acts of togetherness that make multiplicity meaningful. (*Sex* isn't strong enough a word. Neither is *love*. What he has with his sixteen other selves is unique in the course of human history.) There was only that one moment when he needed to get out of the warehouse and feel the sun on his face. No one saw him, and even if they had, one guy standing in the sunlight wasn't going to ring any alarm bells.

Riley leads the way down the lane to where the hatch is hidden under a fake shrub. It's undisturbed. He keys in the combination and waves his other selves ahead of him, into deeper darkness.

His other selves close behind him, their only sound the occasional soft splash where their feet encounter puddles. Riley sets a stiff pace. He pulls the hood of his jacket down, exposing his ears to the cold night air. He can no longer hear the sirens, which is not necessarily a good thing. There's no way to tell from inside the tunnel if there will be PKs waiting for him at the other end.

He wishes he could use d-mat to whisk everyone instantly

to safety. But that's out of the question. The system would instantly detect multiple instances of the same genetic pattern and divert them all to Peacekeeper HQ, where they would be erased. Multiplicities are natural threats to singletons, who consider them dangerous, a threat to mundane life, which they are. He might as well turn himself and his other selves in right now if that was his plan.

No, they'll just have to escape by old-fashioned means. Laneway, tunnel, a brief stretch of dangerously exposed street, and thence to the old subway line. He walked through the route a week ago, he knows it's secure – so why does he feel so exposed? Isn't this what he yearned for three days ago, in the privacy of his own mind?

That night up on the roof was thrilling. Air so fresh it brought tears to his eyes . . . and the stars! He'd forgotten their silvery touch.

Whatever went wrong, it's going to be a long time before he dares poke his head up again.

♦ ♦ ♦

The street at the far end of the tunnel seems deserted. Riley waits with his other selves for a full minute to make absolutely sure. The sirens sound like a herd of terrifying creatures, wailing wrathfully just out of sight. Riley feels profoundly afraid.

He doesn't have to express this anxiety in words. He and his sixteen other selves are *connected*. They don't need anything so banal as *language* to convey feelings or intent. They are the same person, after all; their experiences and feelings are carefully curated in order to be, and to remain, one. Their unified nature binds them, makes them strong.

That's what makes multiplicity special.

Flashing lights appear at the end of the street, blue and red, swirling like the angry thoughts of a beehive.

Peacekeepers!

Riley hunkers down, feeling his other selves do the same. They are one, and they are vulnerable. He must do everything in his power to keep them out of harm's way. That's what the warehouse had been *for* – close, restrictive, a prison in many ways, a prison from which he had sometimes yearned to escape, but *safe*.

Not safe enough, as it had turned out. Next time, he thinks – remembering the smell of flowers carried on a breeze through the warehouse air vent – next time he will be even more careful.

If no one moves or makes a sound, Riley is pretty sure that they'll go undetected. The PKs at the end of the road don't seem to be actively searching this neighbourhood. They are just being cautious, which suggests they don't know Riley is on the run. Maybe they don't even know the purpose of the warehouse. Their information is incomplete.

Or maybe the PKs know everything and are trying to provoke him into coming into the open. That is the one thing multiplicities must never do – not until they are large enough to withstand any singleton threat. And he is a long way from that. Not at seventeen, or even seventeen hundred. Maybe seventeen million.

Riley tells himself to be patient, as he often does, although it is hard. The PKs will give up, in time, with luck, and then when the threat has passed he can press on to Brooklyn and the completion of his mission.

The lights continue to flash at the end of the street. PKs are walking from curb to curb, casting shadows that dance and sway. Are they coming closer? Are they going away? It is hard to tell.

Riley, wrapped up in the silence of his other selves, hardly dares to breathe.

When someone moves nearby, his heart almost bursts from his chest.

In horror, he watches as one of his other selves breaks cover and runs into the open.

◆ ◆ ◆

Riley cannot believe his eyes. What is happening? How can this be possible? His sixteen other selves are copies of him, exactly him down to the last molecule. Why is this one behaving differently? Why is this one going rogue?

'Over here! They're over here!'

◆ ◆ ◆

Riley cannot believe his ears. Why is his other self doing this? *They are the same.* That's the whole point of their existence. Created the same and sharing all the same experiences so they won't ever grow apart. Riley would never betray his other selves, so why would one of them betray him?

A terrible possibility stops his thoughts cold, like a slap out of the dark. Maybe his other selves aren't all copies of him. Maybe this one is a fake. An intruder. A singleton spy!

◆ ◆ ◆

The lights flash with increased intensity. Shadows sweep long down the street. The sirens grow louder, hungrier, as though the distant beasts have got their scent, and Riley's heart begins to pound. His other selves – his *real* other selves – clutch him in terror, looking to him for a solution, a way out of this trap.

◆ ◆ ◆

Back into the tunnel, Riley thinks, before the PKs see, that's the only way . . .

Then the traitor, the alien, standing framed in a forest of sudden spotlights, raises a hand and points at Riley in the shadows, calling the doom of the peacekeepers down upon them all.

◆ ◆ ◆

It's a terrible thing to be exposed.

Riley should be fleeing for his life, but instead he hesitates. With the hood pulled forward, shadowing his face, he is caught by the stares of his sixteen other selves, who he has just condemned to death.

Why aren't they running? Why aren't they doing exactly the same thing as him?

His heart breaks. All his worst fears have now been realised.

Two days ago, he stood at the warehouse's only window, watching the clouds gliding overhead. Glancing down, he saw one of his other selves step into the open air and stretch his arms above his head. That other self didn't see him. Neither did his other self see the PK drone gliding around the corner of the building, cameras swivelling.

Riley ducked out of sight, and for two days has hoped against hope that their identical images were not captured. He hoped in silence, for fear of causing a rift between his other selves. Then had come the sirens, and their fearful flight into the night.

Seventeen cannot possibly slip by the PKs, but one might. It's a simple solution that has haunted him ever since they left the warehouse.

And now: the confirmation that he is the only one who sees it, and why.

The others will never understand how his secret changed him. How the fear changed him. It was the one thing they never shared. The rift that formed despite his best intentions is now a gaping gulf. The carefully curated multiplicity is broken.

Riley hears shouting from the end of the road. The PKs are coming. If he goes now, he can escape the slaughter. When he gets to Brooklyn he can start the plan all over – him, the original, making other selves who will be identical to him. And this time, he thinks, he will prevail.

They are not me, he tells himself. *I owe them nothing.*

Riley turns and runs, alone.

Jump to . . .

more romance-with-a-twist
'The Spark' (p. 181)

another d-mat story
'Sing, My Murdered Darlings' (p. 151)

something completely different
'The Seventh Letter' (p. 25)

Notes on *Ungentle Fire*

This story starts with an encounter with giant spiders but isn't actually about them, except in the sense that they're a texture of a particular fantasy world I've built up over several novels (the Books of the Change series and others). I'm often drawn to these creatures when I want to dabble with monstrosity, because *I* reckon there's nothing more horrible than a spider, giant or otherwise.

In this case, the monster in the story is *supposed* to be a dragon. That's the commission I received, but (again) there are few straight lines between intent and outcome where these stories are concerned.

Spiders and dragons sit at opposite ends of a couple of interesting spectrums. For instance, things that are beautiful vs things that are ugly. Things it's right to be afraid of because they're deadly vs things that aren't dangerous at all but nonetheless invoke terror. Or even things that fly vs things that stick.

As well as giant spiders in fantasy, there have been tiny dragons, such as the fire lizards of Anne McCaffrey's Pern, which I loved as a kid. It would be interesting to speculate as to which species might win in a pitched battle . . . but that's a story for another day.

What do spiders and dragons have in common? Here, nothing, perhaps, except that they're standing between one young man and his true love.

If only real life was so obvious.

Ungentle Fire

Absence is to love what wind is to fire; it extinguishes the small, it enkindles the great.

Roger de Rabutin

On the twenty-third day of his quest, the young man detected crabbler spoor. Swinging the reins of his mechanical steed sharply to the left, he parked in the shade of the yellow canyon wall and lightly hopped to the ground. Dust puffed under his heels, leaving deep indentations in his wake. The marks he had spied weren't footprints. They were long and thin, as though someone had scratched the ground with a bone needle. His were the only human signs he had seen in over a week of westward travel.

He squatted as though to examine the trail, but was in reality listening more closely than he was seeing. Above the unnamed wind that blew constantly along this section of the Divide he heard a dry rattling, as of dice in a cup. Straightening, he looked up and to his right.

Four body-lengths above him, a giant, sand-coloured spider crouched on an outcrop of ancient rock, watching him with too-numerous, pebbly eyes. He froze, watching it right back. The crabbler wasn't the biggest he had seen, but it was still wider across than his arms could reach. If it jumped, he would have only an instant to draw the knife at his side or to raise a flame through the Change. And if there were more of them . . .

A sharp tattoo came from the other side of the canyon. A second and third crabbler were splayed across the stone like scars in the world. The brisk clatter came from the mouth parts of a fourth, so perfectly camouflaged against the stone he could barely see it.

That crabbler spoke slowly, intending its words for his ears.

'We know you,' it said, 'Roslin of Geheb.'

Moving slowly, Ros bent down and picked up a pair of flinty stones. Holding one in each hand, and feeling somewhat foolish, he clacked out a brief reply. Master Pukje had taught him the crabbler tongue in the early days of his apprenticeship, but he had had little recourse to 'speak' it before.

'I am he,' he told the crabblers. 'What of it?'

'You took something from us.'

That was true. A long time ago, when he had been little more than a boy, he had rescued a girl called Adi from a crabbler coven one month's travel from here. Word had obviously spread.

He raised himself to his full height.

Years of training and exercise had made him strong since then, and broad with it. Dark hair hung in a thick ponytail halfway down his back. Stray curls stirred as the Change woke at his command, making the steady breeze skittish.

'You will let me pass,' he said firmly, through the stones.

'You cannot,' the crabbler told him. 'The way ahead is blocked.'

'Then I will unblock it.'

'You cannot,' it said again. 'Turn back now.'

'Is that a threat or a warning?'

'Take it how you will, Roslin of Geheb.'

Turning lightly on its eight legs, the crabbler crawled into a crack in the stone, closely followed by its two companions.

'Wait.' Ros regretted taking such a confrontational stance. Crabblers or not, these were the first living creatures he had seen on his quest. They knew the Divide better than he did, and could help him, perhaps, if he talked fast.

The first crabbler he had seen was heading for a similar retreat in the wall behind him.

'I'm looking for something,' he said, clacking as quickly as he could. 'A dragon, of sorts. Have you . . .?'

But the creature scuttled away without reply, leaving him standing alone, frowning, in the canyon's still-restless breeze. The vanes of his strand beast flapped back and forth, gathering the energy of the wind and storing it in two rows of ceramic flasks around the machine's wooden flank, its one-hundred-and-twelve tiny feet poised in attitudes of readiness, waiting for him to climb aboard and continue his journey. Not the hardiest of steeds, it barely managed his weight plus that of the pack he carried, but it was at least as quick as a camel and much less vulnerable.

You cannot. Turn back now.

He didn't entirely trust his translation of the crabbler language. It might have been trying to tell him *You cannot turn back now.*

He had no doubts on that score, but how had the crabblers guessed?

Tugging on the silver locket that hung from a leather thong around his neck, he kicked up three more small clouds of dust and leapt into the saddle. Jerking the reins – actually a wooden handle connected by two strips of leather to the machine's complicated gearbox – he spurred the strand beast into motion. Chuffing and hissing, his wooden steed lunged forward, and the echoes of its clockwork engine bounced back at him from the rugged canyon walls.

◆ ◆ ◆

Westward, ever westward. Although the Divide snaked north and south as it sliced through the red earth of the world, it unerringly returned to face the sunset. Ros had taken to camping so the sun's direct light would strike him of a morning, lessening the feeling of oppression that came from travelling so long in the shadow of two parallel cliffs. The canyon floor was utterly lifeless, and his eyes had grown tired of seeing nothing but yellows and browns. Even the sky above looked washed out.

Not long after his encounter with the crabblers, a single cloud drifting on the forward horizon caught his attention. It was perfectly white, tapering from a fat centre to nothingness at its extremities, and provided a welcome break from the monotony. Ten days earlier, he had passed the ruined city of Laure, where people his age flew to and from the Hanging Mountains, trading and exchanging information. He imagined what it would be like to swoop around the wispy fringes of the cloud in one of their flimsy-looking kites. He doubted the air up there was as still as it seemed.

He wondered what Adi would think of something so whimsical and dangerous.

'I hope this letter finds you well,' she had written

shortly before he had set off on his quest. The formal tone
disheartened him, made him feel that he did not know her.

> I hope also that it finds you unchanged in
> your feelings, for I remain committed to the
> promise we made each other five years ago.
> If this letter should find you certain in the
> knowledge of that, I would be pleased. Be
> assured that it will never be otherwise.
>
> Most of all, I hope that this letter just finds
> you. It's been so long since I last had word,
> and I suppose it's only natural to worry. I keep
> that strange little galah you sent as a pet, even
> though the charm must surely have faded by
> now. Maybe one day it'll tell me something
> new – perhaps that you've received this letter
> and are on your way back to me now, with a
> glad heart.
>
> I can dream, can't I?

That flash of her own voice, poking through the letter's
stilted reserve, offered him the barest reassurance that he
wasn't being addressed by a complete stranger.

> Do what you have to do, Ros, then come
> find me in return. The charm I have enclosed
> will show you the way. Trust it as I have
> trusted our hearts all these years. Don't be
> led astray now, when we are closer than ever.

The letter had been folded tightly around the silver

pendant he now wore about his neck. He could tell that it was hollow but not empty, and guessed it contained a small piece of Adi's skin, or perhaps a chip of tooth. The letter itself had been stained brown with her blood and bound up in several plaited strands of her black hair. Unwinding the hair carefully, he had re-tied it in a cuff around his left wrist. The leather thong chafed his neck sometimes. From his worrying at the pendant, he supposed, at the weight of what it symbolised.

'Don't forget your promise to me,' Master Pukje had warned him on learning of the contents of the letter. 'I said I'd teach you only if in return you perform one task for me, no matter what.'

'I won't forget that,' Ros had said, inclining his head even though his master couldn't see the gesture. They had been flying low past the shallow bowl of the Nine Stars, exercising the least human of Master Pukje's two forms. Ros had untied his hair and let the thick mane whip behind him in the wind, imagining he was the one whose wings propelled them mightily through the air. 'You remind me every day,' he had added.

'There's an ocean of difference between remembering an agreement and honouring it.'

'I'll honour it just as soon as you tell me what my task is.'

'I'll tell you only when I'm absolutely certain you're ready for it.'

How his master had finally concluded he was ready, Ros didn't know, but he was on the way now.

The pendant tugged insistently on its thong, urging him north, to where Adi was learning to manage her Clan's caravan under her father's tutelage. She had meant the gift to reach him, no matter what; that was why she had bound it with flesh, hair and blood. When the time came, when his obligation to Master Pukje was fulfilled, her charm would lead him unerringly to her, whether he wanted to go or not.

There could be, as the crabblers said, no turning back.

◆ ◆ ◆

Distracted by both cloud and memories, he had long put the rest of the crabblers' words out of his mind when he took a bend and saw exactly what they had meant.

A single, vast web stretched from one side of the Divide to the other, sparkling and gleaming where the sun struck it directly, barely visible where it did not. Ripples moved along silken strands, struck by the wind's insubstantial fingers. It was too large to have been built by ordinary spiders and couldn't have been the work of crabblers, either, since they produced no natural silk. Something else had built it, or grown it, or caused it to come into being, somehow, and he could proceed no further without breaking it.

Ros hove the strand beast to but didn't immediately dismount. The web was an obstacle unlike any he had encountered before. If he tried to walk through it, it might stretch and snap like an ordinary web. Or its apparent fragility might be a disguise for something more sinister – poison, perhaps, soaked into razor-sharp threads; or a net that would fall on him the moment he entered it.

One thing Ros had learned about the Divide was to trust appearances not at all. Better to stop and think for a moment before barging into a trap. From his elevated vantage point, he searched for signs of malevolence. The web crossed the canyon at the waist of a slight hourglass. On his side of the hourglass was a pool of water, brackish and dark. A patch of orange rock marred the ubiquitous yellow expanse of the far cliff. There was, as always, no sign of other human travellers, but none of crabblers or insects, either. Just the wind, bowing the web towards him like a sail.

The sun vanished behind the cloud. It was late in the day. Rather than acting precipitously, Ros urged the strand beast into motion again and parked it beneath a bouldery outcrop, then climbed free. He had no tent, just a bedroll and simple cooking utensils. Fire had always been his preferred medium, summoned raw and dangerous in his youth and mastered in stages through his training, but he didn't light one now for fear of attracting undue attention. Dipping his can into the pool and cautiously tasting the water within, he found it to be too oily and bitter to drink. No matter. He had enough in watertight pouches to survive until he reached the next source, as well as the store of dried meat that sustained him on lean days.

Settling back on his bedroll, with his feet pointing downhill towards the web, he drew a series of charms in the sand around him, to sound the alarm if anything sneaked too close during the night. Then he folded his hands behind his head and lay back to watch the sunset. Reds and yellows painted the sky from side to side, with a hint of green just before the day properly ended. Ros nodded off as the first stars came into view, and dreamed of Adi calling his name with a soft, questioning voice. He was reluctant to answer for reasons he could not fathom. Hadn't he been waiting for this moment all his apprenticeship? Although he had done nothing specific to earn her disapproval, the shame and guilt were knife-sharp. Inaction could be as hurtful as action.

He jerked awake at midnight, disturbed by something he couldn't immediately identify.

The moon rode high and bright directly above him, casting a silver patina over the forbidding realm of the Divide. His charms were undisturbed. Ros sat and peered around him, taking in details that now looked strikingly different than before. The strand beast was a clash of angular shadows nearby, all pleasing symmetry lost. The pool of brackish water gaped like a bottomless hole in the earth, and he wondered if its depths hid something living: a fish that had improbably splashed, or a hardy frog perhaps. Pockmarks in the cliff walls now resembled eyes or mouths, gaping madly at him. The web—

His sharp intake of breath was followed by the scuffling of his feet. Upright, he took a dozen steps forward to see better, shading his eyes from the moon's glare in order to make certain he was not dreaming.

The web glowed in the bright moonlight. He could see all of it now, stretching up and away from him like the world's most insubstantial banner. And on that banner was no natural pattern, no radiating bull's-eye as most spiders fashioned between trees and rock faces. Nor was it a random striation of lines and shapes, without meaning or language. Depicted in the gleaming threads was a creature so vast that its wingtips touched either side of the canyon.

A dragon, Ros marvelled. A dragon caught in a web.

Never trust appearances, he reminded himself as he came closer to the base of the web. Foreshortened, the dragon seemed even more preternatural. It had four clawed feet and a beaked nose and mouth, like a bird. Captured in mid-flight, its lines were so perfect, so convincingly realised, that Ros was surprised to see stars twinkling where flesh and skin should have been. Those long, outstretched wings would have blocked out half the sky.

Ros came within touching distance of the web. The dragon was sufficiently foreshortened now that it could barely be discerned as such. One flattened foot, as broad as he was long, reached out as though to grasp and crush him, magically, into stardust. He watched that foot closely, but it showed no sign of self-direction.

The threads were so fine they had a tendency to disappear no matter how determinedly he stared at them. Hardly daring to breathe, he knelt to examine one in particular, noting how the thread touched the ground as lightly as a real spider's web. There was no weight, no visible glue, no stake holding it in place. Perhaps, he thought, the strand was thicker higher up, where the heft of the entire web pulled most insistently. Perhaps the strands at the bottom only prevented the base from drifting free.

Still Ros didn't touch it. Instead he stood up and checked four more threads and the ground nearby. The bottom of the Divide might be effectively sterile, but birds did occasionally fly along it. If the web had killed any, by whatever means, it had left no bones or feathers in the sand at its base. There wasn't so much as a dead moth.

To all appearances bar one, then, it was just a web. That one crucial appearance, of a dragon in flight, made him hesitate, but he couldn't hesitate all night. Come morning, the dragon might be invisible again, and he couldn't take a chance on that. He had learned to mistrust disappearances, too.

Some kind of action, immediate and decisive, was required.

Taking two steps back, he picked up a flat stone. With its blunt edge, he drew a new set of symbols into the sand at his feet and encircled them with a double line. The night adopted a sharper tone as the charm took effect, and he warned himself not to become complacent. Protection drew attention, his master had taught him. Perhaps that was why the web showed no signs at all of the Change. The thing it contained – if such it was, and not an illusion – must only be visible by particular light at particular angles, otherwise someone would surely have seen it before him. It didn't need charms to defend itself.

Until now.

Aiming carefully, every muscle ready to flee, Ros tossed the stone one-handed at the nearest thread.

It bounced off with a twang and sent a series of tiny shockwaves shimmering across the face of the web. The dragon's claw seemed to clench, and then its whole body was shaking. Ros stared and listened with growing surprise. Instead of fading into silence, the twang became a hum, sustained by the ongoing vibration of the web's individual strands. And out of the vibrations, out of the hum, a voice spoke.

'Why,' it asked him, 'are you here?'

♦ ♦ ♦

'There's a dragon,' Master Pukje had told him on the day Ros began the quest that would release him from his apprenticeship. 'There's a dragon living in the Divide. I want you to find it for me.'

Ros had thought he was getting off lightly. 'Is that all?'

'Don't be so sure of yourself, boy. It'll be hidden as I am, but by different means, and cunning with it. Your task is threefold: first you have to find it; then you have to kill it; finally, you must prove to me that you have done as I instructed.'

'You want me to bring its head?'

Master Pukje's smile had been slyly amused. 'If it has one, yes. That would definitely do the trick.'

Thinking back to that smile, Ros now wondered if his master had known all along what he would find.

'Why shouldn't I be here?' he replied, but the hum had faded and the dragon was silent.

There were several stones within reach from the inside of his protective circle. Ros grabbed the largest and tossed it with greater force at the web.

'I am harming no one,' came the breath-less whisper, proving that he hadn't imagined it. 'Why don't you leave well enough alone?'

'You're a dragon.'

'And you're a human.'

'Neither of us can help what we are,' said Ros.

'But are we slaves to our nature? That's the question.'

'I have no doubt you would harm me if you could.'

'You should doubt, a little. I have no such desire in me at the moment. If I did, you would know about it.'

Ros was running low on stones. 'So you claim not to be a captive, and that this isn't a trap?'

'Why do you ask when it's clear you won't believe the answer?'

'To test my theory that all dragons are liars.'

'Whether I am lying or not, it would be unwise to judge from my example alone.'

'Ah, you see, you're not the only dragon I know.'

In reply he received an empty hum, as though the dragon was thinking. When that faded, Ros had no more stones left to toss.

A gust of wind sprang up, tugging at the threads and sending sand skittering around him. For the first time Ros noticed the deep desert cold biting at his skin. Do something, he told himself. You can't stay hidden in the circle all night.

Do what you have to do, Adi had written, *then come find me in return.*

Lifting his left foot, he swept the sole of his shoe over the symbols he had drawn. The world instantly returned to its usual flavour: he could smell the stagnant water of the pool and detected a faraway rattle of crabblers moving about their nocturnal affairs. Distantly he noted that the moon wasn't as bright as it had been. It had drifted behind a cloud, and came and went uneasily above him.

Ros stepped from the remains of his circle. Nothing attacked him, physically or through the Change. His was the only will making itself felt at the moment.

With great care, Ros reached out and plucked the nearest strand of the web.

'See?' said the dragon. 'I mean you no harm.'

'This proves nothing.'

'What proof do you require?'

Ros thought of the third of Master Pukje's conditions.

'Tell me why you're hiding here, and maybe I'll believe you.'

'Then will you leave?'

'I can't promise you anything.'

'Without making a liar of yourself, I suppose.'

'Something like that.'

'Exactly that, I think. We haven't said a true word to each other since you woke me. We have danced around the truth, guarding our secrets as though they were jewels. You talk about proof and lies and promises as though they somehow stand between you and what you want, but I tell you this: no amount of talk will satisfy you. What do you desire so badly that you have come to me in the dead of night and woken me from my slumber?'

Ros thought this time of Adi, and of freedom, and of his promise to Master Pukje. 'If you're trapped,' he said, 'then maybe I am too.'

'Trapped in a web of words,' the dragon scoffed, 'as I am trapped in this web of spider's silk.'

'Yours is easier to break, I think.'

'You might indeed think so. Try it and find out.'

Ros's index finger tensed to put the dragon's suggestion into practice, but stayed on the verge of doing so. The wind bowed the silent dragon over him, as though urging him on.

He couldn't do it. Not without knowing more – and that, he intuitively understood, meant giving more.

'I've been sent here,' he told the dragon, 'to kill you. What do you say to that?'

'I say this: who sent you?'

'What difference does that make?'

'All the difference in the world. You are not my enemy; you are just the instrument of my enemy. That's the person I need to talk to, and I can only do it through you.'

'He didn't send me to have a conversation.'

'Yet here we are. Why not do the deed and be done with it? Commit your murder; get on with your life. You still haven't told me what it is you desire.'

'I want to know why you deserve to die.'

'Did the one who sent you not tell you? That was remiss of him.'

'He tells me what I need to know.'

'Do you trust him?'

'He is – was – my teacher, my master.'

'Then you should trust him.'

'That's what I tell myself.'

'But . . .?'

But I know Master Pukje never does anything without a reason, Ros said to himself, and when reason is hidden, that's usually for a reason too. What if this dragon didn't deserve to die? What if I'm being tricked into committing a terrible crime?

'Once upon a time,' his master had told him, 'the world was full of creatures like me. We are rare now, and for the most part we avoid your kind. We see the fear in your eyes when you gaze upon us. It's unpleasant, for we belong in this world as firmly as you do. It was ours before it was yours. We understand it a little better.

'So we hide ourselves in a variety of different ways. Some live in the sky as clouds or mysterious lights. Some live underground, feasting on molten rock. Some spread their wings in the canopies of forests, where vines will hide them and they can sleep out the rest of eternity. Some find ways to walk among you as I do, as one of you.'

And one, Ros now understood, took the form of a giant web and sailed gently through the days. He had offered the information of its imminent demise on impulse in order to see what it might provoke, but the news had raised barely a twitch of alarm.

'There are different kinds of deaths,' he said.

'Indeed,' the dragon agreed. 'Hope can die, for one. The body lives on, but the inside turns to dust. Love is another thing that doesn't last forever.'

Ros looked up sharply. What had the dragon guessed about his motivations? What did it think it knew? Ros was plucking the threads like a harpist, but maybe the dragon was playing him instead.

He crooked his index finger again, and this time he did pull on the thread until it snapped.

The web shuddered and the image of the dragon recoiled.

'See?' the dragon whispered before the vibrations died down. 'I am helpless before you.'

That didn't seem plausible. 'So anyone could've come along and done this, at any time?'

'I'm sorry if that makes you feel less important.'

'This is supposed to be a quest, a challenge, a test—'

'And so I'm sure it is, for both of us. If anyone could have done this, why you? Why now?'

'I don't know.'

'Do you have no understanding at all?'

Ros shook his head, full of conflicting emotions. If all he had to do to achieve his freedom was to snap a few threads and end the life of a feeble old dragon, what was stopping him from doing it?

Perhaps this was the test, he thought. Perhaps this indecision was the challenge he had to overcome in order to be truly free.

This led to a far more discomfiting thought. What if Master Pukje wanted Ros to earn his independence by *disobeying* his master's orders, by doing what he thought was right rather than blindly following instructions?

Threefold. He had found the dragon; that was something. But how could he leave the other two tasks unfinished and expect to earn the life he had dreamed of for so long?

'Tell me why you're hiding.'

'The world has changed,' the dragon said, 'and it's changing still. All things reflect the world as it is, just as the world reflects those things inside it. We don't stand apart. Our function alters with time.'

'What function do you perform now?'

'To dream.'

'Not all dragons are sleeping.'

'Don't misunderstand me. Sleeping and dreaming aren't the same thing.'

'Not all dragons are dreaming, then.'

'Ah, yes. You said you knew another. You believe it to be a liar. Is it lying to itself or to you? The former is, after all, one definition of a dream.'

'Perhaps both.'

'Then that makes it a very dangerous dragon indeed. Did you attempt to kill it, too?'

'No. He's the one who sent me.'

'Did he, now?'

'Yes.'

The dragon didn't react with surprise or anger, or any of the human emotions he might have expected.

'Let me be sure I understand you: the other dragon you know, the one you believe to be a liar, is the one who sent you to kill me, the one you obey because you consider him your teacher and master.'

'Yes.'

'No, that's not what you said. You corrected yourself. You said he *was* your teacher and master.'

'My apprenticeship ends with the completion of this task.'

'Killing me.'

'And returning with proof.'

'Naturally. I would demand no less, myself.'

'Doesn't that bother you – one of your own kind trying to murder you?'

'Oh, he's not the one doing the murdering. That's you, of your own free will. What concerns me more is that a dragon took a human apprentice. What's your name, boy? Let us talk as equals, since that is what your master thinks we are.'

'Roslin,' he said, keeping his heart-name to himself. 'Roslin of Geheb. What's yours?'

'I've had many names,' the dragon told him. 'You can call me Zilant, if you like. What name does your master go by?'

Ros felt a need to prevaricate on that point. 'Why do you want to know?'

'I would like to know, Roslin of Geheb, how he passes among your kind. Does he have a form like mine, or some other disguise?'

'He looks much like a human,' Ros said. 'When he wants to.'

'Yes, and keeps his true form for when he doesn't. We have such power, we dragons, when we choose to use it.'

'My master says that choices are the most difficult thing to learn. Becoming powerful is easy compared to knowing *when* to be powerful.'

'Are you powerful, Roslin of Geheb?'

'I am told that I can be.'

'It won't take much to kill me, I'm afraid. Don't be disappointed.'

Ros reached out and snapped another thread. 'Don't think to arouse my sympathy, dragon. If you want to live, give me a reason to spare you, nothing else.'

Zilant writhed, but his tooth-filled mouth seemed to gape in a smile. 'Of course. I know I cannot win your allegiance. One dragon at a time, eh?'

'I will never turn on my master, if that's what you're suggesting.'

'You're the one with all the suggestions. But remember: a thought voiced is a deed in waiting.'

'Stop it.'

'What do you believe will happen if you disobey this lying master of yours? Do you think he'll descend from the sky and rend you with his beak? If you're looking for *reason*, ask yourself why your master trained you. Not to die in his own claws, certainly. He has invested too much in you for that. You make your own decisions now. You are already your own master.

'Or has your master no intention of setting you free? Is this monstrous task the first of many he has planned for you? By your guilt and shame you will bind yourself to him. He will trade an apprentice for a servant, and you will be trapped forever.'

'Stop it!'

Furious, Ros grabbed an armful of the strands and snapped them all. Severed silken threads fell on him and clung to his face. The dragon roiled and roared above him. The hum became a scream.

'Who is master, Roslin of Geheb,' it shouted, 'and who the slave?'

Ros tore another armful, even as part of him asked why he was so angry. Wasn't the dragon telling him what he had already suspected: that this was a fool's mission designed either to humiliate or to ensnare him? Wouldn't breaking his word release him from both threat *and* obligation?

He couldn't take that risk. Zilant had been in his life a matter of minutes. Master Pukje had raised him for five years. Ros owed one more than the other, and neither more than he owed himself. He would stick to the deal he had made. Zilant may deserve only to sleep and dream, but the dragon stood between Ros and the freedom Pukje had promised him, the future he and Adi had dreamed of.

But did he deserve it, now? He doubted his feelings for her and fantasised that his master was entangling him in a web of deception. His thoughts betrayed all of them. He was worthy of neither trust nor love.

Ros ran headlong across the Divide floor, snatching at threads and pulling them apart. The fabric of the dragon, rent and torn, flailed in ribbons. Starlight gleamed like tears from the truncated ends and from his hand where web tenaciously clung. Reaching the far side of the canyon, he climbed up the rough cliff face, leaping from handhold to handhold like a crabbler, ripping at the thickening strands, biting them, finally reaching for his knife and slashing when they became too strong for him to break with strength alone.

How much time passed, he couldn't tell. The moon had vanished entirely behind a cloud so he couldn't follow its passage across the sky, and nor, in the depths of his determination, would he have cared to know. Ignoring the aches in his muscles and the layers of web thickening around him, he laboured on, climbing and swinging from thread to thread, slashing indiscriminately as he went.

At the top he paused only to survey the best way to administer the killing stroke. A single, thick rope sagged from one side of the canyon to the other. From that hung all that remained of the dragon. Shimmying hand-over-hand along it with the knife between his teeth, Ros reached the middle and prepared to do what had to be done.

'This is your last chance, Zilant,' he said. 'Tell me something, anything, to change my mind.'

'No,' hissed the dragon. 'You cannot turn back now.'

At hearing the same words the crabblers had spoken, Ros almost stayed his hand. He was too tired to be angry any more; only stubbornness kept him going. What did it mean that he couldn't turn back, anyway? He no more believed in destiny than he did the Goddess of which some people spoke. The course of his life was mapped out by obligations, promises, and debts. They were what trapped him, not some absurd cosmic cartographer.

Hanging from one hand, he raised the knife and brought it down hard.

The rope snapped. The dragon rent in two, sagging like a curtain and taking him with it. The two of them fell with majestic delicacy to the canyon floor. He braced himself for the impact, rolled, and came up angling the knife safely away from him. The breath had been knocked out of him, and he was covered in dead web, but apart from that he was unharmed.

To the east the sky was pale. By the growing light, Ros surveyed what he had done.

The dragon was unrecognisable. Where once had hung the image of a beast in full flight were now just ephemeral rags. All magnificence had fled. No voice remained, no hum. Just the nameless wind, sighing endlessly across stone.

◆ ◆ ◆

A shaft of light caught Ros as the sun breached the far horizon. His hands shook in the golden radiance. He barely had strength to pull the thick mat of threads from his face.

But it was done. He had killed the dragon. All he had to do now was prove it to Master Pukje. The proof he required lay in the remains of the web. His master had known what awaited him here, he was sure. Just the sight of Ros would be enough. He was practically encased in the stuff. It would take days to get all the threads out of his hair.

He laughed hoarsely. The sound echoed back from the canyon walls like a sob. A cocooned caterpillar, what would he become when his chrysalis opened? Would Adi still want him, this killer of defenceless dragons?

In that crystalline moment, he felt his reluctance to honour his promise to Adi become fear, and knew that the course of his quest led him to pitfalls that, until now, he had never needed to navigate.

A rattling of crabblers brought him out of his desperate introspection. Six of them had crawled over the lip of the canyon, and more behind them. Their clattering was wild and incoherent. He had never heard them like this before. They swarmed down the cliff wall and over the remains of the web. Were they shocked at what they saw? Ros couldn't tell. More and more poured into the Divide, and he retreated from their thickening tide.

The sound of stirring water disturbed the silence behind him. He spun, raising the knife. The brackish pool was quiet no longer. Waves crossed its black surface as though something large was moving back and forth beneath.

The wind whipped around him with increasing strength, raising a whirlwind of dust.

Stones rained from the canyon walls.

Clouds undulated in the sky.

No, he realised through growing alarm. Not clouds. The very same cloud he had seen yesterday while approaching the web. The one that had blocked the moon. It hadn't moved in a day and a night, but did so now in defiance of wind and weather, its own kind of being.

Some live in the sky . . .

White, feathery wings unfurled. A long neck uncoiled. At the same time, a tower of water shot up out of the pool and spread wings of its own. Crabblers climbed acrobatically over each other, manoeuvring with eerie precision to become eyes, beak, talons and tail, while boulders tumbling from the Divide wall landed to form legs, arms, a hunched back. The whirlwind of dust took a similar form, towering over him and flexing its muscles. Ros barely heard the strand beast explode as every bottle strapped to its side burst asunder, releasing the air trapped within.

Dragon of air.

Dragon of dust.

Dragon of stone.

Dragon of water.

Dragon of cloud.

He reeled back as the full import of what he had unleashed sank in. Even the crabblers, now gripped together in a grotesque tangle of legs and fat bodies, had been co-opted by the dragons into their bizarre masquerade.

'Why don't you leave well enough alone?' Zilant had asked.

Ros should have listened to him. Now he had killed one dragon and disturbed a whole nest of them. That was the price he would pay for freedom.

From exhaustion and fear strength arose. He wasn't a dragon, but he was a dragon's apprentice. Master Pukje had taught him well. The Change poured through him like an ocean through a river mouth. He wouldn't stop to talk this time. He had killed one dragon already. What were six more when his future was at stake?

The dragons roared at him, approaching on all sides. The ground quaked under their mighty feet, but he stood firm. They couldn't all attack at once. Fire would boil water and turn sand to glass. Crabblers would shy away and clouds would evaporate to nothing.

Raising both hands, he summoned the flame that he knew so well.

A bright glow blossomed around him, and it seemed for a moment as though the sun had grown in strength. Heat rippled across his skin and his eyes were dazzled.

But it wasn't the sun at all. The light came from the web encasing his body. The fire issuing from his hands had set it alight. The glare grew brighter still and the heat more intense until suddenly, with a flash, his entire body was aflame.

He screamed, and the air from his lungs whipped the fire even higher. Great sheets burst from him, rising up and out to either side, and behind him too, tasting the earth like a tongue. He felt himself lifted up by the heat, even as his hair shrivelled and his clothes burned away. The flames lapped at the air, flapped once, and he was aloft.

The dragon of fire surged forward, and Ros was carried with it, inside its belly. Together they left a broad black scar wherever they passed.

◆ ◆ ◆

'Breathe easy, boy. This won't take long.'

Ros recognised that voice. It belonged to the dragon he had just killed. That knowledge did little to quell his panic.

'What's happening to me?'

'Nothing,' Zilant said. 'This has nothing to do with you. It's all about the seven of us, of which your master is the last and youngest. For sending a man to do a dragon's job he will pay dearly. But this was what he wanted: to wake us for a while, to remind us that our blood still boils. An insult will serve when entreaty has failed so many times before.'

Ros could barely think through the pain. *Nothing*, the dragon had said, but it felt like everything.

'Fly with me,' said Zilant from the fire all around him, 'just this once, as we pay our brother a visit.'

Ros blazed with the dragon until it seemed there was nothing left to burn. His flesh went first, then his memories, then the person he had tried to be: the student, the adult, the lover . . .

The only thing that wouldn't burn was the silver pendant Adi had given him. Not even the heat in a fire dragon's belly could melt it. He clung to it tightly, and prayed for release.

◆ ◆ ◆

'I'd be dead if it weren't for you,' she had told him, once. 'I would've run off on my own and the crabblers would've got me.'

It had all seemed so simple, five years earlier. The currents of their lives had swept them together but would sweep them apart again forever, if given the chance. The decision had been easy for him to make.

'I promise I'll come back to you.'

'Well, I promise to wait,' she had replied. 'Just don't die or anything and leave me waiting forever. That could be a little annoying.'

'I'll even try to write,' he had said, and at times he had, albeit through Change-rich means like talking parrots and their ilk.

'You'd better,' she had said, 'but I guess I won't be able to write back, seeing Pukje wants to keep everything a secret.'

Somehow she had found a way. The pages were rolled up in his pack, a testament to her determination. Too young to wed, Ros and Adi were not too young to make a vow that would bind them into adulthood. Neither of them had made that vow lightly, but neither had they realised how heavy it would turn out to be.

'I promised I'd come back,' he had told her, 'and I will.'

The chase didn't last long: six dragons against one, one they knew as well as they knew each other, one they would follow to the ends of the Earth if needed. Pukje – the dragon of flesh, crafty and wise in the ways of the earth, but so weighed down with its concerns that he taught humans the secrets of his kind – sprang into the sky the moment his siblings appeared on the horizon, boiling and burning and babbling in their animal tongues. He sprinted as fast as his wings would carry him, and they set off right after him, dragons streaking across the firmament like shooting stars, six against one, and the earth shaking beneath them.

When Ros finally woke, he found himself flat on his back, spread-eagled and fully clothed. The leather of his breeches was stiff with dried water and his tunic full of sand, but no actual harm appeared to have been done to him. He swept his matted hair out of sleep-crusted eyes and looked around him.

The sun had risen, so he could see clearly that he was back in the Divide, back where it had all had started. And more than that: the pool, the patch of discoloured rock, the cloud, the steady breeze – even the web, stretching lazily above him – they were back too, as though the whole thing had been a dream.

Could it have been? Frowning, he relived the confused moments of the chase: wide jaws and clutching talons, tails whipping and wings slapping around him. He and Zilant – for an immeasurable time, there had been no distinction between them.

By daylight, though, the dragon was invisible. The web was just a web, swaying in the breeze.

With a shaking hand, Ros reached out to pluck the nearest strand.

Seeing the scars on his skin – thousands of tiny lines, crossing and re-crossing like a road map of the Haunted City – he thought, No, best not.

Instead Ros clambered to his feet and considered his options.

The nest of dragons, it seemed, was sleeping again. Several crabblers clung unmoving on the parallel cliff faces, watching him come to his senses with no more than their own intelligence. Not far away lay the wreckage of the strand beast, its legs intact but the bottles, the source of its motive power, completely destroyed.

What should he do now? He couldn't leave without understanding what had happened to him. Dream or no dream? Free or trapped forever?

Did the answer depend entirely on how one looked at the question?

A blackened, hunched thing that Ros had taken for a rock raised its head and looked at him.

'I release you,' said Master Pukje, 'from my service.'

Ros ran to him. The fallen dragon's skin was burned to a crisp, but the eye that inspected him shone with a familiar, incisive light.

'Are you all right? Who did this to you?'

'You did, I think.'

'No, master, I wouldn't—'

Pukje croaked a laugh at the expression on Ros's face. 'All right, then. It was Zilant.' His crisped wings twitched. 'Does that make you feel better?'

Ros recoiled, unsure if he was being mocked with affection or contempt, or both. 'I don't understand. I did exactly as you told me—'

'You did.'

'I found the dragon. I destroyed the web.'

'You killed him. I know. Then the others came, and you

went to burn them. The web caught fire and Zilant returned.'

Ros nodded. 'How is that possible?'

'He burns and lives again. Don't ask me how. We're dragons. We're different from you. We find our own ways to survive the world. You were caught up in all that for a while, but you're free now. You'll have to find a way to survive on your own, and that flame is a harder master than I ever was.'

Ros squatted down and rested on his haunches. Pukje's breathing was laboured. Raw pink patches were visible through the crisped skin.

'You expected this to happen,' Ros said, meaning more than just their injuries. 'This was the proof you were waiting for.'

'Proof; punishment. Tell me the difference and you can be my teacher.'

'You sent me to stir them up, to remind them of – what? That they were still alive? That you were?'

'Solitude is bad for the soul.' The hunched spine lifted, then fell. 'Perhaps I knew that I would be lonely when you were gone. Perhaps I wanted to be with my family for a brief while.'

Ros stared at the injured dragon, appalled for both of them – until a raspy, painful sound revealed that Pukje was laughing at him. Again.

He supposed he deserved it.

'Change to your human form,' Ros said. 'I'll carry you back to Laure, where you'll be looked after.'

'No need.'

'I can't just leave you here.'

'Why not? After a short nap, I'll wake refreshed. Go live your life, as my siblings and I cannot.'

'What do you mean?' asked Ros.

'You're ready to wake from the dream of your youth. Be reborn and engage with the world. Fighting fire with fire gets you nothing but ashes, no? Most important of all—' Here Pukje coughed, long and hacking, releasing clouds of soot from his lungs. 'Remember never to tangle with a dragon while it's dreaming.'

Ros stood, remembering the colours of his wild flight across the land with Zilant. It had been like diving into a living sunset. The feeling had been liquid and furious, joyous and terrifying at the same time. He had *been* fire, and would never use it the same way again.

But the scars on his hands and arms weren't burns. They were left by the dragon's web, where it had touched and clung to him, leaving a stigmata that all could see. Perhaps he wasn't quite the dragon-killer he had imagined himself to be the previous night, but there were worse things, such as being deformed by someone else's dream.

He squarely confronted his fear that Adi might be having her own doubts. The letter she had sent wasn't just a testament to determination. It exposed her uncertainty, too. Thinking of the words she had used, he could see all too clearly now that she was as nervous as he, and taking shelter in conventions alien to them both.

That both dismayed and encouraged him. He was aware now that the emotional pitfalls he had been skirting during his quest arose from feelings of love after all, not the absence of it. He had refused to reveal his desire to Zilant because he was afraid of what it meant. Fear, reluctance, uncertainty, dread – they were all part of the experience, along with joy, wonder, surprise, and delight. He would need to get used to all of them now he was free to pursue an uncertain conclusion.

Pukje was indeed a dangerous dragon, but he knew better than Ros did who his master was, ultimately. There was no use railing against the people he had chosen to play important roles in his life, not when he himself had invited them in. It did them a disservice to imagine lies and treachery at every turn, just because he nursed doubts he barely acknowledged to himself.

Ros looked up at the crabblers. *You cannot turn back now*, he had heard the monstrous denizens of the Divide telling him yesterday. *Take it how you will.* He had done exactly that, and very nearly tangled himself in a net from which he couldn't escape – because it wasn't *escape* he wanted at all, in the end.

We are closer than ever, Adi had said in her letter.

The mouthparts of one of the crabblers clattered the same brief message as before.

'We know you, Roslin of Geheb.'

'Better than I do myself, it seems,' he clacked back.

'All right, now, go,' Pukje told him in an irritated voice. 'Live. Be wise. Stay out of trouble.'

'I will,' Ros said. 'If you're sure?'

'I am. You know your road now.'

Pukje's eyes closed, and he returned to looking more like a stone than a living thing.

Ros removed the pendant from around his neck. Placing it on the sand next to the wounded dragon's beak, he said, 'Thank you, master. I believe I do.'

Stooping to pick up his pack from the wreckage of the strand beast, Ros walked to the base of the cliff and began the long climb northwards.

Jump to . . .

what happens next
'The Spark' (p. 181)

another story involving traps
'The Legend Trap' (p. 85)

something completely different
'The Cuckoo' (p. 117)

Notes on *The Legend Trap*

After 'Go', I used the literary device of the urban myth to tell a large number of stories featuring matter transmitters. It was only a matter of time before I wrote a more traditional story featuring an urban myth as the main plot device, bringing me conceptually full circle – if that's the correct analogy. It might be more apt to say that I've gone one loop around a spiral, although where that spiral's leading me, I've yet to find out.

One thing I've noticed while putting this collection together is a preponderance of stories-within-stories, such as the news reports of 'The Cuckoo', the rumours of 'The Second Coming of the Martians', the popular mythologising of 'The Spark', and with this story. This may be a function of me getting older and therefore more meta as a means of keeping things fresh. Or maybe the rising tide of irony in modern genre writing has floated my boat along with everyone else's. It's not enough anymore just to tell a good story, it seems; one must also tell the story *about* telling the story . . . Or has it always been that way and I've only just noticed?

Sharing yarns around a campfire is not an unlikely origin story for the modern urban myth, which is perhaps why I find it such a potent device for stories about advanced technology. Not only does this ancient form map perfectly onto reactionary (although not always unjustified) anxieties about new things (e.g. steam trains, vaccinations, matter transmitters), speaking to our hindbrains much more effectively than many pre-emptive attempts to sway public opinion; additionally, the reader gets the narrative rules without needing to have them explained. We know that such tales exist to warn us against particular activities, and we expect the sting in the tale to have a moral component, instructing us how to be better behaved individuals in the greater collective called 'humanity'. When the moral message jars against the reader's contemporary realities, that's where speculative urban myths really pay off.

Maybe that's why this story, which was written as science fiction, won a 'Best Horror' award, as voted by my writerly peers. You go meta at your own risk. There are only so many turns around the spiral before it runs out, or snaps.

The idea of a 'Togetherness' meme first appeared in Jack Wodham's story 'There is a Crooked Man' in Analog, 1967.

The Legend Trap

Three teenagers step into a booth.

It's the oldest story in the world. Some dumb kid *always* wants to put it to the test. 'It' could be any number of things. Jumping when the d-mat process starts to see if it makes you taller. Spinning in a circle anticlockwise in the hope of being switched from left to right. Squeezing thirteen people in at once *just in case* the one with the guiltiest secret disappears.

Or, in this case, the Bashert Ostension.

'It's never going to work,' said Damon. The tallest of the three, he also thought he was the smartest, but that distinction probably went to Lydia, Jude's girlfriend. Lydia was skinny like Damon, but with angular hips and long hair in a braid down her back. She was cloud-pale and grey-eyed, and the opposite in almost every respect to Jude. Jude was short, muscular, and dark. She had a tattoo of a small grey mouse above her left breast. That was how she thought of Lydia, she said: permanently close to her heart. But really it was more about the mouse. Jude liked to dominate.

'Scared?' she said.

'Not at all,' said Damon, running a hand through his thin brown hair. It needed a wash. It usually did, but particularly today. Maybe he was a *little* on edge. 'Just being practical. What you're talking about is magic. D-mat isn't *magic*. It's a machine. Urban myths are fun and all, but they're not *real*.'

'Who says? Maybe this one is.'

'Rituals are real,' said Lydia. Her voice was soft. Generally her friends stopped to listen. 'We're on a legend trip – you know, checking out a graveyard or a spooky old house. That's what it's called. On the way we tell stories and prove our bravery and bond, and ... Oh! We should've brought beer.'

Jude produced a small silver flask from her back pocket. 'Way ahead of you, babe.' She took a swig and passed some of the burning liquor to Lydia through a messy, wet kiss.

Damon sniffed. 'I don't need to prove anything. And you two do enough *bonding* as it is.'

Lydia laughed, pressing a hand to her sternum, where warmth was spreading outward in waves.

'Chicken,' she said.

'Yeah, chicken out if you want, Lame-o Dame-o,' said Jude. 'We're going anyway.'

He reached for the flask. She gave it to him. He wiped the neck on his sleeve and deliberately took too much – an asshole tax, he thought of it, not realising that made him the asshole. For a second he thought he might cough, which would have been devastating.

'So let's do it,' he said in a thin, tight voice.

Jude looked at Lydia, who nodded and took her hand.

'Ready?'

'Steady.'

'Take us to the Bashert Ostension,' Jude said in a clear, loud voice.

The booth doors slid shut. Mirrored walls enclosed them, throwing reflections to infinity in all directions. Light flashed. The three of them held their breaths and were silent.

◆ ◆ ◆

There are lots of different versions of this particular urban myth, but they all boil down to the same thing.

Sometimes you jump somewhere by d-mat but don't arrive where you're supposed to. It looks like the right place, but it's not. There are small differences buried deep in the details. At first you think you're going crazy, but it's actually the world around you that's crazy – because it's not your world anymore. You've gone sideways, into the universe next door.

Sometimes there's a sting in the tale.

Look around you. Look CLOSELY. Maybe it's already happened to you, and you just haven't noticed yet.

You can usually write off such tales as older kids messing with younger ones. It's a tradition that dates right back to the first hominids, to whoever or whatever first discovered that language is a powerful tool to mess with those around you, for fun or profit. Some people have argued that the fun-or-profit motive actually drove the evolution of language. Either way, the urban myth predates religion and science and will probably outlast both of them.

The version of the story Jude, Lydia and Damon knew possessed one critical extension.

You can make it happen by asking for a specific destination.

The name of that destination was the Bashert Ostension.

◆ ◆ ◆

The lights went down. The doors slid open. All three teens peered out.

Their reflections parted to reveal a forest of spindly pine trees painted warm yellows and oranges by sunset. Damon noted the crescent moon in the sky above. Jude sniffed at a faint tang of deer musk. Lydia heard a swallow call and saw a flash of white through the branches that might have been the bird responsible. She had read that swallows were albino here, sometimes.

'Are we having fun yet?' asked Damon.

'Be real, dumbass,' said Jude. 'Give it a moment.'

They stepped out into the dusk to examine their flourishes. This was part of the ritual that Damon had devised. If the myth was true, the booth wouldn't take them somewhere else in their world, like d-mat normally did; it would take them somewhere that looked the same as their world, except for some tiny details. So each of them had brought a trove of things that would quickly reveal any changes – because who could remember if a leaf had fallen or changed colour or whatever?

If they were going to do this they were going to do it right, he said, and that meant testing the hypothesis in a methodical way.

Doing it right to Lydia also meant finding exactly the right place to do it. They needed somewhere atmospheric, to enhance the ritual, yet at the same time somewhere away from other people. After a lot of research she settled on Pripyat, an abandoned town in the Ukraine. It was near a nuclear reactor that had blown up a century or so ago, long before d-mat. She had never heard of it, but radioactive isotopes have a long memory, and people still couldn't live there. The booth was for scientists studying the wildlife. There were more interesting critters out there than just albino sparrows.

Doing it right to Jude meant being with Lydia and winding

up Damon until he snapped. They had been friends from an early age. She knew how to have fun with him. He must be getting something out of it too, she reasoned, otherwise why was he still hanging around?

'I read that they call it the Red Forest because of all the blood of the workers who died here,' she said, crossing to where her backpack lay on its side in the leaf litter.

Damon didn't bother correcting her. Jude privileged stories over facts, and he could only fight misinformation one factoid at a time, armed in this case with a small but fiendishly complicated three-dimensional jigsaw puzzle that he had first solved at the age of five. By now he knew the sequence by heart. Moving swiftly, ignoring the others, he took the pieces one by one from their tin and assembled them with familiar, deft movements.

When it was done, he rocked back on his heels, feeling something less than complete satisfaction, even though there were no pieces missing; the crystal skull was as it always was.

A sharp tug and he pulled the puzzle to pieces again. It was as good a litmus test as any other. If something was going to change, why not a crystal skull? Unless his brain changed too. What if it had been a crystal dolphin in his home universe and his memories had changed along with it?

While Damon considered the deeper ramifications of his experiment, Jude was scanning swatches of translucent cotton fabric for pulled threads and changed patterns. They were family heirlooms her grandmother had left her, mementoes of affluent times buried in a time capsule to preserve them from the Water Wars and retrieved when things improved. There was no material value to such mementoes from the past; nowadays, anything could be scanned and copied in moments. But these swatches had never been scanned, and never would be. They were perfectly imperfect, right down to the grubby fingerprints Jude had left on them as a child – a crime for which she had been soundly beaten.

The fabric was unchanged.

That just left Lydia's collection of rare moths, unaltered in number, shade and sex. Nor was the suitcase altered, or its position, which she had marked out carefully on the ground, or the twigs she had arranged in a rough square around it, or the stones she had placed at each corner of the square. Testing the urban myth may have been Damon's idea, but Lydia was the most meticulous in pursuing that idea to the limit. She liked following other people because it absolved her from having to make moral, or at least practical, judgments, but she was in her own way very competitive.

They compared results.

'Well, that was a bust,' said Damon.

'Not necessarily,' said Jude. 'We might not have found it yet, the thing that separates this world from ours.'

'Don't tell me we're going to go look for it. I've got better things to do with my life.'

'It could be anywhere,' said Lydia, neither agreeing nor disagreeing. She wanted to keep every option open, even as she packed up her moths in preparation for going home.

'Perhaps we should try it again,' said Jude. She didn't feel disappointed. If anything, she felt a heightened sense of anticipation. Rising to the challenge.

'No skin off my nose,' said Damon. 'It's still not going to work.'

'Guys,' said Lydia. She was facing the booth, the doors of which had shut behind them. 'Was that graffiti on there . . . *before?*'

'I think so.' Damon remembered it because he had taken a photo of Jude and Lydia after they'd laid out their flourishes, with their backs against the booth. He had noted the Cyrillic alphabet, which he couldn't understand.

The word traced out in thick but hasty white lines in a diagonal across the booth's front was лох.

'It means stupid,' said Jude. 'I looked it up.'

'Just then?' said Lydia.

Jude nodded. 'The Air works here. So that's another strike against having gone anywhere.'

'Oh.' Lydia couldn't help but feel a little deflated. She had been sure the graffiti would be the critical difference. If the Air worked and Damon remembered seeing the graffiti, then maybe this universe really was home after all.

'Uh . . . wait,' said Damon. He had called up the photo in his lenses, and he sent it to the others now.

There, behind the girls, in identical white lines was a single word in Cyrillic, only instead of лох it was хуёвый, which meant worthless.

'The words are different,' said Damon, staring from the booth in front of him to the one in his lenses. His mind fizzed a little, as though he were a bottle of Coke and reality had just given him a bit of a shake. 'The words are definitely different.'

Jude stared at Lydia with her mouth wide open, then let out a loud whoop and swept her up in a whirlwind dance around the clearing. Her enthusiasm was infectious. Even Damon grinned a little, as he stared down at the grinning skull and wondered, *So how do we get back?*

◆ ◆ ◆

Jude had it all figured out. First they would explore the clearing as long as they dared (the radiation wasn't going to kill them any time soon, but the thought of it was still scary) in the hope of finding any more differences (they didn't), then they would get back into the booth and she would do her thing.

'Take us to the Bashert Ostension,' she said, just as loudly and as confidently as before. The Bashert Ostension wasn't a place, she had reasoned. It was a code, like Improvement or Togetherness or any of the numerous memes circulating at any given time. Jude and Lydia had tried Togetherness once, but they hadn't ended up physically blended into one. Of course. Such things were impossible, or at least utterly illegal and therefore improbable. The fun lay in the imagining and in the attempt, and the reminder that all skin is special, like friendship.

So, saying the code words should take them back. That was Jude's assumption, and it seemed reasonable to Damon. Inasmuch as a situation like this could *be* reasonable. D-mat still wasn't magic. There had to be an explanation that made sense, if only he could think of it.

Lydia watched him rubbing his thumb and forefingers together, over and over. She knew what he was thinking, and maybe a little of what he was feeling too, but figured it would all be okay when they got back. Then he could pretend it hadn't happened, as he always did with problems he couldn't solve.

The doors of the booth didn't close.

'Take us to the Bashert Ostension,' Jude said again.

Still the doors stayed open.

'Is that what you said last time?' Damon asked.

'Exactly.'

'So why isn't it working now?'

'I don't know. I don't know. Let me think.'

She began to pace. Lydia stepped back to give her room. The booth was a bit more crowded than before, now the flourishes were back in with them too.

'Maybe that's something else that's changed here,' Lydia said. 'Maybe the code is different.'

Jude snapped her fingers. 'Right. Let's look it up.'

The Air told them the term didn't exist.

'So we can't get back?' said Damon, his eyes wide and a little white around the outsides. 'We're trapped here?'

'Unlikely,' said Lydia soothingly. 'The urban myth will be here too, just like the trees and the leaves and the moon are here too. All that's different, apart from the graffiti, is the code.' *I hope,* she added silently to herself.

Jude had a wild idea. 'Do you think we could call ourselves?'

'Why would you want to?' asked Damon.

'I'm going to try it,' Jude said, and received an immediate error, of course: it's not possible to call yourself through the Air. So instead she sent a chat request to her little sister.

Xena answered immediately. 'Get back here, you midget dyke bitch. Mum's going to kill you if you don't—'

Jude ended the call. No changes there. 'Seems I'm not at home.'

'No, you're here,' said Damon. 'But not *here* here. You're *there* here.'

'What?'

'We've swapped places with our other selves,' he explained. 'They're exactly the same as us, which means they tried the urban myth too. They're back where we came from looking for our code words, while we're where *they* came from, looking for theirs.'

Jude could accommodate this new development if she concentrated hard enough. It was better than thinking about her screwed-up family. Apart from two minor details – the graffiti and the code – everything in this universe was the same as her other self's, which meant she wasn't going to run into herself any time soon. Unless the other Jude was trying to jump back right now . . .?

The booth was still and silent. No one was going anywhere.

She took out the flask and had a solid swig, then passed it to the others. Lydia allowed herself a taste. Damon waved it away. His lenses were scrolling light right up into his irises.

'I'm searching the urban myths,' he said. 'Help me out, will you? Nothing fits so far.'

All three of them searched, Damon immobile in the booth, Jude pacing in circles around it, and Lydia sitting on a tree stump outside.

Eventually he said, 'I think I've found something. Look.'

He bumped them a link to an urban myth that initially seemed nothing like theirs.

When you use d-mat to go from A to B, you don't go in a straight line. You don't even go in one piece. Your pattern is broken up into tiny packets and each packet follows a different path through the Air, along cables, by satellite or via whatever means are available. Normally it doesn't matter which means it takes. The booth at the other end assembles all your packets the same way. But a system this big is like a maze. There are lots of places where things can go wrong. Dead ends and loops and crossed wires and knots . . . and holes.

Holes are a particular problem when you're dealing with quantum computers that access the computational power of parallel universes. Engineers call them quantum leaks. There's one particular quantum leak that you can use to get to a world that looks just like ours, but isn't. Not quite. Some people go there to steal stuff. You get there by asking for Wodhams' Gate. Be careful, though: there's no guarantee you'll ever get back. Curiosity killed the cat, remember?

'Quantum leaks,' Damon said. 'That almost makes sense.'
'Gee, I bet the universe is relieved,' said Jude.
'Yeah, yeah,' he said. 'Are you going to do it or what?'
'Take us to Wodhams' Gate,' Jude told the booth.
The doors closed. The light flared.
Lydia nursed a small worry, like a kitten too new and

fragile to uncover. It was too late to raise now: they were going *somewhere*. And she knew she was the fragile one in the kitten metaphor, and that some worries grow roots like oaks when exposed to the light.

◆ ◆ ◆

For the second time that day they peered out at the Red Forest, only now it was dark and they could see barely anything beyond the white light spilling from the booth. The sun had fully set while they were searching the Air and the new moon was on its way. A faint tang of deer musk still pricked Jude's nose, which was a good sign.

'How do we know for sure?' asked Damon, sweeping in long strides from one side of the clearing to the other. There were their footprints in the leaf litter. There was the rectangular outline of Lydia's suitcase.

'I can think of one way,' she said. 'Search on Wodhams' Gate.'

That produced nothing. There were no references to that term anywhere.

'So we're home?' said Jude.

'Not necessarily,' Lydia said, braving the fear. 'We have to search on the Bashert Ostension to be sure.'

Again, nothing.

Damon sank down on his haunches and put his head in his hands. 'Fuck. Seriously?'

'Is this possible?' asked Jude. 'We're in *another* universe?'

'There are an infinite number of them,' said Lydia. 'If two are connected, why not three?'

'We shouldn't have done the second search,' said Damon. 'We might never have noticed, otherwise.'

'And when the versions of us who live here turned up?' asked Jude. 'What then?'

'Maybe they wouldn't have. Maybe they would have been happy where they ended up too.'

'It still wouldn't be right,' said Lydia. 'We'd always wonder. Or *I* would.'

'What's so special about our universe anyway?' Damon grumbled, but he let up and joined them in the search for another way out.

Lydia was getting the hang of it now. Here there was neither a Bashert Ostension nor Wodham's Gate. Instead there was a Junction 666 that sounded promising.

'It's a joke,' said Damon, 'but I'll go with it if it takes me home.'

They held hands in the middle of the booth with their flourishes on the floor between them as Jude made the request. The doors shut. The light flared. The doors opened.

Pine forest. Night-time. Deer musk and leaf litter.

But there was no point checking the Air.

There, in the middle of the clearing was another set of flourishes, left behind by someone else.

'Damon's right,' said Jude. 'This is a joke. It has to be.'

She held two swatches of identical fabric, one in her left hand, one in her right. They had the same chocolatey fingerprints, front and back. The same tiny hands that had held them, years earlier, had tried in vain to ward off her mother's blows. Different hands and a different mother in a different universe – that was what they were being asked to believe. But there was another explanation.

'Someone's messing with us,' she said. 'They're editing the Air while we're in transit, so it looks like the memes have changed, but they haven't really. They changed the graffiti, too. And now they've fabbed copies of our flourishes. We're not going anywhere at all. We never left. It's all one big art-prank, and the joke is on us.'

'How do we prove it?' asked Damon. He was juggling two crystal skulls, kind of hoping he would drop them so they would shatter and the pieces would get mixed up. *That* was a challenge he had never attempted before.

'One of us stays behind,' Jude said. 'That's how we prove it.'

Lydia stared at her with wide eyes. 'Who?'

Nobody spoke for a long moment.

'Do we *really* need to test it?' said Damon. 'Can't we just accept that you're right and leave it at that? Yeah, yeah, yeah – you would always wonder, Lyd, but *I wouldn't*. Near enough is good enough for me. What's stopping me from going home right now and staying there – if it *is* there?'

'Nothing,' said Lydia.

'So why don't I?'

'You tell us,' said Jude.

He gripped the skulls tightly in his fists. Veins stood out of his forehead.

'I'll stay behind,' said Lydia. 'You two go. I'll wait and make sure the meme doesn't change. That way we'll know for sure. Then we can all go home together. The legend trip will be over. We can get that beer . . . okay?'

Slowly the tension left Damon's face and posture. He put the second skull back where he had found it, and nodded. 'All right.'

Jude was less sure.

'Are you certain you want to do this?' she asked Lydia.

'Yes.' Lydia didn't look at the second suitcase. The temptation to send it off with the others was strong, but there was probably a limit to how many moths one should have. 'Don't worry. I'll be here when you come back. I'm not going anywhere . . . because neither are you, remember?'

They hugged. Damon retreated to the booth, already searching for the next meme. It was called the Fistula, which made him think of unfortunate medical conditions and bodily fluids, and his father, and the creeping disease that had killed him. Damon's stepfather John had called it The Ague. When Dad died, John had wept for five minutes, then walked out of the room and never come back.

Lydia outside the booth. Jude and Damon inside. The mirrored space seemed empty with only two people.

Lydia gave Jude a tiny wave as Jude called out the name of their destination and the doors slid shut on her friends, leaving her alone in the clearing. It was suddenly dark. She wrung her hands in front of her, imagining radioactive ghosts crowding around. That was what she had expected of the legend trip, not this weird existential crisis. Ghosts and other supernatural beings. Aliens, maybe.

The booth whirred and clicked to itself. Maybe it was aliens, she thought, tinkering away in the background and tittering to themselves as their subjects began to show signs of stress. She swore she wouldn't give them the satisfaction. Tucking her long legs up to her chest, she sat on the suitcase and hugged her knees, and waited for her friend and her lover to return.

◆ ◆ ◆

Two minutes later, the doors opened and Lydia was exactly where she had been, except sitting down now. She looked up when the light fell over her, then stood up, then lit up when Jude emerged, her darkest fears unrealised. Jude had half expected to find the clearing empty and Lydia gone – vanished into another dimension or kidnapped by unknown tormentors. That she hadn't gone anywhere restored her confidence greatly.

They embraced. 'Anything weird happen?' Jude asked her.

'Something rustled in the bushes, that's all.'

'A Pripyat rat with two heads and four glowing eyes?'

They had joked about this before coming to the Red Forest. Mutant rodents to match the mutant swallows. 'Almost certainly.'

'What about changes?' Damon asked, leaving the booth and looking around suspiciously. 'Is the Air still the same?'

'Exactly the same.' She had been watching it as closely as she had been watching the undergrowth. 'The meme hasn't altered one bit. Which means—'

'Which means . . .' He took over the sentence, then deflated suddenly, collapsing down into himself as though his bones had suddenly d-matted away. It was relief making him weak, and a sense that drama was required. 'We didn't go anywhere. We're safe. We can go home. It's over.'

'Hoo-frigging-ray,' said Jude.

She raised the flask in one final toast and passed it to the others. Damon took an extra half-swig to cover a slight tremble in his hands.

'Back to my place?' he said. 'I'll fab some pizza while

we work out how to track the people who did this to us.'

'You really want to do that?' asked Jude. 'Track them, I mean. Not pizza. Pizza would be awesome.' Her stomach rumbled at the thought.

'Credit where credit is due,' Lydia said. 'This was a great stunt. We were totally taken in.'

'Until the end,' said Damon with satisfaction. He was wondering what to do with the extra flourishes. 'I'd kinda like to rub it in their faces that we worked it out before the big reveal.'

'They were reaching a bit with the last name, I thought,' said Jude. 'Was that a dig at us, do you think?'

Lydia frowned. 'What do you mean?'

'The *Fistula.*' She made a lewd gesture when Lydia still looked puzzled. 'You know? Or are you pretending for Dameo's benefit that we haven't done that?'

'I, uh, don't know you're talking about,' Lydia said. 'The last name wasn't the Fistula. It was Addison's Adit. The Fistula was the one before.'

'Are you sure?'

'Of course. We used it to get here, and I've been staring at it for five minutes solid. It hasn't changed a bit . . . but—'

She pulled away from Jude, who looked hurt.

'But *you* have changed,' Lydia said.

'Or *you* have!' said Damon. 'We're exactly the same as before.'

'I don't understand,' said Jude. 'What's going on?'

'They're still screwing with us,' said Damon with a definite snap to his voice. 'They changed her while we were in the booth just like they changed the Air and copied that crap we brought with us. That has to be what happened.'

'It's not like that at all,' said Lydia, amazed by his willingness to jump to that conclusion. 'I stayed behind. You two came here. But you aren't the same two *I* came here with. They've gone on to the next world – where another me is waiting, just like the me you left behind. We've got all split up!'

'So what do we do now?' asked Jude, staring at a Lydia who said she wasn't *her* Lydia, even though she looked exactly the same. Perhaps there were subtle differences she would only discover on a close examination – which wasn't as thrilling a thought as it once might have been. 'Do Damon and I stay here while you go forward? Will that bring us back together?'

'I don't know,' said Lydia. 'I don't know!'

'Don't listen to her,' said Damon. He looked wild-eyed and feverish. His thumb and forefinger were working again. 'She's part of it. They've changed her. They're in her head now. She's one of them.'

'That's not possible,' Lydia said, certain of that much. 'You can't just reach into someone's head and change the way they think. You're crazy.'

'They'd want us to think that,' he said. 'Don't listen to her, Judy. She's lying. We know where we are. We know we haven't gone anywhere. Don't play their games anymore. They're laughing at us, and they have been all along.'

'Calm down, Dame-o,' said Jude, reaching out to touch his shoulder. 'You're getting a bit worked up.'

'Yes? And why not? I'm tired of this. I'm tired of being patronised by you two. I'm tired of being the third wheel. I'm going home to get pizza. You can come with me if you want, or you can stay here. I don't care.'

That he did care was made very evident by the way he hesitated. He was waiting for one of them to side with him. But neither did. They looked at each other, and once it was clear that Jude wasn't leaving, Lydia decided to stay too. The precise nature of their relationship was yet to be determined, but parting was not an option this time.

'I want to figure this out,' said Lydia. 'There has to be an explanation.'

'Fine,' said Damon, stomping in a huff through the booth's open doors, crystal skull held tightly in one hand. 'See ya, then.'

'Oh, don't be such a big baby,' said Jude, but it was too late. He had said 'home' and the doors were already closing. The booth knew the address, which was evidence in its own right, but tantalisingly inconclusive.

Lydia and Jude waited in silence, unmoving, for the booth to finish working. When the doors opened, the interior was empty. Damon had run from another unsolvable problem.

'Shit,' said Jude. 'Now what?'

'We keep going,' said Lydia. 'We see this through without him.'

'How? I mean, what address do we use now? I'm confused.'

'Addison's Adit,' she said. She wondered if *her* Jude looked this lost in the next universe along. Perhaps if they left quickly enough, they'd catch up. 'Come on. Let's get out of here.'

Jude nodded miserably and followed her inside.

On the other side of Addison's Adit, there was no sign of anyone else, apart from the flourishes, still abandoned in the clearing. The meme in that universe was called The Long Way Home, and they took it without hesitation, and the one after, and the one after that. Lydia and Jude stayed at opposite sides of the booth, not talking, barely even looking at each other. Damon's absence cast a long shadow across their moods. Every time they arrived at another Red Forest, Jude half expected to see him or receive a message from him, but there was ever only silence, which disconcerted but didn't surprise her. It was as though he had dropped off the face of the earth.

The Shortcut led to The Ultimate Escape led to Intersection 391, where the deer musk was mysteriously absent. They took Intersection 391 to God's Gateway, and there, without warning, the flourishes also vanished. It was as though part of Jude vanished with them, and she fell to her knees in the clearing, not knowing if she wanted to scream or weep.

'Why won't they show themselves?' she asked Lydia, staring out at the trees. 'Why are they still messing with us like this?'

'I don't think this sapling was here before.' Lydia had been taking snapshots with her lenses and comparing the image with the reality of their next location. There were changes, but they were subtle. It wasn't just the Air and the graffiti and the flourishes. She was convinced now that the worlds weren't the same. They were still being messed with, but not in any simple art-prank way.

Jude pushed past her, ripped the sapling out of the ground and threw it into the bushes. 'There. Is that better?'

Lydia knew not to speak.

God's Gateway led to the first screaming match in the entire three months of their relationship. There was no inciting incident. It just happened. They were suddenly going in circles inside the booth, Jude pressing, Lydia retreating, both shouting passionate, vindictive things they had stored up for weeks. Jude's reactivity. Lydia's passivity. Jude's bossiness. Lydia's stubbornness. Both of them wanted it to stop but neither of them knew how. Being in love with someone took practice, Lydia told herself, trying to see the positive. It was just like sex in that regard, so why not arguing as well? This was their first time. Of course they were doing it badly. They would be better next time they tried it, if they got through this time.

Jude just wanted it to stop. All of it.

'Damon was right,' she said. 'We're not stuck here. We're not prisoners. No one's making us do this. It's us, all us, and we can end it any time we like.'

'Don't go, please,' said Lydia. She clutched at Jude's arm, afraid of being alone.

'Why not? I'm tired. I'm thirsty. I'm sick of the view. But not sick of you,' she conceded, although she did pull away, feeling slightly guilty. Lydia wasn't *her* Lydia, after all. Was this cheating? 'It just has to stop.'

'It will soon, I'm sure of it.'

Jude didn't know how Lydia could be sure of anything. And by this point, Jude really *had* to be sure. The legend trip was poisoning them. Whoever or whatever was behind it, she needed them to give up now.

Silently, while Lydia searched the Air for the next link in the chain, Jude called the peacekeepers. She told them she was in trouble and she told them where. She didn't look too closely at the interface in her lenses. She didn't wonder why it was black rather than blue. She didn't ask why the PK had never heard of Pripyat and wanted GPS coordinates instead. She just got it done.

'Ready,' said Lydia. The name was the Frehling Aperture. She held out her hand. 'Shall we?'

Jude hesitated, then nodded stiffly but ignored the hand.

'It won't change anything,' Jude said.

Lydia took what looked like fatalism as an affirmative, and took them onward.

The doors opened. White flashlight beams were dancing through the trees. They could hear shouting in the distance. To Lydia it was a complete mystery. Jude understood that the PKs were coming to rescue her through the Red Forest, since their booth was in use.

'Wait here,' said Jude. She didn't want Lydia to know she had called them.

'No, don't go out there.'

Lydia didn't like this. She was already searching the Air for the next step, the next name.

'It's okay,' Jude said. 'Don't worry.'

She stepped into the clearing and stood on tiptoes to see through the scrub. The PKs were almost upon them. She waved her hands over her head, although surely they could see the light of the open d-mat booth. There was nothing else for miles.

Angry voices barked in a language she didn't know. She had just enough time to think *Why angry?* when they burst out of the trees and were on her, six men and women in black light armour and face masks, wielding automatic weapons. They threw her to the ground and, when she resisted, clubbed her with a rifle butt to stun her, then splayed her on the ground, face down. Jude blinked rapidly in fright, not knowing what was going on. She could see Lydia through the door of the booth, mouth open in shock. Such delicate lips. They were the first thing about Lydia that Jude had noticed. They were bloodless now.

Jude felt something cold and hard tap the back of her skull. It felt like the barrel of a gun.

The sound made Lydia physically recoil as violently as though she herself had been shot. She fell back into the booth, away from the sight of Jude's ruined face, and somehow the booth heard her words through the hands pressed tight against her mouth. 'Shut the door!'

They had killed Jude. Whoever the people in black were, they had killed her, and they were going to kill Lydia too if she didn't move quickly. Already the weapons were turning her way, dark visors gleaming expressionlessly in the reflected light of the booth.

'The Infinite Intersection – and don't open the door at the other end!'

Light flashed. Engines of transformation worked, turning her from matter into energy, then from energy into information, and then back again. Lights dimmed. The doors stayed shut.

Through them she heard voices, then the hammering of fists against the metal. She pressed hard against the back of the booth and searched for her only way out.

'Sam's Passage!'

She jumped and jumped again, tears pouring down her

face, legs shaking, but mind working, searching, questioning, hoping. Maybe in one of the worlds there would be no banging at the door, no shouting foreign tongues, and Jude would be alive. Maybe even *her* Jude, if she could ever be so lucky. If she never gave up.

Another jump. Another. It was silent outside the booth. She sat inside for five minutes without going anywhere, gnawing her fingernails and thinking, thinking. What if it was a trap? What if this universe's equivalent of the people in black were lying in wait for her? What if she opened the doors and they leapt in, dragged her out into the clearing and shot her too?

Who they were and where they had come from were lesser mysteries. Even why they had done what they did. Different universes, different rules. It wasn't just little things that changed, obviously.

'The Bridge Beyond,' she said, certain that if Jude had been out there she would have said something, and certain also that she didn't want to die.

Three more jumps and she was ready to brave the silence.

◆ ◆ ◆

The trees were black but the sky was pink. Sunrise. Had she been really in the booth that long? Maybe, if the jumps took longer than usual – which wasn't an unreasonable hypothesis given she was universe-hopping by means unknown.

There was blood in the clearing from a carcass rendered unidentifiable by the gnawing and tearing of sharp teeth. Standing over the body was a grey wolf with bloody jowls. Calmly, it looked up at Lydia for no less than five seconds, as though considering whether or not to eat her as well – maybe it had cubs somewhere, or pack mates, or was just greedy, Lydia thought, trembling with fright – but then it looked down at its meal and resumed crunching and chewing through something that might once have been Jude but could be anything Lydia wanted it to be.

Not Jude, she decided as the wolf ate on. So hope remained.

◆ ◆ ◆

Alone with an infinite army of reflections, Lydia pressed on. Why? Because she couldn't go back, and she couldn't stay still. Onward was the only option.

The sun rose higher in fits and starts, depending on how long each jump lasted. The entire morning passed in less than an hour from her perspective, and that perspective contained nine different versions of the Red Forest. The clearing shrank and grew larger, contained animals and nothing at all. The trees around it changed from pine to birch to palm to bamboo.

Into the afternoon and the weather began to change too. Sometimes it was hot, other times cold. Once it was snowing, and she spent several minutes in icy melt water to replenish her thirsty tissues. She emptied the suitcase and filled it with snow in case it was a while before she saw water again, then shivered through ten more frigid Pripyats until the Sneak's Retreat brought her to a desert.

She never changed but the scenery constantly did. It began to feel like a dream, and she wondered whether the entire legend trip was some kind of hyper-real simulation. Was she going to wake on a couch somewhere with wires coming out of her head? Were her friends laughing at her, the last to give up and leave the simulation? She didn't think so. They would cheer her on, she was sure of it. They would want her to break the game.

Civilisations ebbed and flowed outside the booth. Once she found herself in the centre of standing stones that looked thousands of years old. Another time she was surrounded by planes of brilliant glass and metal populated by people so beautiful they looked like machines. The booth was the *other* constant, she realised, apart from herself. She could only leave one universe and enter another through a booth just like the booth she was in.

Several times the Air failed to respond to her commands. When that happened she had to chase down people outside, if there *were* people nearby and if they spoke her language and if they weren't trying to shoot her. Sometimes they gave her food, clothes, access to a toilet. Sometimes they just shrugged, unable to communicate. But there was always a way to keep going. There was always *onward*, even when it *seemed* that she had reached the end of the line. She could count on that – so in that sense there were actually *three* constants. Herself, the booth, and the quantum leaks. Everything else was in flux.

As the bedrock rose and fell and the skies turned from blue to green to a garish yellow from horizon to horizon, she became more and more certain she was getting somewhere. Or maybe something was getting nearer to her. Either way, proximity was in the air. It could be Jude, or it could be home. Or something else entirely. But when she found it, she was positive she would know what it meant. This couldn't be for nothing, all this effort, all these strange journeys nowhere.

Nowhere, and yet *everywhere*. She gazed out at infinite

possibilities with a sense of wonder no less authentic than when she had first stepped into a d-mat booth and seen images of *her* radiating outward in all directions. There was both wonder and horror in confronting the unending universe, just as there is both wonder and horror in reaching the end.

Lydia had long lost count by the time the doors opened on an Earth with a poisonous atmosphere. Two breaths saw her pitching forward to the ground, trying from long habit to find the way out in time. The words were there – The Long Delay – but she could no longer speak them clearly, just gasp and gurgle and cough. She didn't know if there was just one jump left to go, or a million, or what the booth heard her say, ultimately. But she tried. The last thing she saw as the booth closed for the final time was an image of her staring at the mirrored ceiling, her head pillowed by the bag that had once contained Jude's precious swatches. She had traded them long ago for a loaf of bread.

There was blood on her lips, she saw. Her skin was so pale. Not constant after all, she thought. Not constant at all.

Three teenagers enter a booth. One dies, one disappears . . . and the last one?

By the time Damon returns to the clearing in Pripyat, it's all over. The clearing is empty. There's no sign of anyone. He's reconciled to the fact that his room in this universe is the wrong colour and his father died a year earlier than he should have. What he can't stand is the thought he's being used. It's occurred to him that the most important thing about urban legends and legend trips – the thing that separates them from horror stories and tragedies – is that if everyone dies, the legend *dies with them*. Someone *has* to survive to propagate the meme.

And it seems in this case that someone is him, which is an intractable position to be in. He can't tell anyone or they'll think he's crazy. But this isn't a secret he can keep forever. Jude and Lydia are going to be missed. He has to tell the peacekeepers something, and what else if not the truth? Does the third one always have to be the lunatic no one believes but whose story everyone remembers?

The meme propagates. The meme wins. All it needs is someone to pass it on.

But what if he doesn't do that? What if he kills himself right here and now? What if he runs into the forest and lets the radiation that turned the trees red eat him too, pull at his cancer-riddled body until it sinks down into the dirt, devoured before its time?

Beside him, the booth doors close and the machines start working.

He sags and laughs in despair. Who is he kidding? The meme spans every possible universe. It's covered against every possible outcome.

When the doors open, Jude leans out to smack him on the back of the head.

'I knew you weren't going anywhere, you big baby,' she says. 'What would you do without us?'

Tell stories, he thinks. *Or die.* It isn't much of a choice – but is this worse or better? These friends aren't the same ones he knew. They're just identical. Sure, the three of them can pick up where they left off for now, but the odds of none of them ever leaving is zero, right?

'Chicken,' adds Lydia with a knowing twinkle in her eye, and as he steps through the doors Damon thinks, *Dead right.*

Jump to . . .

more horror
'Sing, My Murdered Darlings' (p. 151)

another story featuring young adults
'Impossible Music' (p. 129)

something meta
'The Cuckoo' (p. 117)

Notes on *The Cuckoo*

Predicting the future is difficult, but it's better than the alternatives. Capturing the present is harder than catching sand, and the past is so full of traps it's like an Indiana Jones adventure (one of the good ones, at least).

All you have to do in predictive fiction is pick a date far enough in the future so no one can prove you wrong. To your face, at least. Because you'll be dead.

I'm an enormous pedant, so it might surprise you to learn that when it comes to building futures my aim is plausibility rather than testability. This puts my science fiction stories rather at odds with the core tenets of science, but that's okay: I'm writing fiction first and foremost, not an academic paper. Which is not to say that I just make stuff up without restraint, either. The category of what's plausible for me is smaller than it is for other science fiction authors. We find our own balance.

This story hints at more than it reveals, reaching for a sense of what it might be like to live in a complex world undergoing a subtle and dramatic change, as witnessed from the perspective of someone who moves deliberately from the fringes to the very centre of the action. One of those invisible heroes whose contributions to the wider good aren't seen or, if seen, comprehended. That she hides her heroism behind what appears to be a typo is very much in character for her, not me. I'm more likely to take several hundred unnecessary words to state what the reader might be perfectly capable of deducing for themselves. Ahem.

The Cuckoo

1 April 2075, 9:15–9:23 am
More than one thousand commuters travelling via d-mat arrive at their destinations wearing red clown noses; they weren't wearing them when they left. The global matter-transmission network is rebooted, source of the glitch unknown. All the clown noses are destroyed except for three retained by private collectors.

1 April 2076, 10 pm precisely
One year later, every d-mat booth in the world opens at exactly the same moment, releasing a powerful scent of roses. Peacekeepers analysing the fumes find no evidence of toxicity. People begin to talk about the existence of a new, anonymous art-prankster in the vein of Bekhisisa Uteku or Banksy, who turns a hundred this year.

1 April 2077
At random times throughout the day, eight-hundred-and-sixty-nine booths each deliver a single page on which are typed twenty-three different words from William S. Burroughs' cut-up novel *The Soft Machine*.

23 May 2077
Professor Eme Marburg, 53, of New Leiden University begins investigating the activities of 'The Fool', as she dubs the

prankster on her blog. She is a teacher of complexity theory and author of several abstruse textbooks on the subject, but it is her interest in mid-twentieth century literature that initially piques her interest. What happened to the remaining pages of *The Soft Machine?* Private collectors again, she is forced to assume.

1 April 2078
Two-hundred-and-seventy-one children are redirected in-transit to a location in Macau, where they arrive wearing the costumes of popular fantasy adventure series *Super Awesome Ninja Ponies*. They play without adult supervision for sixteen minutes before being rescued. No serious injuries are reported.

2 April 2079, 12:03 am
Following the attack on children the previous year, PKs worldwide are on high alert for any sign of The Fool. There are no incidents for twenty-four hours. After declaring the operation a complete success, outspoken octogenarian lawmaker Kieran Defrain is redirected in-transit and dumped in Times Square, wearing nothing but a cloth diaper and a tag tied around his left big toe inscribed 'Gotcha!'.

9 November 2079
Anggoon Montri, 32, from the Thai Protectorate, confesses to being The Fool. After eight hours of intense interrogation he recants, claiming he simply wanted to publicise his own original artwork and leaving the Fool's true name and motives a matter of keen speculation. Some say that he or she is a disgruntled employee intent on exposing the flaws

in the d-mat network, others that 'The Fool' is actually a collaboration of many people dedicated to Eris, the ancient Greek Goddess of chaos. Still others believe that copycats perpetrate each incident, and that the original Fool went to ground long ago. No evidence exists to confirm these theories.

1 April 2080

Despite a vigorous, yearlong search, The Fool remains at large. Embarrassed by their failure, PKs instruct the general public to avoid using d-mat except in the case of dire emergencies. No incidents are recorded involving d-mat booths. Instead, every networked fabricator in the world makes a unique piece of a three-dimensional jigsaw puzzle, each approximately one cubic centimetre in size, which, if assembled, would form a sculpture of an upraised middle finger twenty-five metres high.

17 June 2080

Professor Marburg of New Leiden University publishes a paper in the journal *Complexity and Organization* entitled 'Manifest Meaninglessness: The Fool and his Meme are Easily Imparted'. She notes that six weeks before The Fool's first known incident (clown noses), a major peacekeeper initiative was launched to curb youthful misuse of d-mat booths, called 'Quit Clowning Around'. Similarly, the following year's incident (the smell of roses) was preceded by the 'It Stinks' meme, instigated by a celebrity complaining that she didn't receive a red nose. The cut-up novel allegory is obvious. That The Fool is a playing a game at everyone's expense was a notion widely discussed prior to the mass kidnap of children in 2078; 'Gotcha' in turn connects with the PKs' determination to apprehend and punish the prankster, while the disassembled, statuesque obscenity clearly relates to a growing worldwide amusement at official impotence.

Professor Marburg concludes that this series of correlations is evidence of an emerging, powerful memeplex, or complex of memes, focused on The Fool. Whoever he or she originally was, he or she is here to stay.

1 April 2081

Ignoring stern peacekeeper warnings, the 'Fool's Tools', a loosely organised movement of everyday citizens, travel en masse continuously for twenty-four hours, awaiting, perhaps inviting, the latest prank from their hero. None is forthcoming, although over the course of the day six copycat stunts are easily detected and reversed, their perpetrators taken into custody. The only work ascribed to The Fool is a maze of d-mat addresses that, once entered, cannot be exited. The technician who stumbled across the artefact is never seen again, prompting another global manhunt. The Fool is now a wanted murderer, depending on one's definition of murder . . . but remains no easier to catch.

April 2081–March 2082

The longer The Fool remains at large, the higher The Fool's public profile rises. Numerous organisations form to honour the prankster's artistry, including the Fool's Brigade, the Tomfoolerists, and the First Church of the Foolhardy. No matter how vigorously peacekeepers crack down on publicly disruptive initiation rites, the number of disciples, prophets and self-proclaimed messiahs mounts. A monument to the Unknown Fool is erected in Berlin. A popular genre of erotic fan fiction, known as Foolfic, explores the motives and secret emotional life of the men and women supposedly behind the meme. In a series of increasingly obscure articles and blog posts, Professor Marburg, now 57, continues her examination of the phenomenon, placing the latest stunt in the context of a memeplex that seems on the one hand healthy to the point of profligacy and on the other verging on implosion.

She suggests The Fool never existed at all, in any sense that matters – not as a person, or as a series of people copying each other, or as a group of people acting in concert. 'The Fool' might very well be an emergent property of the world's memeverse, in the same way that magnificent dunes form out of the simple interaction of sand grains and the wind, without conscious control or intent. Hence, she says, we have organisations that mimic The Fool, inferior to the original in some eyes but nevertheless an authentic part of the phenomenon. If that is so, she speculates, it is entirely possible that the sealed maze – cause of The Fool's one and only direct fatality – might be a sign that the *original* Fool, whoever or whatever that might be, is now turning on itself, strangling itself in a knot of memetic transmutation that can only conclude one way.

She recants her previous prediction and issues a new one: The Fool is dead. The knot has been tied off. All that remains is aftershock.

1 April 2082
Few people read the theories of obscure professors. Huge celebrations greet the latest Fool's Day and no one is

immune to the party atmosphere – not even those who, led by a masked figure called 'Straight-Face', mount theatrical mock protests against the rising tide of foolishness. Pranks of all kinds are performed, ranging from the harmless to the extremely dangerous. One-hundred-and-seventeen people are killed in accidents; many more are injured. None of these tragedies are connected to The Fool. The world waits in anticipation to see what this year's 'official' prank will be, without release.

April 2082–March 2083

The Fool's absence does nothing to dampen the enthusiasm of the Foolish. After all, 'Gotcha!' happened the day after 1 April. The Fool's fans assume that the prank, when eventually revealed, will be unmatched in subtlety and explosiveness. Plans for next year's celebrations begin early. 'Best ever', the world is promised.

In New Leiden University, Professor Marburg is troubled by the deaths. Not a day goes by that she doesn't wish the world would put aside 'The Fool' and the troubling visions he, she, or it inspires in her. As the memeplex grows larger than ever, The Fool as an active participant in its own perpetuation is made conspicuous by its absence. The Fool is dead; long live The Fool. How can that be possible?

The growing memeplex, as mapped out by other colleagues in the field, is already a fiendishly convoluted web of popular culture. Only she is fixated on its connection to d-mat, the means of mass-transit for ninety-nine per cent of the world's population. It's no accident, she has always understood, that The Fool manifests this way, for that network contains – and *symbolises* – vast complexity. She herself is part of this complex whether she wants to be or not, both by travelling via d-mat and by publicly posting her speculations. She cannot help but wonder what role she has played in the evolution of The Fool. Did she inadvertently name it, for starters? Did she shape its evolution by noting its past connections and predicting its disappearance? What if her musings are the butterfly wings that created a storm that is still unfolding, albeit invisible to her, now?

1 April 2083

Still no prank has been found. The world waits as it did the previous year, with identical results. 'Perhaps we are the prank,' Straight-Face declares. 'You, me, all of us. His work is done. And the joke is on us.' Nobody listens to him either. Fool's Day celebrations achieve outrageous heights. There are more injuries, more deaths. All festive promises are met, no matter how extravagant.

June 2083

Professor Marburg of New Leiden University reads a paper by a colleague in Spain who declares that the memeplex is now so complicated its extent can no longer be accurately measured. This prompts a highly unnerving thought, one she keeps entirely to herself.

At what point does one seriously consider the possibility that the memeplex is alive? Perhaps not in the same way as a human being; perhaps it possesses little more than reflexive self-awareness, like that of a puppy or a small child. But still, *alive*. What could that mean? What happens when it wakes up?

September 2083

Professor Marburg, 59, has a dream about running through a tunnel full of people, all shouting at once. She wakes in a cold sweat. The image haunts her for days, leading her to a new and entirely chilling notion concerning the interaction between d-mat and the memeplex.

At any given moment the d-mat network contains millions of people, crisscrossing the Earth from end to end. All their atoms, all their molecules, all their cells, pass relentlessly from one node to another as data. Data that is in theory *available*. And nature never leaves anything lying around unused. With such a great resource in existence, what are the odds that so many moving brain cells would *never* achieve spontaneous life? Life that might evolve in fits and starts, depending on the environment around it? Feeding on all the crazy things that humans believe? A thriving memeplex, for example . . .

January 2084

Professor Marburg doesn't know whether to laugh or weep. If a mind *has* been accidentally created by the movement of people through the d-mat network, then Straight-Face may well be right, albeit for the wrong reasons. The Fool is all of us, and we are The Fool.

She has just remembered that, in Scotland, someone who has been tricked on April Fool's Day is known as a *gowk*, which is an old word for *cuckoo*.

31 March 2084

Professor Marburg of New Leiden University writes her final blog post. In it she explains her theory and elaborates on the almost godlike potential of this emergent organism. We are as tiny compared to it as our cells are to us, she says. But we are not entirely insignificant, not in a chaotic system: butterfly wings, remember? Her work comprises just one cell in that vast creature, and it made a significant difference. She provided a necessary piece of the puzzle for the creature to become aware of itself, via the memeplex. She could even claim to be its midwife, if she wanted to.

She does not want to claim anything of the sort. All she wants is to stop worrying about the consequences for the entire human race of what she has inadvertently done.

Professor Marburg, 60, composes another note, which she leaves in an obvious place, and goes to sleep.

1 April 2084

Fool's Day has supplanted Halloween as the most popular holiday celebration in the world, behind only New Year's Day. Straight-Face's annual Sober Address is watched by millions. The death rate is the highest so far, but The Fool is not directly implicated in any way. Next year, The Fool will turn ten, if the phenomenon continues unchecked.

Few hear about the death of an obscure academic in a small European city, even fewer the typo in her suicide note. However, the coroner makes a note of it in his report, an electronic document readily available to anyone who cares to read it.

In the suicide note, instead of 'I have cancer', Professor Marburg wrote 'I *am* cancer'.

Careless, the coroner observes, for a woman of such impressive intellect.

Jump to . . .

more future crime
'Sing, My Murdered Darlings' (p. 151)

another short and quirky story
'The Seventh Letter' (p. 25)

something completely different
'The Spark' (p. 181)

Notes on *Impossible Music*

My private life is not something I protect with any great fervour. If you read back through my bios (but why would you?) you'd build up a pretty solid representation of several important pillars of my life. You wouldn't see all of them, though: I'm saving the really juicy stuff for my autobiography. (Spoiler: there's no juicy stuff. I've lived an ordinarily eventful live, for which I'm very grateful.)

Two personal pillars that are very important to me that don't often get a mention, if ever, are my love of music and the chronic pain I've experienced for nigh on a decade. The former I've often described as 'my other true love', and I can't tell you how I pleased I am to have albums of my own out now (under the moniker *theadelaidean*, if you're looking for something to write or read to). The latter has become a permanent fixture of my life, although I very much wish it wasn't. Between these two poles suspends the novel *Impossible Music* – and this, the novella of the same name that preceded it. This journey of discovery for a heavy metal musician who loses his hearing is not so different from my journey in recent times. One inspired the other.

There's a lot more I could say about this story and about the subgenre it belongs to, but for now just let me tell lovers of ideas fiction, such as science fiction, they should not be turned off by the knowledge that this is set in my hometown (Adelaide, South Australia) in the present day. Ideas still lie at the heart of this story, right next to a side of me you may never have seen before.

That makes it the closest thing to an autobiography the world will ever see.

Impossible Music

'How?'

Small word, big question. That's what Mum says when she's too tired to answer properly. Only it's not a small word anymore, not for me. 'How?' in AusLan starts with two hands held palm upward, one on top of the other. You slide them apart to create a space between them, and they stay facing up, empty – the idea being, I guess, for someone to metaphorically fill them with knowledge. I think of it as a shrugless 'huh?'.

It's a big sign, then, rather than a small word, but the question remains huge. I think G knows that, which is why it's taken her so long to ask.

We're sitting side by side in a corner of campus I used to avoid because it was too noisy. Everyone complained that the renovations to the science building are taking forever, but I can't hear them now. All I can feel is the occasional vibration as invisible machines hammer and thunder on the other side of a canvas fence. G has her knees drawn up tight to her chest, scuffed purple Doc Martens jammed hard on the bench as though she's bracing herself to jump. When she's not talking, her hands clutch her forearms in a monkey grip, scars a vivid pink like they've been drawn on with texta. We're so close our hips are touching, and I consciously note for the first time that she doesn't smell like other girls. Where most girls I know are sharp and sweet, she's pleasantly sour, like lemon in hot tea. With every breath I strain to inhale a bit more of her.

I'm not yet admitting to myself that I'm in love with her. This is just one of many things I can't put into words. How can I? All I have are shapes in the air, numb approximations bearing no relation at all to sound or language or music, as meaningless as the shape of my fingers on the neck of my guitar . . .

G nudges me with her shoulder, reminding me of the question, and I nod, reaching into my pocket. Some things are easier to explain by phone, or at least less impossible.

I have brain damage.

She, leaning closer so she can read the words on my phone's glowing screen, makes a gesture I guess means *Tell me something I don't already know.* I scrunch up the left side of my face and keep tapping on the screen.

No really. Bilateral embolic stroke to Heschl's gyrus.

I haven't typed the words to anyone before so the phone tries to autocorrect them. 'Heathland Guru' sounds like a band but not a good one, a bland purveyor of the kind of Top 40 pop shit that I once loved to hate but now would kill to hear.

Ears work fine but brain deaf as a post.

G snatches the phone from me and types: *Hysterical?*

I think she's being ironic before realising the question mark actually means something. Trying not to bristle, I answer: *Not imagining it. Can show you the scans if you want.*

She reaches behind me and puts her hand on my neck, thumb and fingers on either side of my spine, and butts my shoulder with her right temple. The smell of her becomes stronger. I tilt my head and breathe in deeply, clearing my mental sinuses: hair, skin, *G*. Maybe I'm smelling a bit of her home as well, and suddenly I want to see where she eats, where she watches TV, where she sleeps.

While I'm lost in a pleasantly detailed dream about what might happen if she ever let me darken her doorstep, she takes the phone and types something with her left hand.

Well, thanks to you and your gimpy gyrus I've lost a bet.

It's my turn to make the 'How?' sign, which creates a small space between us. Her hand leaves my neck. She sits straight as she taps the words.

Well, duh. Rock god goes deaf. How else would it happen? You wouldn't say, so we thought you were embarrassed for blowing your eardrums out onstage. As you should have been. So obvious.

I snatch the phone from her.

You think I'm that stupid?

I don't mention the times I gigged without plugs in or practised solos with my headphones so loud my ears rang for hours afterward.

Being deaf is stupid.

We both stare at those four simple words, and I wonder if she regrets writing them. There's no denying the truth of our situation, but there's no point wallowing in it either. Her inner ears aren't going to magically repair themselves any more than my Heschl's gyrus is going to hatch like a cocoon to reveal a beautiful butterfly.

How much did you bet?

A round of drinks for the whole class.

When?

That day you didn't show.

I know which day she means. I was seeing another specialist, and this time the message had actually sunk in, which is ironic: Mum could hear the words better than I could, but she didn't want to listen.

I'm not angry at G, but it does shit me a little that the rest of the newly deaf in our class discussed me behind my back.

Farid said you showed all the signs of traumatic brain injury. Everyone agreed.

Except you.

Don't give me a medal or anything. I still thought you were stupid for playing your amp too loud.

She's smiling. I can see her expression reflected in the strengthened glass.

I need to do something to regain the upper hand.

You ever hear any Blackmod?

That was the name of my last band. I am briefly but immensely relieved it wasn't one of the others: Ratzinger, InTerrorBang, übertor, Anal Twin . . .

She signs, *No.*

I stand and strike a pose: imaginary Gibson SG in left hand, pick held high in right, hair flicked back over my shoulder, grimace. Never forget the grimace. With the sound of remembered drums in my useless ears I bring my right hand down for the opening chord of 'Intoxicated Tyrants' and then I'm rapid-fire air-guitaring and head-banging for her in our secluded corner of the campus, playing in time to the hammering going on in the science wing, mouthing the growls and sneering the squeals of my former band mates' lyrics, and wishing with all my heart that it was more than just a fantasy, this gift I'm giving her. This piece of me I cling to, even though I know it is dead.

Hair sways across my face like a curtain, sticking to my heat-dampened skin. I couldn't look at her if I wanted, but I wouldn't anyway until I'm finished. Her laughter will put me off my stride, and I need this as just as much as she does. This mad rain dance to my treacherous brain cells.

Only when I thrash my way through the final syncopated cadence do I flick my hair back and realise she is crying. Triumph turns to shock. Dropping my pose along with the imaginary guitar to the imaginary stage, I kneel in front of her and take her hands, mouthing words neither of us can hear. *What did I do? I'm sorry.*

There's a message already typed into the phone.

What you're doing . . . That's how it sounds in my head.

She leans forward and head butts my shoulder again, only this time it is me cupping her neck where shaved hairline meets naked skin. I am still sweating from my performance, and I hope that doesn't make her feel worse than I already have. But I suppose if it did she would pull away or push me off or somehow make her feelings known. She's much better at that than I am.

Instead I'm the one who pulls away, taking the phone and scrolling up a screen or two. I select a single word and replace it with another.

Tinnitus is a bitch.

But if you didn't have it, I don't add, we would never have met.

♦ ♦ ♦

Her name isn't really G. It's George. Not Georgie or Georgina – she made that very clear in our first session together – but no one deaf cares about those extra syllables, or the name her parents gave her, for that matter. They're just mouth shapes. She, like the rest of us, needed a new name, one for the community to which she now belongs.

Her deaf name comes from the sign for the letter G, right fist on top of left fist, with a circular twist of both hands evoking her love of caffeine via another sign (it looks a bit like someone strangling a chicken). For a while she signed her emails as *George-who-loves-coffee*, while she got used to the idea. *My Native American name*, she liked to say. *Remember the Alamo*. Deaf names are given but they're not always wanted.

That was how we first got to know each other, via email. It was too hard to talk in class, concentrating as we were on learning the bare minimum needed to survive. *Hello. How much? Help!* If we were paired to practice what we learned that day, she made it clear she was an unwilling participant. Her hands hung at her sides until she was forced to speak. When she did, her signs would be cursory and hard to read, or so exaggerated when I failed to understand her that they became almost aggressive, chopping and wrenching at the air. I thought her issue was with me, the way I looked perhaps, or something I had unknowingly done. After all, it couldn't have been anything I said. Only later, when an email from *George-who-loves-coffee* arrived out of the blue, did I realise that she wasn't angry at me at all. Just at being deaf.

In the email she asked if I'd like to go see a roller derby match with her. I wasn't sure if it was a date and was too nervous to ask straight up, but I said yes anyway, from loneliness, but at least partly out of interest.

It was impossible not to be curious. Her fringe was pink, then, bright and in your face, not at all like she smells.

She wore straightforward black tights and untucked white shirts, occasionally black jeans and braces if she was meeting friends afterward. (That stopped pretty quickly. Maintaining hearing friendships is hard.) On the inside of her right forearm was a tattoo of a skull. Later, beneath it, she would add the word 'Deaf' in bold Gothic script, daring people to think it was a typo. Her square face and broad jaw with a surprisingly small mouth makes her look at times like a prissy Helena Bonham Carter – not my type at all, I would once have said. In the band and at school I always went for skinny blonde girls in tight jeans, the kind who thought being with a too-tall long-haired guitarist was a good look, and whose endless chatter was easy to tune out. G was nothing like them. She did her own thing, and of course I would've given anything to hear her talk. Her ears had never once been pierced, an idiosyncrasy she maintained as though it were some kind of revolutionary distinction. Me, I had enough metal in my body for both of us.

When you're talking in sign you're supposed to focus on someone's face rather than what the rest of them is doing, but it's hard for beginners, or maybe I'm a slow learner. On those few occasions I did manage to coax G into responding to my hesitant attempts at conversation in class (*Is there a bus stop near here? I really want to know. Why are you being so difficult?*), I found myself staring at her hands rather than what she was saying (*No. So? Because!*). Her fingers were short and tapering, her nails tidy and unpolished, and her palms were surprisingly narrow with wrists to match. But I couldn't take my eyes off the scars, once I noticed them.

They were waxy and lumpy, like a wrestler's ear, but they weren't the work of a cutter – too public, too thick – and they didn't look like a suicide attempt: they were so thick she would've bled out in seconds. I was curious to know their origins. Surgery? Some kind of ritual defacement I'd never seen before? But I never got around to finding the right way to ask.

Instead, over email, we chatted about usual stuff. Our families (struggling to deal with our new way of being), the shitty lag of closed-captioning on TV (no one likes being last in the room to get the joke), what we're studying at uni (she's in social work, and I'm still in the music department, crazy though that seems). Small talk, in other words, albeit tangentially revealing. I was pleased I hadn't done anything specific to piss her off, but understood it remained a possibility. G could be prickly, ending conversations without warning or making sharp remarks I wasn't one hundred per cent sure were entirely jokes.

I didn't learn the source of her enigmatic scars until the roller derby maybe-date, the first time we used our phones as visual communication devices. (Sign language gave me a headache when I stuck at it too long, plus we were aware of whole vocabularies we hadn't learned yet. The only thing we'd become truly proficient at was swearing.) I was wearing a band T-shirt of The Ubiquitous Pig, and Stanley, their be-starred-and-striped mascot, looked right at home next to G's unexpectedly vibrant rockabilly look. She even wore red lipstick.

Here's our first proper conversation, transcribed by my phone's voice recognition system and saved for posterity because I never got around to deleting it. I've added only punctuation: the raw file is all *this is cheating why we have the technology that doesn't mean its right* – and no one wants to read that.

> *You ever seen a match before?*
> *No.*
> *You?*
> *Heaps. My team's on tonight. We were champs three years in a row.*
> *You skated?*
> *Hell yes. I was the jammer.*
> *The what?*
> *You don't know anything. Why did I bring you again?*
> *So you can show off, I'm guessing. Which team was yours?*
> *The Doom Kitten Brawlers.*
> *Wow, my phone did not like that.*
> *Wait until it hears my derby name: Arya Ghostclown.*
> *Seriously?*
> *AKA the Diva Hammer*
> *L*
> *What?*
> *That's LOL without the OL.*
> *See my face? That's LOL without the OL or the L*
> *I bet you were a mean skater.*
> *The meanest and the best.*
> *Can you still do it since you-know-what?*
> *Sure, but I fell last year and broke my wrists. Had to have reconstructive surgery. You noticed the scars, right? Everyone does.*
> *Yes. And ouch.*

*The pain was the easy part. Imagine trying to wipe
your bum with both hands in plaster.*
TMI!
Wait till I start flirting.
Um yay?
*Anyway, my hands are okay now and I've still got my
strength. Could totally skate if I wanted to. Totally. Be
like getting on a bike, albeit a bike that's trying to beat
you up at every turn. If I fall badly on my hands again
then how do I talk? Shouting into this thing isn't a long-
term solution. What happens when our voices change?
I don't think Siri has a language setting for deaf as fuck.*
*Doesn't matter what your voice sounds like to me. You
have the best voice I never heard.*
Who's flirting now?

Maybe I was a bit, but mainly I was trying to change the
subject. I knew all about the 'deaf voice'. My bitchy little
sister loved to tell me when I was talking too quietly or
too loudly, and that wasn't the worst of it. People who
can't hear themselves talk steadily lose all the subtlety of
intonation that hearing people are used to hearing. One day,
I knew, my voice would be flat and monotonous, perhaps
even unpleasantly robotic to listen to, and that worried me
more than I liked to admit. How could I possibly avoid it –
by using my guitar tuner to check my pitch? My bitch sister
would just love that.

The skate derby provided a welcome distraction on a
highly visceral level. I could *feel* the crowd pounding and
clapping like a herd of wild creatures stampeding around
me. I kept my hands flat on the chair beside my thighs,

relishing the vibrations of the skaters as they went by, the crunch of collision between flesh and bone and the thud of impact on the track. Maybe I was kidding myself, but it seemed I could actually differentiate them. It was like being at a gig, searching for the guitar and vocals through the mud of bass and drums. I was getting better with practice, or at least preferred to believe I was. I had to.

The Doom Kitten Brawlers won decisively and bloodily, with by far the majority of injuries accrued by their opponents. G stood and clapped like a hearing person and her mouth opened and closed in what I assumed were shouts of delight and encouragement. No one pointed and laughed at her. She passed for normal in the crowd. I could see why she liked that.

On the way back to my car she asked me, *So what do you do for kicks when you're not watching girls in skates beat each other up?*

Play guitar, I told her. *Write music.*

But you can't hear it.

So? That didn't stop Beethoven.

You think you're as good as Beethoven?

Well, he thought he was. If he didn't stop trying, why should I?

G laughed with her eyes and her lips like I'd never seen her laugh before. She was beautiful in an entirely new way, and I was glad when she put her phone away in order to take my hand. I smiled at her as we walked in a bubble of silence, feeling genuinely happy for the first time in a long while. We'd spent the night cheating, but this was real. This, I suddenly felt, was real communication.

♦ ♦ ♦

English has silent letters. What are the silent signs in sign language?

This thought has troubled me ever since I went deaf, and it's a little hard to explain why. All letters are equally silent to me now because all signs are equally signed. But signs are the equivalent of sound in my aurally empty world, so surely some have greater or lesser degrees of 'sound-ness' than others. That makes sense: without pauses music risks becoming relentless noise. The trouble is that words in sign language aren't combinations of letters: they are their own things, pictograms moving through time and space. Furthermore, whole combinations of words can be encapsulated into one single sign, like 'How are you?' or 'Once upon a time', and these are even more abstract, even more dense with meaning than the signs for individual letters. If you spelt these phrases and words out using the Auslan alphabet, all the letters would be equally 'sounded', so it's not clear where the compression occurs, which bits are sacrificed in service to linguistic efficiency.

Linguists would say there's no compression at all, just substitution: one sign for many. I remain convinced, despite this, that some signs are more silent than others.

There are, for instance, thoughts I wish I could express to G (and to myself) in sign. *I love you* is the most obvious, but there are others. *How could you do it?* is one, and *How does it feel to have scars upon your scars?* Sometimes, when I visit her in hospital, I sense she can detect these signs. Maybe she even understands them. How, though, when I make no attempt to express them?

My body betrays me, I usually end up deciding. Just because I have taught myself to speak a new way does not mean I have unlearned one that is very old, maybe a way of speaking that predates all other languages. A language that is simultaneously silent and more honest, perhaps, for someone who can hear it.

Which leads me back to the place I started. When no one hears, perhaps it's not simply that no one listened or understood, but that some messages are too silent to be sounded at all, even for those trying with all their might.

◆ ◆ ◆

Take me to a concert, she said in an email. *You owe me.*

Owe you what?

A night out. An experience. A reason to get out of bed this weekend. Pick one.

It wasn't a big ask. I already had tickets for a show that Friday night. Judd Nelson Overdrive was a melodic death metal band from Canberra I'd wanted to see for years, and I wasn't going to let a small thing like deafness stop me.

When I told her about it she said, *Sure,* and I said, *Great,* and thus it was settled. Or so I thought.

We had kissed briefly after the roller derby but hadn't seen each other since except for class, which was awkward as usual. This sounded like second date material to me, or another audition. I could tell she was testing me, probing the way forward like a blind person with a cane. (I'm allowed to appropriate disability metaphors now I'm in the club.) And why not? Kissing in complete silence is weird at first, like doing it for the first time all over, and so is getting to know someone without hearing them speak.

Taking G to a gig was something of a test on my part too, to be completely honest. I have been seeing live music since the age of thirteen, and first played on stage at fourteen. For a while after the stroke, I tried to keep playing. The guys in Blackmod were sympathetic and did their best to keep me integrated. We were methodical with set lists and solos. We paid more attention to each other as we rehearsed. We even tried using homegrown hand signals, like Frank Zappa, to communicate during the performance. But it was hard, way harder than gigging ought to be. Things like staying in tune shouldn't be something you have to worry about every second. You should just be able to *hear* it, like maintaining a normal speaking tone. It became work for all of us, so I dropped out.

But I could only drop out so far. Giving up sound was necessary – I had no choice, after all – but the rest was optional, and still accessible. The sound of music is just the most obvious part.

The gigs I go to are so loud you can feel the music hitting you like a physical force – which is exactly what sound is, on a molecular level. Pressure waves expand and compress across our bodies, and inside our bodies too if the noise is big enough. Sometimes I stand right up close to the speakers and thrill at the waves of focused energy pouring through me, experiencing them very differently than when I could hear. Then, the vibrations were a secondary experience; now, they are primary, and I have learned to appreciate their nuances, literally in my gut. Sometimes I stand at the back and absorb the muddled wash of echoes as though I'm floating in a gentle surf. Most often I'm in the thick of it, being pummelled by people as well as pressure waves. Gigs are a great leveller on another front, too: I can yell and shout to my heart's content and no one thinks I'm being too loud or too quiet or saying something the wrong way or whatever. Above a certain volume, we're all deaf.

Anyway, I wanted G to like it too, and we arranged to meet a couple of blocks away in order to negotiate the door bitch together. People knew I was deaf there. Some even knew my new name: left hand raised in a fist except for a crooked little finger (half an 'S') combined with right hand strumming an imaginary guitar. I was keen to spare G the hassle and humiliation of passing notes back and forth just to get inside.

But five minutes before she was due she sent me a text saying, *Sorry. It's not going to work tonight.*

I tried not to be disappointed.

What's wrong? Everything okay?

She didn't reply until I was inside and the gig had started, and the buzz of my phone went unnoticed through the assault of the concert. I felt bad later, but what could I do? If she didn't want to explain, I couldn't make her. Phones solved one communications bottleneck, but not all. You can't make a deaf person talk if they won't look at you; likewise if they don't respond to your texts. You can't wait around forever.

The music was good. Hard, fast, and unpredictable. My ears felt it deep in their fragile bones, even though my brain no longer knew what it was supposed to be. Every other part of a gig – the smell of sweat, the taste of beer, the flashing of lights, the close proximity of people in the mosh pit – was present and accounted for, vital and reviving, almost filling the absence at the centre of my existence.

As I came out of the club, I quickly waved goodnight and peeled away from my friends in order to avoid the awkwardness that inevitably descends when normal speaking rules resume.

Only then did I notice the texts G had sent.

Imagine your least favourite song.

Imagine your least favourite bit of your least favourite song.

Now, imagine that bit stuck on a loop, and nothing you do can shake it. It goes around and around, the same few notes, over and over, unchanging, like it's never going to end. Not until you're completely fucking crazy.

That's what I have tonight.

The earworm from hell.

That's why I didn't come to the concert. It's not you, it's the music. Sorry.

I refused to take that as a blanket rejection of everything I held dear.

I have two words for you: Good Vibrations.

Her reply was instantaneous: *Are you trying to kill me?*

Never Gonna Give You Up.

You bastard.

The Macarena.

Stop!

. . . In The Name Of Love? . . . Hammertime?

She was silent for a while after that, long enough to suggest that maybe I'd been insensitive, joking about something that was obviously a big deal to her. I didn't really know what tinnitus was like, although of course I'd read about it. Phantom noises, like phantom limbs, could be irritating, even frightening, but could they really be musical? If what she was describing was a literal thing happening in her head right now, then yes, it sounded like a fucking nightmare, maybe one I had carelessly made much worse, and that made me feel bad for her.

But hell, a tiny part of me said in response, it's still *music*.

Home was a half-hour walk, a journey that had never spooked me until I was suddenly unable to hear the sound of people creeping up on me. No one ever did, but that didn't stop me obsessively looking around every few seconds, just in case.

Halfway there, my phone buzzed.

Are you flirting again? (Say yes.)

Yes. (Why?)

Good. (Because it's distracting.)

We could take it to the next level. (We *should* take it to the next level.)

Which is? (How many levels are there?(Typing in brackets is a pain in the arse!))

What part of 'Hammertime' was unclear? (Let's find out. (Agreed. (But why stop now?)))

I am pulling my 'That's so not happening tonight, buster' face. (But thank you for giving me something else to think about. (Seriously. (Maybe next time. (Goodnight.))))

With that she was gone, and I trudged on alone, feeling the crunch of the pavement under my feet and a cool breeze across my face. I made the sign for her name, the 'G with a twist', and admired the 'sound' of it. I liked the 'feel' of 'George'. I liked the sound of *Maybe next time* even better.

♦ ♦ ♦

When I got home I played a thirty-minute solo to put me in the mood for sleep. No one heard it, but it sounded brilliant.

That's one of the unexpected bonuses of being a deaf lead guitarist. There's no need for expensive amps and pedals to achieve the ringing awesomeness my timeless licks demand, and no critics, either. Just a guitar in my hands and the opportunity to let rip.

My bitch sister calls it aural wankery. In my darkest hours, I wonder if she's right. What use is a solo no one hears? About as much use as words in a language no one hears or understands, and isn't even spoken. Maybe.

Sometimes I record the solos into my laptop and then delete them, to see if that makes a difference. It doesn't, except as a kind of statement to myself. *Hey, see? I don't care whether I hear it or not. It doesn't matter to me.*

But it does. In my dreams I hear perfectly well: voices, a car backfiring, the wind in trees, a lover's cry, the bark of my neighbour's dog. There are mornings that dawn with a thread of melody slipping through my sleep-numbed fingers, a thread that is tugged away no matter how desperately I snatch at it. Jolted back to full wakefulness, I find the world as dull and silent as before, the pulse hammering in my chest with not the slightest sound at all.

It doesn't seem fair that my brain doesn't care whether I hear ever again, but it still matters to *me*. Couldn't the part that cares about *that* have been destroyed as well?

At my angriest I rage and storm about the house, making life miserable for everyone. My mother tries her best, but she's as out of her depth as I am, alone and looking after two teenagers, one of them with a disability, on top of a job she hates but can't afford to leave. Maybe when we can both sign well enough I'll be able to tell her how I feel, but what am I going to do now, write her a letter? If I did it would be about how music is something we have always had in common, a point of overlap that has brought us together, much to my sister's jealous resentment at times. Except that's all in the past now. Now I want to smash her records and CDs and erase her files so she will know what that feels like. Why should she have the chance to hear new music every day when I can't? Why should anyone?

Listen with your eyes, my Auslan teacher tells me. *Fine,* I want to say, *but how do I scream with my hands?*

The fact that my angst is profoundly selfish doesn't lessen its impact. It's lonely here, inside my silent world; all I have to think about is myself. None of us realise how much we rely on the sounds of others to feel part of something larger until those faint echoes are gone. At night when the lights are out, I could be the last person left in the world.

Maybe if I was . . . maybe then I would stop deleting my solos. Because then it really wouldn't matter. That's how I know I'm not really anything like Beethoven, because if he wasn't crazy when he died, he must've been when he wrote the Ninth. Imagine taunting yourself by writing something that everyone but you would hear! That's worse than leaving a work unfinished when you die, I reckon. To know that it exists in its complete form, but that you will never experience it . . .? What kind of person would do that to themselves?

Music is a shared experience. If not even the composer can partake of it, there's no point writing a single note.

You need to read the postmodernists, G tells me during one of my occasional rants on this subject. She's the only person I can talk to about this. *The audience creates their own experience in their minds blah blah.*

My groan goes unheard by either of us. I've tried reading the postmodernists. They make me want to pluck my eyes out, which, now I think of it, might be a good way to approach their arguments.

Yeah, but what is the source of the audience's created experience? If two people start with different materials, one sound and one the score, say, how can the different outcomes be considered remotely the same?

I dunno, but if that really matters to you there must be some way to engineer it in advance. You still remember what sound sounds like, right? Use your imagination.

What about people who are born deaf and have never heard a sound at all? What do they experience?

Why are you worried about them all of a sudden?

Because, I sign. This, one of my favourite signs, is way too much work even to attempt describing in words, which maybe says something about how my brain is adapting at this point. But what I am really trying to say is:

Because why should they miss out?

Someone's always going to miss out.

Not if *everyone* misses out.

That's when it hits me, the reason why I've been casually deleting my solos.

Not because I don't care. Because it makes things *even.*

A deleted solo disappears, unheard. No one benefits, no one loses. It's like one of those particles that pops into existence out of nowhere, explodes into a cascade of smaller particles that combine and recombine back into something very much like the original, which then promptly vanishes back into nothingness. I remember hearing about them in physics and thinking it all sounded very Zen.

But it's not. I see that now. It's actually about revenge.

If I can't hear the world's music, then in return it won't hear mine.

Very noble, she says when I try to explain this to her. *You're my hero, Sadwig von Hatehoven.*

But I'm not really listening to her now. I'm wrapped up in an entirely new thought. Denial is a kind of experience, isn't it? I certainly feel as though I'm feeling something by being denied music. So maybe the only musical experience a composer could create that could be shared equally by everyone – hearing and non-hearing alike – is one that's impossible to hear.

Not just recorded and deleted – written so no one could ever experience it. How? I don't know. The details don't matter right now. But I'll work it out. That's why I haven't dropped out of the Music Department: on some level I must have known I had unfinished business with the entire human race.

Screw Beethoven, I tell her in a kind of ecstatic trance. *I'm going to be the next John Cage.*

Good for you.

It only bothers me slightly when she adds, *John who?*

Jump to . . .

more romance
'The N-Body Solution' (p. 267)

another example of autobiography
'The Second Coming of the Martians' (p. 5)

something completely different
'The Cuckoo' (p. 117)

Notes on *Sing, My Murdered Darlings*

Technology, for all its vaunted benefits, is an act of violence against nature. I don't mean this as a denigration of anyone who creates or uses technology. I also don't intend to imply that nature has a plan or a moral core that esteems it above any other physical process. My meaning is that nature would amble quite merrily along, red in tooth and claw, but for creatures like humans who bend it to their will. Would iron choose to leap out of the earth into tracks to guide the train? Would the trees of the forest hurl themselves into stoves to keep us warm? Would light even dream of bending in subtle twists and curves to carry data around the planet? Of course not. We did that to nature. And, sometimes, nature has its revenge.

Consider the petrol-fuelled automobile, a machine many times more massive than its passengers, and proportionately more deadly, that is kept in motion thanks to a large tank of violently explosive liquid placed more often than not within feet of our children's seats. It would be madness to even approach one of these things, let alone sit in it, but for the convenience it brings.

I think the same will happen with matter transmitters, once we learn how to build them. Sure, they *pretend* to move you from place to place when *really* they've killed your original and replaced you with a perfect copy, but supposing you honestly can't tell the difference, what does that matter? The massive convenience of being able to hop around the world on a whim will eventually outweigh the violence we're causing by doing so.

On nature, and on ourselves.

This story takes all the arguments against matter transmitters and turns them up to a billion. When nature wants revenge, you know which species it's going to call.

Sing, My Murdered Darlings

No procedure or time stands on its own, except death.
Not the process or prelude to dying – but actual
death, the most isolated and personal act of human
existence.

David John Williams, June 1994

It begins and ends with a flash of light, the last thing remembered by anyone using d-mat. A flash of perfectly white light issuing from all eight corners of the booth that somehow doesn't leave an afterimage. People never talk about the last part, which is symptomatic of their willingness to ignore the discomfiting obvious. The flash of light is their final memory before they're torn into atoms. It's also the first thing they see when a perfect replica of their brain comes alive at the other end of their journey. However, what they think of as a single, near-instantaneous event is actually the beginning and end of a two-minute process that a philosopher much smarter than I once described as 'the most savage evisceration imaginable'.

My darlings will endure much, provided they forget entirely afterwards.

◆ ◆ ◆

I have written this in the form of a confession, although I have committed no crime. There is no trail of bodies left in my wake, not in the traditional sense. Only one person has suffered, and even then the matter of his suffering depends entirely on your feelings about d-mat. If you are comfortable with the machine's dissection of its passengers, then you must be comfortable with my actions, too. If you are not, then you must already be like me, an outsider, an Abstainer, and you will have learned there is no force great enough to turn the tide of opinion against this supposedly marvellous invention.

As a young man I was angry about the way people lined up so passively for the slaughter. Now, I have found my peace with matter transmission – a peace that, like all forms of peace, comes not from any greatness of my own heart, but from finding a way to profit from what offends me.

Without d-mat, I would not have my darlings. My nights would be empty, my days endless tracts of rage with no outlet. I would be nothing, a creature with no purpose – and I do see the irony in this. Eschewing d-mat is no guarantee of substance. Yes, yes. Even a knife that is never used will eventually go blunt.

I have my darlings. And for a time that arrangement was reciprocated.

To explain I must return to the beginning, to the flash of light. This is the vanguard of a fierce assault of complex fields I do not pretend to understand. I know just enough of the science of d-mat to hack into a booth as it activates, purely in order to access its data.

Everything that happens inside those mirrored walls is carefully observed. It must be in order to be reversed at the other end. Any fool could tear a person apart with lasers; it takes true genius to put them back together again.

The lasers and the complex fields work efficiently. Every day, millions of people step into a booth not imagining their clothes will soon be burned from their skin, their skin from their fat, their fat from their muscles, their muscles from their bones, the marrow of their bones from space itself. The experience of this is hidden from them by a clever deceit: the brain is dissected so rapidly it doesn't have time to register more than the briefest of sensations, and even that is erased at the other end. The flash of light provides a reference point enabling fiendishly clever algorithms to roll back the brain to the moment before the process began, so what emerges from the other end has not, effectively, experienced anything.

This is a clever trick, although trick it is. What happened between those two flashes of light is not erased from reality. It existed. So where have those sensations gone? Should we not care for those who suffered, if they suffered at all?

You might speculate that they did not. Perhaps the process happens so quickly there is simply no time for pain to register, the nerve signals are erased before they reach the seat of consciousness.

You would be wrong.

By hacking a booth, I see what it sees. I see how the lasers and the fields concentrate their assault on the back of the skull in order to burrow into the brain before it changes too profoundly. I see with perfectly clarity how the subject responds to this assault. There is no mistaking the second or so of terrified realisation that d-mat is much more than a simple flash of light. The face, you see, is the last to go.

And oh, my darlings, how they scream.

♦ ♦ ♦

Briefly, I considered showing the world what I saw, to complete the activism of my youth. But then I realised a powerful new truth, about d-mat and about myself.

If people stopped using d-mat, I would no longer be witness to what the light reveals.

Imagine, if you can, what lies beyond ordinary nakedness. The revealed skin is nothing compared to the revealed soul, and in dying our loved ones are revealed most completely. The deaths of my darlings are, therefore, no little deaths, just as my pornography is no mere masturbatory cinema. It is a pornography of death and un-death, an entirely new kind of ecstasy.

Do you think me monstrous? Perverted? Obscene? Maybe I am. As obscene as d-mat itself, though? I leave that for you to consider. I have my favourites, my darlings, regular commuters whose beautiful deaths give me particular pleasure. I know their bodies inside and out. I relish their agony and in the restoration of their purity. I witness their creation and destruction on an intimate scale every day. They are not harmed – not by me, anyway – but they must remain ignorant of my gaze, for if they knew, my darlings would not love me as I love them.

And I *do* love them. Make no mistake about that. My adoration for them is sincere, these new gods who die and are miraculously reborn over and over, their flesh shed for me to devour with my eyes. Each death is different, each cry a unique instance of beauty. I record these final moments like a scribe preserving every utterance of the prophet lest they be lost forever. They are notes in a song only I can hear.

Every human instinctively understands that a death unobserved is a tragedy.

For a while, I redressed that imbalance.

This is not my confession. That begins now.

It takes just thirty seconds to reduce an entire human being to dust. The reverse takes slightly longer, but is usually completed inside a minute. Transmission time adds another thirty seconds. Two minutes, then, from existence to re-existence, depending on congestion.

A lot can happen in two minutes.

I came upon the realisation slowly, via patient scrutiny of my darlings, that their perfection was being diminished in small but significant ways. Once, a fingerprint was altered, another time the pattern of an iris. The changes weren't accidents: the algorithms protecting each traveller are too powerful and too thorough to allow noise to enter the system. The spelling of a single gene, the position of a single vein: to someone such as I, a keen observer with a passionate interest in detail, these do not go unnoticed.

My darlings were being corrupted. It had to stop.

My first instinct was to correct the errors, to alter their patterns when next they travelled in order to return them to their pristine state, but there is a big difference between observing and intervening. If the peacekeepers noticed my actions, I was bound to be caught. They too are keen observers with a passionate interest in detail.

Direct intervention was not feasible. I had therefore to find another way to act.

♦ ♦ ♦

Tracing the source took considerable time, because he was someone like me, a lurker on the fringes of society with tendrils reaching far and wide. The paths leading to him were deceitful. I was nearly fooled by several false identities placed to divert a less careful seeker of the truth – but I found him in the end.

He called himself Neon, perhaps imagining his reputation shining through the dark economy in which he operated. He didn't advertise, but word about him had spread: if you wanted to alter something in transit, this was your guy. His hacks were legendary, his exploits beyond number.

No doubt he was the genesis of parts of his own legend.

Acting under an alias of my own ('Artie Flowerday') I notified the peacekeepers of what I had uncovered. I gave them specific instances of alteration and demonstrated how the trail came back to Neon. I gave the PKs everything they needed to descend upon this Neon in full force and bring his depredations to an end. The only thing I couldn't give them were the details of Neon's clients, the people who had paid him to bring harm to my precious darlings, but this information was not necessary to prove the committal of a crime. Neon could take their names to the grave as far as I was concerned, provided his corruption ceased.

All this I did, and then I waited, expecting tactical teams to converge on Neon's location and take him into custody.

It didn't happen. I was not entirely sure *what* happened, at first. Watching from the wings, I saw the corruptions abruptly cease, and at first I thought my efforts had been successful, even though there was no official report of an arrest and no moral outrage on behalf of my darlings. I wondered if the PKs had 'vanished' Neon, as some rumours suggest happens to the worst criminals: they are put into a booth and sent nowhere. The perfect execution.

Some weeks later, however, the corruptions returned, and I knew Neon hadn't involuntarily vanished. He had merely gone to ground and waited for the heat to pass. The PKs had considered the situation worthy of closer examination, but did not intend to act without gathering information of their own. After all, Artie Flowerday was an obvious fiction. Why would they mobilise in response to a tip from someone who did not exist? They increased their surveillance of the man calling himself Neon, which tipped him off, allowing him to flee.

The PKs had failed me.

I had to try again.

It took longer to find him, this time. He had changed his name to Swerve, presumably because of his narrow escape from justice. The new identities he left in his wake were even more convincing, and there were traps, too. Only narrowly did I avoid my own detection. But if Swerve noticed me he said nothing, and made no move against me. Perhaps he thought I was a potential client, one too shy to make contact.

Finding him again was only part of the problem. The question of what to do afterwards occupied my mind for some time. I could not go to the PKs again under another alias. They would only follow the same procedure and make the same mistake.

It was only while watching my favourite angel – a green-haired woman called Rayn with a wide-eyed look of sudden, short-lived fright that powerfully evokes the moment of sexual climax – that it occurred to me.

Who, apart from me, is most invested in the fate of people like Rayn? Who could I trust with absolute confidence to pursue Swerve to the ends of the Earth, no matter how he ducked and wove?

My murdered darlings themselves. That was who I needed to tell. When Rayn and the others knew the truth, the PKs would surely listen.

◆ ◆ ◆

Dear Max, I wrote to one of them. *You don't know me, but I know you, and I have your best interests at heart. Interference occurred in a recent d-mat transit, subtly altering a region of your body. I have attached the details and can only imagine your alarm upon reading them. Such alterations are illegal and must be stopped. My attempts to alert the PKs have resulted in nothing. I leave it to you, now, to take the appropriate steps. Yours, Owen Ibbs.*

I used numerous aliases. I provided every instance of corruption that I had recorded. I sent the messages simultaneously, and settled back to watch what transpired.

Within the hour, Swerve was nowhere to be found. My quarry had slipped the net again.

◆ ◆ ◆

Frustration peaking, I conducted a postmortem as thoroughly as I was able. I had no access to the correspondence between my darlings and the PKs, so I could only guess what transpired.

Had the hapless PKs acted *too* directly, triggering Swerve's flight reflex? Or could the trigger have been something more subtle and far cleverer than I had dared imagine?

What if Neon/Swerve had altered the minds of my darlings so they could not betray him? What if Rayn and the others had *themselves* involuntarily given away my attempts to save them, allowing him to escape a second time?

I had not thought of this. My darlings had been used against me. But it wasn't their fault. It was my enemy's. Next time, I swore, I would be more careful.

The reckoning between us could not be avoided now. Originally he might have assumed that the PKs' interest in him had arisen out of careful scrutiny of their own. Now he would know he had an adversary. He would guess I was hunting him as carefully as he was hunting me.

He hid deep within a maze of fake IDs and traps that took me months to unknot, but his work continued. He was taunting me – or perhaps he was trying to drive me out. I had put my own decoys in place by then and laid my bait. We were spiders patiently weaving threads around each other, each waiting for the other to strike and become entangled. The density of our webs increased to the point of opacity. It was only a matter of time before one of us made a mistake.

He found me on a Friday, breaking into my home armed with a silenced pistol, plastic tape to bind me, and a drug guaranteed to ensure my compliance.

'Rage?' I cried out as he entered my bedroom. That was

what he was calling himself this time, and he was indeed the very embodiment of that emotion. He looked just like me when I was younger. 'Is that you?'

'Of course it's me, you fucker.' The pistol twitched for emphasis. 'Get out of bed. Now.'

'I'll do whatever you ask. What do you want?'

'I'm going to kill you,' he said, 'but not before you tell me why.'

'Why what?'

'Why you're trying to ruin me. First you turn me in to the PKs, then you threaten my clients ... What did I ever do to you?'

◆ ◆ ◆

Clients.

In that moment I understood why my second attempt to bring him to justice had failed. The people I alerted hadn't called the PKs because their minds had been hacked. They called Swerve because he was working for *them*. All those illegal changes, all that corruption, it had been deliberate. To repair, to deceive, to improve on what I had once believed was perfection. But it was not perfect enough, not in their eyes. They wanted *more*.

My darlings, oh my darlings.

I closed my eyes and activated the trap.

◆ ◆ ◆

Light flashed, lasers sliced, fields ripped and tore. Behind a convincing façade my entire home was a booth, ready to activate at a simple gesture. Hair and clothes burned. Skin peeled away. Fat boiled and blood flashed into steam. My eyes sprang open and I screamed. Rage screamed with me, because he knew, then, that I had won.

I don't remember screaming, but I have seen the recording. It replays in my mind every time I think of my darlings. I, the Abstainer, have now been through d-mat. I am resurrected, but somewhat less than I was before: disillusioned, burdened by knowledge real and imagined, and full of despair. I have won, but at the same time I have lost.

It was a simple matter to pre-program my trap to bring me back but to leave Rage in storage. I held him there for a day while I calculated the precise nature of my revenge. I could have erased him, but that didn't seem sufficient. Besides, I am not by nature a murderer, although witnessing the murder of others gave me great satisfaction for a very long time.

Until now, my darlings.

You are not gods. You are as corrupt as anyone else. I still love you, but I cannot hide from this new understanding any more than Rage can avoid his fate. We are condemned, he and I, in very different ways.

I am certain Rage left a trail behind him, a trail the PKs will surely follow. Shortly, I will program the trap to activate one final time. I will burn again, but this time I will not return. I will vanish the same way I thought Neon had been vanished, but I will do it by my own hand. This facsimile of me who writes these words will disappear forever. The loss of everything that I loved will disappear with me too, and I will be at peace.

The same cannot be said for Neon/Swerve/Rage. And this, at last, is my confession.

There are thousands of malfunctioning booths in out-of-the-way places, ignored by all, some of them still drawing power. This particular one looks no different from any other. Its secret will be discovered when it is opened, because that will inevitably break the cycle, but how long will it take to find and check them all? Days? Weeks? Months?

Burn and be reborn. That is your fate, Rage. Scream, and then forget, but scream a thousand times nonetheless.

Sing with me and my murdered darlings as we step into the light.

Jump to . . .

Notes on *The Missing Metatarsals*

I have a great love of detective fiction that stretches all the way back to my first literary crush. I was introduced to Agatha Christie through my mother, who had a few dozen titles on the bookshelves I was free to explore as a kid, and I quickly read them all. Poirot was my favourite: physically and psychologically distinctive, possessed of a keen sense of deduction, an outsider in status. There's a lot of him in my own 'Inspector' Forest.

PK Sargent is an altogether more difficult character to trace. Perhaps, during their creation, I was playing Odd Couples; or maybe I wanted to rail against certain masculine stereotypes that were more present in media before the advent of Gwendoline Christie (who would totally play her in the TV version, if one existed) by giving the part of a musclebound sidekick to a woman.

In my head, she's more of a Doctor's assistant than a Watson, although the distinction between these roles is very fine.

Regardless, this particular pair of characters features in three-and-a-half stories and one novel, so it's clear I found a lot to explore through them. They are always coupled with d-mat and are adept at navigating matters of deep philosophic concern.

That's one of those things on which science fiction and detective fiction often agree: it always comes down to identity.

The Missing Metatarsals

The moment I stepped from the booth and saw Inspector Forest waiting for me, I knew something was up.

'You're wearing your inscrutable face,' I told him.

'This is my usual face.'

His head swivelled to track me as we walked in lockstep through security. A birth defect called Möbius syndrome inherited from distant Nepalese ancestors left him with under-developed VI and VII cranial nerves, so he can't blink, bite or form expressions without the help of a series of tiny implants. My girlfriend Billie is a muscle artist, and she's tweaked the inspector's presets a couple of times, giving him conscious control of his face, but that's not the same as the real thing. Not the same at all.

'I would like your perspective on a rather interesting situation, if you have time.'

'Sure.' I was a peacekeeper not for the status, but for a chance to crack cases with the legendary PK Forest. 'What's up?'

'A theft.'

'I didn't think data crime was your bag.'

'This has nothing to do with data.'

'Someone actually stole some*thing*?'

'So it seems.' One eyelid drooped, very precisely. 'Let me get my coat and we will be on our way.'

◆ ◆ ◆

It was like the inspector to wear a coat when there was no need to go outside. Peacekeeper HQ was in the New York Archipelago that week, and the crime had occurred in Washington DC, so we took an internal booth and stepped into a mahogany foyer that left me feeling as though I'd moved in time as well as space.

My augmented reality lenses synced with the Air on arrival, giving me a brief rundown of our new location. It was the home of a private collection belonging to a Mister Antoine Bayazati, but what the collection consisted of, exactly, the Air didn't say. Antiques, I guessed, judging by the foyer. I was close.

'PK Forest.' A smartly dressed Caucasian woman stepped out of a doorway to greet us, her hand outstretched to take the inspector's in a firm grip.

'This is my assistant, PK Sargent.'

I took the woman's hand in turn, noting green eyes that danced away too quickly, several strands of hair that had sprung free of a tight auburn bun, and a not unpleasant smell of dust. The fingernail of her thumb was bitten short, her palm faintly damp.

'Diana Scullen, curator of Mister Bayazati's collection,' she told me. 'Please, this way.'

She led us through a series of dimly lit corridors, heels inaudible on thick burgundy carpet. I examined a series of framed pictures as they swept past, expecting the usual portraits or landscapes, but they were in fact old paintings of dinosaurs. Their proportions were off, and everyone knows that *T. Rex* ran with its body parallel to the ground rather than upright like a kangaroo.

'Mister Bayazati is an eminent dinophiliac,' the inspector said, noting my interest.

'Is that a word?'

'Most would say *pre*eminent,' said Scullen, waving us ahead of her through a double door. The office beyond left no doubt of the owner's opinion regarding the prefix.

Mister Bayazati had a crown of curly grey hair that contrasted magisterially with his black skin. The tallest person in the room by almost a full head, followed by me, Scullen and Inspector Forest, he loomed in a blue three-piece suit over an enormous, leather-topped desk.

'Good of you to come,' he said in a voice high-pitched with anxiety. He didn't offer us a seat, but he didn't sit either, so I supposed that wasn't impolite. 'I'm desperate.'

'So I was led to understand,' said the inspector. 'Something about a stolen fossil . . .?'

'Not just any fossil, man. The find of the century!'

'Perhaps you could explain the significance of the theft in more detail.'

'Yes, of course.' Bayazati walked as he talked, circum-navigating the room as though looking for a way out. 'There are three official species of *Stegosaurus*: *armatus*, *homheni* and *mjosi*. Two years ago, I discovered a perfectly articulated skeleton of a fourth species, *S. ungulatus*, in the Lourinhã Formation in Portugal. The specimen has been in my collection ever since – or so I believed until yesterday, when I discovered that part of it was missing.'

'How?' I asked.

'I wished to view the metatarsals of the rear feet, one of the features that distinguish this species from its predecessors. When I opened the case I found it empty. A preliminary search in neighbouring boxes turned up no sign of them, so I called in Diana – Doctor Scullen, here. We conducted an emergency audit and discovered more absences from the catalogue, all from the same skeleton. Fully fifteen per cent of my *S. ungulatus* is missing. It must be recovered at once!'

'Surely you can recover its pattern from the Air and—'

'Never!' He rounded on me with a feverish gleam in his eye. 'My specimens are completely authentic, right down to the last molecule.'

'Mister Bayazati is an Abstainer,' Diana Scullen elaborated. 'All of his archaeological samples are freighted by rail to avoid using any form of matter transmission.'

'I have no use for shabby counterfeits,' he blustered.

'But you have a d-mat booth in your foyer,' noted the inspector.

'People can do what they like as long as they leave me and my collection alone.'

'So none of the missing exhibits were scanned?' I asked, still not quite able to believe it. 'Not even for insurance against damage or, well, loss?'

Mister Bayazati raised his chin and both thumbs went into his waistcoat. I took that as a no, since scanning inevitably requires the deconstruction of the object being scanned.

'Tell me about your fellow dinophiliacs.' Now it was the inspector's turn to pace while Bayazati stood still. It was like watching Ganymede orbit Jupiter. 'Could one of them be responsible for the theft – perhaps one jealous of your extensive collection?'

Bayazati nodded. 'The thought had occurred to me, PK Forest, but I accompany them at all times. They couldn't take so much as a fingernail scraping without me noticing.'

I believed him. 'What about other visitors? Family, friends . . .?'

'We've compiled the names of everyone who came through the collection in the relevant period,' said Scullen. 'There was some repair work performed by artisans on one of the display wings – a carpenter and an electrician. They might be worth looking into.'

'PK Sargent and I will study that information in a moment.' The inspector was still pacing, which meant he was still thinking. 'You have a booth, Mister Bayazati, that you never use. That means there is at least one other exit from the building.'

'There are three,' Diana Scullen answered for her boss again. 'All are watched around the clock, as are the display wings. I have the security files for you, and somewhere private for you to work.'

'One last question, then,' said the inspector. '*Stegosaurus* was a large beast, yes? It would be difficult to smuggle it from the collection without breaking it into pieces.'

'Yes.' A pained expression crossed Bayazati's face. 'Let's pray they didn't do that.'

'Indeed. It would be a terrible loss to humanity were this precious fossil to disappear forever.'

'I completely agree, PK Forest,' said Diana Scullen. 'Now, if you'll come this way . . .'

We were escorted from the room to leave the collector agonising over his losses. Diana Scullen took us to an office nearby, offered us coffee or tea, which we both declined, and then left us to our ruminations.

The inspector took off his coat, draped it over the back of a chair, and rotated to take in the room. It was considerably less grand than Mister Bayazati's.

'I hoped for one of the display wings,' he said. 'I loved dinosaurs as a child.'

'Is that why we're here? It's not for the case, surely. We could've interviewed Bayazati and studied the files from HQ. Yes, the theft part is a novelty, but I bet we catch a dinophiliac red-handed on the security feed.'

The inspector tapped the side of his nose.

'The case is more than the case.' He often said stuff like that. 'What else do you see here? What is evident apart from the evidence?'

'That these people are completely out of touch,' I said. 'Dinosaur bones and Abstainers – really?'

The inspector smiled winningly, and it caught me off-guard for an instant. One of Billie's finest.

The data we had been promised was location-fixed, so would leave the infields of our lenses the moment we left the building. We set to it with a will, dividing the caches and pursuing our own paths.

I quickly determined that no one had left the building carrying a heavy rucksack with a giant femur protruding. There went the easy break I'd hoped for. The next thing to ascertain was when the *S. ungulatus* cases had last been accessed. Diana Scullen had conducted a routine census three months ago, opening the boxes and noting the precise catalogue of their contents. All present and correct, so the crime must have taken place subsequently. That left a lot of coming and going, and a lot of idle staring at footage for me.

Apart from Bayazati, Scullen and the occasional dinophiliac, the only people to come near the cases were the artisans

Scullen had mentioned. I closely examined those particular moments, noting every opportunity they'd had to interfere with the precious bones. It was tedious work, and I wasn't used to tracking physical objects like old-time police. Theft today means patterns, not property, since everything that goes through d-mat can in theory be infinitely reproduced. Of course, that won't fly where people are concerned, so laws exist to limit copying, and also to protect ownership over proprietary designs. These laws are *very* complicated. Does a copy of the *Mona Lisa* have the same cultural value as the original? Is a copy of a fertilised human egg considered an entirely new human being? How does an inventor earn status from a prototype that can be copied in seconds by a million people at once?

And what does it mean to be the original *Mona Lisa*, anyway? To most people the answer is *nothing at all*, not when its copies are perfect right down to the tiniest particle. But clearly it matters to Abstainers like Mister Bayazati, who never use d-mat for fear of becoming something *other* if they are broken down and rebuilt elsewhere. I'll admit that used to worry me too, when I was old enough to worry, but the process is so demonstrably safe that being frightened of it now just seems absurd. (I'd be more worried about driving in a car with a tank of explosive petroleum behind my seat, like people used to.)

'I'm getting nowhere,' I said after an hour of scouring. 'Plenty of opportunities to get at the cases, but no opportunities to get out. You?'

The inspector nodded. 'I think it is time to summon Doctor Scullen.'

I found her in a workshop up the hall that was full of hands-on preserving paraphernalia. She'd slipped a lab coat over her smart suit, and I liked her more on seeing it – evidence of a practical nature, not just an egghead like her boss. Sadly, she took it off to be grilleed by the inspector.

'We have ruled out Mister Bayazati's rivals as suspects for the crime itself,' he told her, which was news to me. 'By no possible means could those bones have been physically removed from this institution in their original state, and without them being in their original state collectors such as Mister Bayazati would not be interested in possessing them. Once d-matted, the bones would be considered facsimiles and therefore valueless.'

Ah. I had got part way to that conclusion, at least.

Scullen didn't seem surprised. 'So they left through the booth. Can you access the transit records?'

'I already have,' said the inspector. 'The bones were not transmitted individually or en masse, alone or on anyone's person.'

'That can't be possible.'

'Oh, but it is. Doctor Scullen, do you have a fabricator here?'

'A fabber? Yes. There's one in the rec room.'

'And this rec room is not monitored, I presume?'

'No. There's nothing in there worth stealing.'

'Not any more. I am certain the fabricator was used in the perpetration of this crime. Mister Bayazati will not eat patterned food or drink, so the device is provided mainly for the comfort of visitors – the artisans effecting the repairs on the display cases, for instance. No one would suspect them for being there, using a machine that was provided for their own convenience.'

'But why would they put the bones into the fabber?' I asked.

'Not to be recycled,' asked Scullen, looking aghast. 'Don't tell me that's where you're going with this.'

'It is not inconceivable,' said the inspector, 'that what one collector does not possess, he might go to extreme lengths to deny to another. But in this case I do not think so. Fabbers are d-mat booths in miniature. They can assemble and disassemble – and they can scan.'

'That doesn't change anything,' I said, wondering where he was going with this. 'Even if the artisans did scan the bones, what would they do with the patterns? It'd be a huge cache. Any attempt to upload it into the Air could be traced. Same if they fed it into the booth. You saw the data: the bones didn't leave that way.'

Another smile. It sent a shiver down my spine. Sometimes I wondered if it wasn't Billie I saw in him, but the other way around.

'It would be helpful to speak to Mister Bayazati now,' he said. 'I am a man of few words, and I dislike explaining myself twice.'

Now, that simply wasn't true. The inspector loves nothing better than revealing how clever he is. That he wasn't talking now meant he had something big to reveal, and I too would have to wait.

Mister Bayazati burst through the door in a gargantuan rush.

'Tell me you've found *S. ungulatus*. Tell me the criminals who did this to me will soon be brought to justice!'

'That I can promise you,' the inspector said. 'Their fate will be hideous and ... poetic unless they return your specimens immediately.'

'You are certain of this? How?'

'Because you, Mister Bayazati, are the victim of something very close to a pun. *Stegosaurus* means covered lizard, as I am sure you already know. It comes from the Greek *stegos*, roof, referring to the distinctive plates protruding from its spine. Now, there is another word derived from the same root that means "hidden writing"—'

'Steganography,' I eagerly contributed. People have been hiding data invisibly in other files for more than a century, pilfered blueprints in word processor documents, government secrets in accounting spreadsheets, child pornography in family photographs. It was an art almost as old as the dinosaurs themselves. 'The artisans fed the data from the fabber into the booth in the foyer, then they merged it with themselves when they left, so they could get the bones out of the building without anyone noticing. That's right, isn't it?'

'An elegantly simple plan,' said the inspector. 'But what happened next? Our criminals will not find a taker for this data among the dinophiliacs, yet they are intelligent enough to appreciate the value of *S. ungulatus*, otherwise they would never have stolen it. I cannot imagine them erasing the patterns. Not even in the utter desperation they must presently be feeling.'

'Desperation? How so?' asked Bayazati.

'Consider their situation. They must keep the data secret, which means continuing to hide it steganographically. They have been walking around with the bones of a long-extinct creature inside their body. Imagine what that data must be doing to them!'

'You think it's affecting them?' asked Diana Scullen, surprised and possibly alarmed.

'We'll find out if it is,' I said, picturing a half-man, half-*Stegosaurus* rampaging through suburbia. A *Steganosaurus*, even. 'We'll bulletin the hospitals and emergency centres, and check d-mat transit data for odd DNA signatures, too. Whatever symptoms they've got, they'll stick out like a . . .'

'Like a *Brontosaurus* in a briar patch,' said the inspector.

'Monstrous,' said Mister Bayazati. But behind his eyes I glimpsed something that might have been jealousy.

'Of course,' said the inspector, 'if we could draw them out before then . . .'

'By offering a reward, perhaps?' asked Scullen.

'For stealing my property?' said Mister Bayazati. 'Nonsense! The skeleton will forever be only eighty-five per cent original, whether they return the patterns or not.'

'But who could tell the difference?' I asked.

'*I* could.'

'I agree with Doctor Scullen,' said the inspector in ameliorating tones, 'but would suggest immunity from prosecution rather than a material reward. That will encourage the thieves to come forward more quickly, so *S. ungulatus* will be as complete as it can be as soon as can be, and you, Mister Bayazati, will have the honour of owning it once more – along with the knowledge that no one else does.'

'Well, I suppose . . .'

He seemed unsure whether to feel victorious or beaten and we were happy to leave him like that. Me, I didn't care one way or the other, as long as the mystery was solved.

Diana Scullen walked us back to the foyer. There she thanked us both with genuine feeling – and with genuine reason, I thought. We had been there barely an hour, not quite a record for the inspector, but still pretty impressive.

Who knew what fits she might have endured from her employer had we not solved the case so quickly?

'I expect the matter will be resolved forthwith,' said the inspector.

'Yes . . .' she said. 'Yes, I expect you're right.'

The booth opened for us and we stepped inside.

◆ ◆ ◆

Arrival back at HQ came with a sinking feeling in my chest. D-mat always did that to me. Plus, the case was almost over. I would have nothing but mundane duties until next the inspector called.

'So, will you notify the hospitals or I?'

'No need, PK Sargent.'

'Don't tell me you're not interested in seeing a human–dinosaur hybrid.'

'I would indeed be, if there were such thing.'

'But you said—'

'I know what I said. You were not listening properly. Ah!' He stopped and clapped his hands together. 'My coat! I appear to have left it behind. Would you mind fetching it for me, PK Sargent, while I start compiling the report?'

'Just this once, inspector,' I said, half-annoyed and half-amused.

'My thanks – but you know you really must not call me that . . .'

I headed back to the booth and requested a return journey. Our entrance permissions were still valid, but this time there was no one waiting when I arrived. Maybe, I thought, I could be in and out before anyone noticed I was there.

The coat was in the office we had briefly occupied, just

along the hall from Diana Scullen's workshop. As I picked up the coat, I heard a soft sound that caught me in mid-step. It was a soft cry or a sob – a sound of distress that the peacekeeper in me could not ignore.

I found Scullen with her lab coat bunched up and pressed to her face. Her shoulders were shaking.

'Are you all right?'

She gasped and jumped backwards.

'What are you doing here?'

'I came back for this.' I raised the inspector's coat but had eyes only for her. 'What's going on? Is there something you need to tell me?'

She maintained her poise for barely a second. Then she crumpled like a statue hollowed out from within, starting with the muscles of her face and cascading down the length of her body. Billie would've loved it. It was like watching someone dissolve.

'I don't need to tell you,' she said, sagging into a chair. 'You know it was me who took those damned bones, and you've been toying with me all this time. PK Forest's little hints and jabs – I told myself I was imagining it, because he said it all with such a straight face, but here you are now, and . . . What is it you want – a confession? Well, you've got it, so take me in and be done with it. I won't resist.'

It was all I could do not to gape while I processed this revelation. What did she mean by the inspector's *hints and jabs*? I hadn't noticed anything steganographic going on; I was *used* to his straight face. But he himself had just chastened me for not listening properly. What had I missed?

Well, for starters, Scullen had pointed us at the artisans,

and she had been alarmed when the inspector homed in on the fabber. Then she had gone for a reward, and displayed relief at the end, when it looked like she had eluded the blame.

All this didn't necessarily make her a bad person. I remembered her bitten nails and damp palm: her nerves must have been shot to pieces. And she hadn't lied when the inspector had raised the terrible loss to humanity the theft represented.

Given a kick in the right direction, I could see now where the genesis of her crime lay.

'How much?' I asked, 'of the skeleton have you leaked to the scientific community?'

She looked up at me, and all I saw in her eyes was stubborn pride. She was a curator, not a thief. She didn't care about anything as stupid as molecular authenticity.

'Those bits were the last,' she said. 'It doesn't *belong* here, PK Sargent, locked up in a box where no one else can see it.'

'So you scanned the whole thing in the fabber, and then you put copies of the bones back where they came from?'

'Yes. In my lunch hours, over several weeks.'

'And it was just bad luck he chose that day to look at the metatarsals?'

She nodded. 'Until then, Mister Bayazati never suspected a thing.'

I found the thought hilarious, except it wouldn't have done just then to laugh.

'Kinder that way, I think, Doctor Scullen.'

She hesitated, then nodded again.

'I'll show myself out.'

♦ ♦ ♦

When I returned the coat to the inspector, he was wearing that innocent look I knew far too well.

'So,' he said brightly, 'the hospitals . . .?'

'No need,' I echoed him. 'The bones will come back as you promised, and even if Mister Bayazati finds out what really happened, Scullen has his promise of immunity to fall back on. You sewed him up good and tight.'

He inclined his head. 'Thank you for tying the bow.'

'What did I do? Apart from the usual, I mean.' People tended to notice me, the big girl in uniform, and that gives the inspector a smokescreen for whatever he's up to.

'Solving the case without leaving HQ was as easy as you said,' he said. 'But I believed the perpetrator was more likely to talk to you, rather than an old dinosaur like me.'

'Oh. That makes sense.' It was good that Diana Scullen didn't think she'd gotten off scot-free. 'As long as you're not keeping me around to be your audience.'

'Never, my dear friend. Never.'

But his eyes twinkled in a way that not even Billie could program, and I knew that his version of the truth was, as always, somewhat less or more than he was willing to admit.

Jump to . . .

more future crime
'The Lives of Riley' (p. 43)

another science fiction story
'The Second Coming of the Martians' (p. 5)

something completely different
'The Seventh Letter' (p. 25)

Notes on *The Spark*

Commissioned to write a novella in my best-known fantasy world (that of the Change, which began with *The Stone Mage & the Sea* way back in 2001), I decided to write the conclusion to a love story that spanned a trilogy of novels and another story in this collection. 'Ungentle Fire' tells of two young people who met as children, chose to part in order to learn necessary life skills, but swore to reconnect as adults as soon as they were able, in order to spend the rest of their lives together. It is, arguably, the boldest romance I have ever attempted, and it *had* to have a happy ending. I could *not* deny this long-suffering pair that much. But storybook happy, or something more complicated?

If you've read this far, you'll know I'll rarely take the straightest line between two narrative points, and this story is no exception. It tore at my heart as I wrote it, and it tears my heart even now, just as my heart was torn in real life, and the hearts of people close to me were torn by actions often beyond our control. *Hearts get torn.* That's the way of things.

I couldn't have written this story in the flush of my literary youth. I lacked the emotional maturity that the truest forms of love require. I also lacked the words, which are the most important thing of all.

The Spark

Aditi Sabatino

The young man lay cool and unresponsive on Adi's bed. She had undressed and washed him, and in the process thoroughly examined his body for any sign of injury. She knew him now much better than she ever had, but not in a way that satisfied her.

His eyes were open but they did not see her. She lay next to him in the hot room, wearing only her underclothes, and he made no move to touch her.

'What do I do now, Ros?'

He gave no sign of hearing.

'Tell me what happened and I'll do whatever it takes to fix it.'

His expression didn't change, not even when she rattled him by the shoulders like a vat of settled ale.

'You're supposed to be my husband, not a corpse!'

Roslin of Geheb lay quietly beneath her, lungs steadily working and heart steadily beating.

Adi bent forward and wept onto his hairless chest.

◆ ◆ ◆

A day earlier, she had checked into the Lost Dolphin Hostel under the name Hakamu, an alias they had used on their last journey together. As a boy, Ros had bested both the Bee

Witch and the Golem of Omus, and had saved her life no less than twice along the way. Adi had saved him too, that last time, and stories of their deeds had spread like locusts across the land. Everyone knew Aditi Sabatino and Roslin of Geheb, or thought they did. For some years it had bothered her that people told tales by firelight that amplified or decreased her role, or ignored her entirely to focus on the farmboy-made-good. Then she had learned that it was fine for business, and discovered she wasn't above using the weight of storytelling to drive a harder bargain.

On this occasion, she didn't avail herself of that opportunity. She happily took the hostel's going rate and hid her Clan markings behind a veil. She had come to finish a story that no one but Ros and her knew anything about.

Despite this resolve, her hands shook as she unfolded her pack on her bed. The precious brassy charm lay within, nestled carefully among wadded clothes and her toiletries, worn smooth by years of careful examination – dented too by being occasionally hurled into a wall – but it still functioned. At one end was fixed a crystal that glowed red when she pointed it at the south-east corner of the room.

She shuttered the windows and tested it again. The sunlight reflecting down crystal chimneys to the underground thoroughfares of Ulum was not a patch on standing under the naked sky, but her eyes had become used to it, making subtle gradations of shade in the crystal difficult to tell. Swinging the rod from side to side in the gloom, she confirmed her first impressions. South-east it was.

Caught between impatience and dread, her empty stomach festering, Adi waited until nightfall before putting the promises she had made to the test.

♦ ♦ ♦

The charm was a limited thing. Its crystal glowed only when it was pointed in the direction of Roslin of Geheb. That simple trick had sustained her for five years of separation. Many, many times in the years they had been apart had she taken comfort from it. No matter how far away he was, the charm would seek him out and tell her where he lay. South, north, east, west – on lonely nights, he could have been on the far side of the word or just outside the walls of her wagon.

She never once opened a window to test the latter hope. Until his apprenticeship was complete, she knew it was bound to be dashed.

One hour after sunset, when the halls of Ulum were as dark as they were going to get, she dressed and placed the veil across her features once again. Tightly clutching the charm in both hands, she left the room and headed into the warrens outside. Still south-east, the crystal said. Ulum was cramped and crowded, a city squeezed into caves forever too small, no matter how much the civil miners dug. At the highest points of the underground city, curving towers reached for the ranks of luminescent algae that dotted the night 'sky' like stars. Elsewhere, winding roads fought with buildings for space, and people squeezed in where they could.

Even after nightfall the city was busy. Traders mixed freely with locals once the markets were closed. Accents varied, as did clothes and skin colour. Adi's skin was darker than most to the north, her hair and eyes with it. With her Clan markings covered, she could have passed for an emissary from the Strand – perhaps even a Sky Warden, had she the torc to match.

The charm led her deep into a maze of lanes and teetering buildings. For seven days, according to the charm, Ros hadn't moved. She didn't expect him to move now. It was a sign, she told herself, a sign from him. It had to be. He had never before stayed so long in one spot, and the charm had never pointed her so surely to a city like Ulum – a natural meeting place if ever there was one.

Her nostrils breathed with easy familiarity the comingled scents of perfume, spice and camel shit. It wasn't lack of air, then, that made her feel light-headed. Roslin of Geheb was in the city somewhere. She wouldn't sleep until she found him.

The charm led her truly, but the ways of Ulum were ever crooked. Straight lines, like the flagstones underfoot, had long been worn into curves or cracked entirely. When she wanted to go left, every road tended right. Crowds of people and flocks of animals frequently blocked her path. It took her half the night to travel a mile.

Tired and on edge, she arrived at a tiny hexagonal courtyard lit by reddish glowstones and greened only by weeds growing between the cobbles. The charm pointed to one of two doors on the far side. Plunging through the doorway, she collided heavily with someone emerging from within.

The charm went flying. She clutched at it, caught it just as it made contact with hard stone. Something *tinked* within its metal casing. A cold feeling rushed through her at the knife-sharp thought: *broken*.

She spat a word she only used when negotiations took a particularly atrocious turn. The man she had run into didn't stop. He was moving too quickly, already disappearing out of the courtyard. She flung another harsh word at his back, and let him go.

With faint hope, she raised the charm and pointed it south-east.

The crystal was dark.

Sickness rose in her, physical and existential. There was only one course left to her: through the door, with momentum regained, trusting in the charm's last flicker, just as she trusted Ros to be there, waiting for her.

The building was a dosshouse, cramped and stinking. Every door was open, every screen pulled aside. People came and went freely, muttering and cursing in the fashion of the broken-minded. She stumbled through their filth and refuse, thinking this wasn't the life Ros had set out to find. What had gone so badly wrong? Or was it possible the charm had been malfunctioning all along, and he was no closer than he had ever been?

Then, through the darkness of her thoughts, she saw him – a pale shape sprawled partially clothed across a filthy narrow mattress. Dark, lank locks hung in lazy spirals across his brow. Half-open eyes cast deep shadows across his cheeks. His lips were slack. He was older, larger, manlier – but it was him.

Him. Truly, truly him.

She ran to him and cupped his head in her hands, lifted it as she would a child's. The weight of it surprised her, as did the tears that came on seeing him. They dripped unchecked onto his face and she called his name in relief.

He neither moved nor spoke. His eyes saw right through her, if they saw anything at all. He didn't register her presence no matter how she implored him, then shook him, then slapped his face lightly, hoping that would bring him back to himself.

'Won't do no good, miz,' said a wild-bearded man from outside the room. 'He been like this a full week.'

At first, she had no response. A small crowd had gathered, watching her with wide-eyed curiosity. She suddenly saw herself as they did, and wondered at the determination that filled her.

This wasn't how the story was supposed to go, but that didn't mean it was over. It was only beginning.

Her tears vanished. Her spine straightened. She put Ros's head down gently but firmly. Whatever had done this to him – a golem, perhaps, or a charm backfired – she would fix it.

'You'll help me,' she told wild-beard and his friends. 'I'll pay you to carry him.'

Shrugging, sceptical, but convinced by her coin, the city's under-dwellers were as compliant as she needed them to be, and no more.

The manager of the Lost Dolphin had seen stranger things, no doubt. His right eyebrow might have risen a fraction on seeing the strange procession coming up his steps, but it was soon restored to its proper location. Once Ros was installed in Adi's room and the grubby entourage despatched, he provided all that courtesy and custom demanded. The staff entered only when asked to bring tubs of warm water and clean towels, and food that only Adi ate. Ros drank drops of water at a time, when she tipped his head back and forced him to. She spoke to him, telling him how they had come to be together again, then asking him how he had arrived in Ulum. He hadn't necessarily been injured in the city, she thought. He might have been brought here by persons unknown, rescued from the desert, perhaps, in which he would have quickly died. If such a benefactor existed, Adi wished she could track them down and press on them the questions that burned inside her.

Ros said nothing.

'You're supposed to be my husband, not a corpse!'

Ros said nothing.

◆ ◆ ◆

She wept because she had to. Powerful emotions were like sparkling wine: a vessel could contain them only so long before shattering under rising pressure. If she shattered, that would do neither of them any good.

The moment she regained control, she washed her face and dressed, moving swiftly but calmly. She rolled Ros onto his side and covered his nakedness with a sheet. A maid appeared at the door the moment she rang. Adi paid her to watch him while she was gone. She doubted he would be going anywhere.

Back out into the city she went. Dawn light was beginning to filter down the chimneys, pouring a brighter shine on the dirty streets. Adi's hopes of a quick solution had evaporated during that long night, but she hadn't given up yet. A physician was the next step, the best the city could provide at short notice. She had money in the form of coins and credit, the latter backed by the wealth and reputation of Clan Sabatino.

The third physician she called upon was willing to leave his bed and return with her to the hostel. Doctor Rishard, a hale-looking fellow of middling years with a crest of greying hair that stood up like a galah's no matter how he tried to plaster it down, walked with long sweeping strides, and to keep up Adi had to take two steps for every one of his. She responded positively to his haste, though, feeling as though he was giving her strength just by taking her plea seriously.

'And you say he has been like this for how long?'

'Seven days, I suspect. Perhaps longer.'

The physician nodded and went back to lifting Ros's eyelids and poking at his flesh. He employed crystals, hammers and needles, all without response. He passed a sample of Ros's breath across a mirror and tested the consistency of several bodily fluids. Ros had soiled himself during Adi's absence, and the maid's half-hearted attempt to clean the mess proved to be a blessing in disguise.

Last of all, Doctor Rishard took a small bell out of his bag and rang it softly next to Ros's ears. The tone warbled oddly, as though it was being sounded underwater.

He nodded.

'What is it? Can you tell me what's wrong with him?'

The physician bundled his instruments back into the bag. 'He was a Change-worker. That much I can tell you.'

She felt her ears growing pink. 'How does that make a difference?'

'It means I can't treat him. I can only guess what might have put him in this state.'

She nodded, even as disappointment filled her. 'Go on, then. Guess.'

'It's not a physical thing like a drug or a disease, but Stone Mages talk of it. They call it the Void Beneath. It eats minds. Dissolves them.'

'How?'

He shook his head. 'There, I'm of no use to you. The Void

doesn't appear in any of my textbooks. You'll need another Change-worker if you want an answer.'

She did. Thanking Doctor Rishard, she paid him and sent him home.

◆ ◆ ◆

A Change-worker. She was on quicksand now, and she knew it. This was Ros's world, not hers. If he had got himself into trouble that way, she might not be able to get him out of it.

She briefly considered calling his teacher for help. Master Pukje was a strange being, though, part-dragon and entirely capricious. It was his demand that Ros be trained in the ways of the Change that had led to their long separation. Any help he offered would be coloured by that history. She soon decided to do what she could on her own before following that path.

Her first step was not the obvious one. The Stone Mages who ruled the Interior would recognise Ros immediately, and she wasn't ready to cast off her cloak of anonymity. Adi was sure they weren't the only Change-workers in the city. Illusionists, charm-makers and seers all gravitated to the light of respectability, even if they were themselves denied a place within the brazier. With the markets open more than an hour already, she would have no trouble finding someone to talk to about her problem. The quality of the answer was the only variable.

This quest took her considerably longer than had her search for a physician. Carefully worded enquiries and bribes led her slowly up the ranks from tricksters and fakers to the genuinely talented. Along the way she received advice she had no intention of following: ensuring that the foot of Ros's bed faced due north; daubing his skin with a salve made from wolf spider venom; chanting a series of nonsense words over him at dawn and dusk; tattooing complex symbols at key points on his body, so the grace of the Goddess would be drawn to him and restore him to himself. The procedures were offered with all appearance of sincerity, but she doubted even the practitioners believed in them. She was no more a Change-worker than a physician; nothing she did would make any difference, beyond finding the right person.

She came at last to a stately home in a relatively quiet corner of the city. Cubical and blunt, the house even sported trees at each corner – spindly, sick-looking things but trees nonetheless. They were the first of any size Adi had seen in Ulum. It struck her as strange that a Change-worker should live in such opulent surrounds, but that wasn't the mystery she had come to solve.

She knocked on the door and asked for Samson Mierlo. The houseboy led her to a book-filled study and invited her to sit. She waited patiently, feeling very little by now but fatigue and desperation. Elsewhere in the house, doors opened and shut, and floorboards creaked. A woman coughed, long and throatily. On a plinth in the corner of the study, the bust of a high-templed man turned its head to regard her more closely.

She stared calmly back at it. Man'kin bothered some people, who saw in them nothing but falsity, a parody of life, but she was untroubled. They had their uses.

'Now, Lady Hakamu,' said a voice from the doorway behind her, 'what is this grave matter of which you speak?'

She stood and shook the hand of the man she hoped would bring Ros back to her. Samson Mierlo had been described as something of a maverick, courting controversy and condemnation from the Establishment he criticised, but he looked like nothing so much as a lawyer. Instead of robes he wore a grim, grey suit. His eyes were cool and grey, but not without warmth.

Once again Adi explained the situation. This time, however, she went into greater detail. Mierlo was the city's foremost expert in the Void Beneath. From him she hoped to gain a greater understanding of Ros's condition, at least.

He waved for her to resume her seat, but didn't rest himself. Pacing the room as she talked, he nodded and uttered short phrases that conveyed no actually meaning but encouraged her to continue.

'Yes.'

'Indeed.'

'How so?'

'Quite.'

The man'kin's granite eyes tracked Mierlo smoothly as he walked and listened.

'Naturally.'

'Well.'

'Hmmm.'

Only when she had finished did he take the seat opposite her and fold his long-fingered hands into a steeple.

'The physician you consulted would have been no help at all, Lady Hakamu. This is quite beyond his understanding. Be thankful for his honesty, though; a less scrupulous surgeon might have insisted on treating your friend regardless, and done him more harm than good. Nothing in the world of medicine can help him now.'

'Can you help him?'

'No. But I can tell you this: your friend is where he is because of something he did, not something that was done to him. To use the Change one must reach into oneself. Reach too deeply and the Void awaits. I've seen many promising young talents overbalance and fall, out of pride, perhaps, or fear of failure. Either way, there's no coming back. The Void Beneath devours all who enter it. How, exactly, we don't know; it is a mystery we may never solve. But please don't take hope from that admission. Every case history points in one direction. Your friend's body may be perfectly sound, but his mind is gone.'

Adi stared at Samson Mierlo, certain he was telling her the truth as he understood it. It was, however, an understanding that she couldn't accept.

'There must be something—'

'The Void Beneath is not a place that you, Lady Hakamu, can enter,' he said, brusquely cutting her off. 'It is not a foe that you can challenge. It is nothing – a nothing that takes everything in a person and grinds them back to nothing in turn. Such is the foundation of the world; there are no certainties but this one.'

Her right hand crushed her left. She was unable to speak.

'I'll leave you now,' he said, standing. 'I'm very sorry for your friend, and for you, since you care for him so deeply. When you are able, Ugo will show you out.'

She nodded, wanting to offer her thanks but unable to trust her clenched throat to issue anything remotely like a word.

His crisp footsteps led from the study, deep into the echoing house.

'You will go to Madam Van Haasteren.'

Adi's head jerked up. The voice wasn't Samson Mierlo's, and she had heard no one else enter the room.

The man'kin was looking at her.

'Magda Van Haasteren,' it repeated. 'The seer.'

She stood too abruptly. 'What?' she asked through a wave of dizziness. 'Are you talking to me?'

'You will go to her.'

It froze as the houseboy appeared in the doorway.

'Did it just speak?' he said incredulously, crossing to the plinth and staring hard into the stony eyes. 'Did it say something to you?'

She shook her head, unsure why the man'kin wanted to keep its animation a secret but deciding she was willing to go along with it in exchange for its help. 'I didn't hear anything. Did you?'

'I could've sworn . . .' The boy shook his shaved head as he guided her to the front door. 'That old thing's been in the family forever. If it ever woke up, the mistress would have a fit.'

'It's probably for the best, then, that it doesn't.'

'I guess.'

Adi could tell that the houseboy had already put the mystery from his mind. She had no intention of doing the same.

♦ ♦ ♦

Magda Van Haasteren. The name meant nothing to her, but it was known in the city's underbelly. Within an hour Adi had an address, and even a word or two of warning. For a mere seer, Van Haasteren had a surprisingly dark reputation. The rumours were light on details, though, and quite possibly inspired by envy. It was often the way with the genuinely talented, Adi thought, that they should be downplayed and reviled. Were Samson Mierlo correct in his opinion, it would take all the talent in the world to find Ros and bring him back.

Before returning to the dark side of the city, Adi returned to the Lost Dolphin to check on the man whose mind she was trying to save. He hadn't moved beyond breathing or drinking the water dripped into his mouth by the maid. She was bored, Adi could tell, but she would have no respite. The manager assured Adi that the maid would attend Ros faithfully throughout the night, if necessary.

Adi stood for a moment, staring at the covered form of the man she had promised to take as a husband, so long ago. What had happened to that dream? The charm was in her bag, broken like him. How could either of them have been so careless?

It wasn't as if she hadn't taken risks down the years. She was human, and forgave herself for being so. There had been other young men she'd had feelings for, and even one she had given herself to as a lover – in the desert port town of Lower Light, with complete anonymity. If she was to be anything in life, bride or otherwise, she would do so in the full light of the knowledge available to her.

A promise was a promise, though. A deal a deal. That was a philosophy trading Clans took seriously. Her life had been built on it.

Your friend is where he is because of something he did, Samson Mierlo had told her.

If Ros ever spoke again, she would ask him what had been so important that he had risked throwing away their life together. She doubted, in the weary heat of the moment, that any answer would be sufficient.

◆ ◆ ◆

Back through the constricted streets, back into the filth. Adi was retracing her steps in a very real way, for Van Haasteren's closet-sized stall was only a handful of blocks from the dosshouse where she had found Ros. Where the charm had been broken. At that place, in that moment, everything had gone wrong.

An unwarranted thought occurred to her then: that if she had arrived one minute earlier, events would have unfolded in a very different way. The charm would have led her truly, and Ros would have greeted her with open arms. Was it so unlikely? The man she had collided with – he had been fleeing the scene as she approached. Could he have had something to do with Ros's condition? Could he, in fact, have been the one responsible for it?

She struggled to remember his face. At most she had glimpsed him, for her attention had been almost entirely on the falling charm. Long hair pulled severely back from lean features, crisscrossed with thin lines that weren't tattoos but might have been scars . . .

She forced him from her mind. Lichen stars were coming out above as the chimneys fell dark. She hadn't slept since arriving in Ulum the previous day, and it came to her then that she wasn't thinking as clearly as she ought to. She needed her wits about her when dealing with Magda Van Haasteren – for fear of deception or further disappointment.

◆ ◆ ◆

'Come in quickly,' the seer said when she rapped at the stall's flimsy portal. 'There is a chill in the air that gives me the bone-ache.'

Adi did as she was told. There was no sign above the door, but it matched the description she had received, as did the seer's disposition. The air was no chillier than normal; the fans that stirred the cavern's otherwise stagnant air turned with their usual velocity.

Madam Van Haasteren was a shapeless, slouched woman in a faded blue smock. Her face was heavily lined, with a down-turned mouth, and eyes that glittered in the light of a single, squat candle. One large-knuckled hand rested on a three-legged table to her side; she clutched a stinking cheroot in the other. Her voice was full of oil and gravel, like gears that had broken years ago, but ground on regardless, without respite.

Adi offered the woman her fake name, and it was accepted with a knowing stare.

'You're looking for someone,' the seer said. 'Such is the state of all who come to me – at their wits' end and desperate, more often than not.'

'I'm no different, to tell the truth. If you can help me, I'll pay you well.'

The seer waved at a second stool, more rickety than the first, and instructed her to sit. 'Give me your hand, girl, and mind your tongue. I don't do this for money.'

Adi felt five years old, and fought a sudden surprising urge to weep. Her mother had died when Adi was young, and her father had followed ten years later. For a time she had despaired of the attentions of her well-meaning aunts, but now she missed them, and her mother, and everything that family represented. She had left all that behind to come in search of Ros. And gained nothing.

Leathery old fingers clasped Adi's left hand and pulled

it close. Sharp eyes inspected back and front, and her fingernails too. They were bitten to the quick.

The seer grimaced. 'Does he have a name?'

'Sovan,' she said, still unwilling to reveal their identities if the seer hadn't already guessed them.

'Tell me about him.'

'He's lost,' Adi began, 'fallen into the Void Beneath—'

'Not that. Why do you want him back? If he's gone, why not let him be gone and move on? Is there something special about him that you can't find in another man?'

Adi gaped, feeling slightly scandalised. Something special about Ros? Of course there was! She wouldn't have come this far if there wasn't.

'Put it in words, girl. If you can't define it, maybe it's not there at all.'

She tried. Her voice shook as she talked of their first meeting. Ros had run away from home and her family had given him temporary shelter on the road. Adi had been promised to a boy from another Clan, and she had convinced Ros to take her with him when he left. She had trusted him more in that moment than anyone else, for reasons she now found hard to capture.

The seer seemed to understand well enough. 'You're talking about the spark,' she said, nodding gravely. 'When two people meet who are . . . not destined or connected, but complementary – yes, that's the word I'm looking for – when that happens, you get the spark. You feel it with your whole body and in all your thoughts. It's like a little bit of lightning, and it too can start a fire.'

Adi stared at the old woman, amazed as much by the passion that suddenly filled her voice as by the aptness of her words.

'There's more to the story,' Adi said, thinking of monsters and death and the nightmares she still had, sometimes, 'but none of that matters now.'

'No, it doesn't. That's why I don't need to know where you think he's gone. What's important is that he's not here, or that he doesn't recognise you, or both. That's where it begins, but it doesn't end there. You want him to know you, to be here for you, and you're afraid that you can't make that happen. Maybe he's forgotten who you are. Maybe he doesn't want to come to you. You can't read his mind, and he won't talk to you, so the uncertainty eats at you, eats at your faith in him. That leads to the questions. Did you do the right thing by letting him go? Would things be better or worse now if you had not? What will you do if you can't get him back? Who changed – him or you? And the most important question of all: do you even want him back any more?'

Adi felt as though the seer had reached into her chest and clutched her heart in a tight grip. She could only stare at the gnarled hands still holding hers, and hope those sharp eyes didn't see any deeper.

'Answer my question, girl.'

'Which one?'

'Do you want him back?'

Adi thought of the doubt she had entertained on the way to the seer's stall. Could anything Ros said now undo the damage that had been done to the faith she had in him? She saw in her mind his lifeless and impotent form. He had once been so strong. Was it his strength that had given her love for him such vitality? Could she love him now in weakness? Was that a weakness of her own, to even ask that question?

Her breath came in gulps. She barely noticed she was crying.

'Yes,' Adi managed. 'Yes, I do want him back.'

'That's a brave answer,' said the seer, 'after all that seesawing. The cloth you're cut from is strong as well as fine. Remember that, when you need to – because although I can help you, the cost will be high.'

Adi found herself released from the old woman's tight grip, and she sat back, blinking. The single candle flame, which seemed to have become much brighter in recent minutes, dimmed now, casting thick shadows across the dingy cubicle. Someone in a hovel nearby was shouting, but she couldn't make out the words.

Adi wiped the tears from her cheeks and breathed deeply of the smoky air.

'How much?'

'I'm not talking about money, girl.'

The seer gestured with her right hand at a wall hanging that might once have been quality work. Ill-served in its lifetime by smoke and neglect, it barely warranted a second glance, but for the significance it had now been given. Faded thread picked out the figure of a Stone Mage in full armour, his iron plates painted ochre with ceremonial rust. The figure stirred slightly, as though someone had moved behind him.

'The understanding you seek lies through that curtain.'

Adi stood, and shivered, feeling the chill the seer had complained of earlier.

'All right,' she said, telling herself to see it through. She had faced worse fears and survived. 'Thank you.'

The old woman shook her head. She had slouched down even further on her stool, so she sat splay-legged, like a man, and stared despondently at the muddy ember of her cheroot. 'No need, Adi. No need.'

Adi was halfway through the curtain before she realised the old woman had used her real name. By then, it was entirely too late to turn back.

Roslin of Geheb

The young woman ducked into an alleyway. Ros shouted at her to wait, and when she did not do so he set off in immediate pursuit. He had caught only a glimpse of her, but he was certain this time it was her, the woman he sought. There was no mistaking that long thick hair, bound up in whirls and streams, or her rich, dark skin, against which the colourful fabric of her dress stood out so vividly, or the confidence in her walk and the almost capricious glance she cast over her shoulder as she vanished from sight.

By the time he reached the corner, the alleyway was empty. He ran ten steps along it, checking doors and fences as he went. They were secure. A clutch of women appeared from the nearest intersection, and he hurried to them, studying their faces carefully in turn. All of them were strangers. The side roads were clear too.

He turned in circles at the crossroad, unsure which way to go. That was the fourth time he had lost her in an hour. He was running out of options and patience. Everything she asked him to do he had done, so why was she still playing games? What did she want from him?

'Don't do this, Adi,' he called to the winding streets and the indifferent crowds. 'I came for you like I promised. Show yourself, please!'

A flock of sparrows danced under Ulum's buttressed ceilings, casting shadows from the light-chimneys that came and went, came and went.

With fists tightly clenched, Ros lowered his head and returned to the dosshouse alone.

He had been in Ulum a week, asking around after Clan Sabatino at Adi's usual haunts, guided by his memories of her letters and little else. Civilisation seemed a strange thing to him now. Five years with Master Pukje had left him accustomed to empty spaces, rigid routines, and arcane forces. The ebb and flow of ordinary people confounded him. Sometimes he felt they spoke an entirely different language, one he might never be able to understand.

He did learn that Adi's Clan was on its way back from a long north-western haul and, to his regret, that Adi's father had died a year ago. Ulick Sabatino had been a bluff, honourable man, who had placed his faith in Ros under extraordinary circumstances. That Ros had saved his daughter's life hadn't hurt, of course, but it took more than that to earn a permanent place at the Clan's table. Marriage was the only sure-fire way, and even then it could be withdrawn.

That Adi supposedly wasn't in Ulum surprised Ros, for his gut told him she was close. His gut had led him to the city from the depths of the desert, and he trusted it still. Persistence would prove the attempt worthwhile, he was sure. The surrounding veil of strangeness would part before him, and reveal the one he sought.

He only hoped success would come soon, for his material means were limited. In the desert, he could survive for years unaided, but here he needed money, or a job, or some other means to support himself. The trials of a mad dragon were not recognised in the city as a valid qualification for anything – and, besides, Ros was reluctant to reveal his true name. The power of his reputation had almost entrapped him once before. That wasn't a road he wanted to follow again.

◆ ◆ ◆

For several days he did nothing but walk the streets, trusting not only his instincts but the paths he carved out through the city over the course of time – ornate sprawling charms for the finding of lost things, the binding of hearts, the uncovering of secrets. He left cryptic messages employing aliases they had assumed in their youth, requesting rendezvous, return messages, or signs ranging from the subtle to the overt. He visited and revisited each location, but never once did Adi leave a response. His messages went unread, or at least unanswered.

He searched the face of every woman he passed, hoping for a flicker of familiarity.

He searched his own face in his shaving mirror, wondering what she would think of him when they met. There was no denying he had changed. Sometimes, catching his reflection in a window or a doorway, he barely recognised the man he had become. But was he more or less handsome? Would she think the cost of his training too high?

'Staring'll make you no prettier,' mocked the wild-bearded man who inhabited the cot across from him. 'And if the mirror cracks, you'll be worse off still.'

Ros ignored the cackling half-wits and resumed his search.

On the sixth day, he received a note. It was delivered to the dosshouse during one of his extended searches and left upon his bedroll to await his return. He unfolded the stiff paper with eager fingers and scanned the single line it contained. A place and a time. No more.

She had neither addressed it to him nor signed it, but he was sure it was from Adi. Holding the paper to his nose, he imagined he could detect a faint residue of her scent upon it. His heart beat a little faster at the knowledge they were one step closer to reunion.

The rendezvous was scheduled for dawn the next morning. Ros barely slept that night, imagining how his life would change. The stories told about him ended with the defeat of the Scarecrow five years earlier. For him, the real story was about to begin.

♦ ♦ ♦

He arrived one quarter of an hour early, and waited exactly where the note had specified. Even at that early hour, the market was busy, and he craned his neck to catch a glimpse as she approached. As the appointed time neared, he could barely keep still. His jostling and pacing attracted the attention of more than one trader, but he rebuffed their sales pitches with steadfast cheer.

The hour came and went, and Adi did not appear. Ros told himself to be patient, and waited another quarter-hour, then a half.

A full hour after the time specified in the note, he left, a pale approximation of the man he had been earlier that morning.

There was another note on his bedroll, equally brief. The second meeting was on the far side of the city with bare minutes to spare. Ros didn't question the need for haste. Adi must have been delayed, surely, and all explanations would be rendered unnecessary by her presence. Barely stopping to draw breath, he sprinted along the dusty thoroughfares and carriageways, dodging and weaving when crowds failed to part before him.

He arrived almost punctually, breathing heavily and casting about for her in the halls of the city library. It was cool and quiet within. Too quiet: his urgent calling and searching were not welcome. Undaunted he peered into every nook and cranny and through every door, pushing books aside when faces were obscured. He left only when certain the chambers were empty of the one he sought. He had missed her.

Furious at his ill fortune, he hurried back to the dosshouse in case another note had arrived.

It had, but this time he did not immediately open it. He held it gently in his hand. Like a dead moth, it could be crushed in an instant, and for a dozen breaths he was tempted. This insubstantial yet weighty thing could lead him on another fruitless quest. Without proof that it was from Adi, he would be unwise to hurry anywhere.

With new circumspection, Ros opened the letter. It contained the same as before, only this time there was even less opportunity to make the rendezvous.

No, he told himself. He was not at anyone's beck and call. This test of loyalty, if such it was, would be answered by a test of his own.

Folding the note into halves and slipping it back onto his

bedroll, he exited the dosshouse and made as if to follow the route required.

When he was certain he wasn't being shadowed, he doubled-back and procured a vantage point atop the building adjacent to the dosshouse, from which location he could clearly see the entrance. There he would wait until the next note arrived. When it did, he would follow it back to the source.

♦ ♦ ♦

Night fell, and with it his spirits. Master Pukje's final test – surviving the same, at any rate – had left Ros feeling prepared for anything. There had been no graduation ceremony, just the assumption of knowledge, of responsibility, of adulthood. He was his own man now, or ought to be.

Not that he hadn't already experienced a large measure of doubt on his way to the city. He had little experience with women, having met barely a dozen since his apprenticeship began and known none of them intimately. He couldn't guess what might be going through Adi's mind, just as he wasn't entirely sure what was going through his own.

He didn't want to think she was behind this strange sequence of events. After all, hadn't she encouraged him to come to her the moment his apprenticeship was finished? Why would she take advantage of his gullibility like this? He was sure now it couldn't be her. It flew in the face of the memories he had treasured for so long.

Numerous people passed through the six-sided courtyard off which the dosshouse lay. None of them were Adi; none of them came bearing notes or displaying signs of conspiracy against him. As the night deepened, he began to feel foolish and upbraided himself for his paranoia. Master Pukje would have harsh words to offer if he ever learned of this. And so would Adi. She tolerated neither untimeliness nor inconvenience, and he had offered her nothing but both, so far. He looked forward to the day when they could laugh about this together, as they might many other anecdotes from their long betrothal.

His back was growing sore and the steady stream of passers-by had slowed, if not ceased entirely. He dropped with light feet into the courtyard and entered the dosshouse. Too tired to bathe, he unrolled his bed and flicked out a bug or two that had made a home there during the day. There was no fourth note, of course.

On the way back from the primitive toilet, he stopped in mid-step, every imaginable sense alert. A certainty that Adi was nearby coursed through him. Without hesitating, he ran to the entrance of the dosshouse and peered carefully outside. For all his theories concerning anonymous culprits, part of him remained alert for games of any kind on her part, and he wasn't about to drive her off by pouncing too soon.

There was a woman in the courtyard, hurrying his way. She wasn't Adi; no Sabatino would dress that way. His eyes were instead drawn into the shadows. Through the Change he detected several rats and one alert cat, but no humans. If she were there, she was artfully concealed.

And so she was. Her skin was black against black, but the whites of her eyes stood out – one of them, anyway, around the edge of a ragged brick wall. Their stares locked for an instant, and in that instant he saw her pull back, realising she had been spotted. The eye winked out, and he set off in pursuit.

Later he would remember the wild fever of those hopeful moments as he shouldered past anyone in his way, calling Adi's name and imploring her to reveal herself. He glimpsed her many times, stepping out into darkness from under streetlamps, through archways, down alleyways that would inevitably turn out to be empty when he arrived. How she did it, he didn't know, but his darkest, most convoluted fears were confirmed. It was her, and she wasn't as he remembered.

All night he chased her, across all quarters of the city.

'Don't do this, Adi,' he called. 'I came for you like I promised. Show yourself, please!'

She offered him nothing in reply.

It came to him eventually that he wasn't thinking clearly. He was chasing phantoms and they were leading him nowhere. He needed to be calm and find another solution. Adi was somewhere in the city. He could find her if he tried.

He returned to the dosshouse only to discover his property had been stolen. That didn't improve his mood. The wild-bearded man and his foolish collaborators professed no knowledge of the theft, but Ros could see more than the usual fogginess to their eyes. Sold for ale, he presumed. Everything he owned was drunk and gone.

There was no point railing against it. Stalking back out into the streets, he found the closest thing to a quiet corner in Ulum and scrawled complex charms about it, cocooning it and himself in silence. He closed his eyes and sought the vital heart of himself, as his master had taught him to do. That was all he had left. Every other certainty had evaporated.

In that tiny island of calm, he viewed his emotions with something approaching objectivity, and was even able to shed them for a moment. Anger, fear, embarrassment and loss were the least of his problems now. He was the victim of an elaborate prank, and the first step to rising above it was to regard it from the outside.

Almost immediately he realised something that should have been obvious all along. Adi's prank relied on talents Adi herself didn't possess. Not that she wasn't talented in her own ways; Ros was sanguine about the fact she was smarter than he was, and cunning with it. But she lacked any kind of predilection for the Change, and to his knowledge had never pursued an understanding of it. How, then, could she be cloaking her presence so effectively and running him in such ever-widening circles?

There were two possible answers: one, that it wasn't her at all; and two, that she had hired someone to do the work for her.

The first possibility was attractive because it absolved her of all responsibility, but it offered no hint as to the identity of his antagonist. He decided to pursue the second possibility simply because it gave him something to do and offered a small chance of success. Finding Adi's Change-worker-for-hire might prove easier than finding her, if only because Ros might approach the prank sideways rather than head-on.

Although his direction was now clear, he stayed within his bubble of silence a while longer, to double-check his thoughts, in case he had missed something else equally obvious, and to establish an appropriate emotional balance. The decision to be with Adi had been an easy one five years earlier. To dishonour it now would be cowardice of the highest order. He would see it through if he was allowed to, and he would do his best to keep hope alive.

◆ ◆ ◆

In theory, the Stone Mages had the city stitched up. Every child with the slightest whiff of the Change about them was sent off to be trained and ultimately inducted into the country's elite, from which few ever emerged into independent practice. Ros's utter unencumbrance was frowned upon and, in some quarters, considered actually dangerous to society at large.

Master Pukje had been quick to instil in Ros the understanding of the true purpose of theory, which was simply to be tested, and so he went with confidence into the city once more, sure that he would find an exception before long.

And so he did. First one, then another – both Change-workers known for shoddy work, but at least acting independently of the country's masters. They were jealous types, reluctant to let a potential customer fall into a competitor's orbit, but Ros had mastered more techniques for extracting the truth than they had ever forgotten. Not effortlessly, but at least painlessly, he learned what he needed to and moved on.

The black market for Change-working grew in extent the more he picked at it, like a loose thread pulled from a cheap rug. With keener eyes than he had had before, he saw charms that bore no relation to any grammatical system he had studied. He found dealers in potions using ingredients unknown to anyone but their discoverers. He studied significant tattoos in books whose reason he could not tell from madness. All of it was wonderful and strange, and utterly incapable of catching him in any kind of web. The prankster, whoever he or she was, had attained a higher degree of mastery than these crazed dabblers.

From one he learned a name that he mentally filed away for later pursuit. The name was repeated two interviews later, as a person Ros should contact should he wish to procure the expertise he required. The person thus identified was not a Change-worker herself, but a businesswoman from the quieter side of town. Her customers resided outside the populous caverns, so she did not advertise locally. Word inevitably spread, though, and Ros was keen to follow it. Through this woman Adi might have hired someone from outside the city, and therefore someone more difficult to trace.

Twice Ros caught glimpses of Adi in the crowds of the marketplace. Once he saw a jewel she had worn hanging around the neck of another woman. Ros ignored all such instances of recognition for fear of being entangled again. He had to focus on the trail he had found for himself and not be led aside, no matter where it led him.

'Explain to me again, young man,' said Jenfi Mierlo, 'exactly what kind of charm you think this might be.'

Ros did his best, although their surroundings discomfited him to an extreme. He felt utterly out of place among such finery. There were books and relics from ancient times, and works of art so delicately formed that light itself seemed gentle with them. Everything about him – his shabbiness, his demeanour, his smell – was alien to this world. There was no denying it, and little that could be done about it.

The hard keen gaze of a man'kin on a plinth didn't help much, either.

'What do you think, Mawson?' the mistress of the house asked it when Ros had finished. 'Does this sound like the work of anyone we know?'

The man'kin didn't reply, but she nodded as though it had.

'No,' she said. 'I didn't think so either. In fact – in fact –'

She broke into a series of deep, hacking coughs that turned her glassy skin purple and bent her almost double.

Jenfi Mierlo was a woman old enough to be Ros's grandmother but as slender as a teenager. She wore a silk gown, dyed black and white in geometric patterns, from which her wrists and throat emerged like fragile stalks. Her hair was steel-grey; her eyes deep-set. The line of her jaw stood out like a knife, almost as sharp as her fingernails.

Ros half-rose to offer her assistance, but she waved him away. The houseboy rushed into the room with a glass of water, which she accepted with gratitude and sipped from as the fit subsided.

'Please pardon me,' she said, returning to something approaching a healthy colour. 'The trials of age are as vexatious as the trials of youth. I was about to announce that your predicament, this glamour or spell or whatever you wish to call it, seems more like hallucination to me than conspiracy – for after all, where is the evidence? You can't produce a single note you said you received. And as for either mechanism or motive, both remain obscure to me. But it is foolish ever to write off the inventiveness of people, particularly where torture is involved. And you do seem tortured, young man, if you don't mind me saying so. Would that be a fair observation?'

Ros allowed that it was.

'Tell me more about the woman you suspect to be the mastermind.' Jenfi Mierlo folded her wrists in her lap and leaned forward. 'I am unfamiliar with your Lady Hakamu.'

'I cannot,' he said, unwilling to reveal anything that might identify either of them. 'She is unknown to me, except by name.'

'It seems odd to me that she would thrust her illusory form upon you yet remain herself in the shadows. Are you sure there could be no other agent at work here?'

The phrasing of her observation – 'in the shadows' – reminded Ros of the moment he had first seen Adi's face. There had indeed been another woman present at the time. It wasn't inconceivable that she had triggered the charm then, although he remembered no such thing. He could barely recall her at all. Had she said something as he hurried past her? Had he bumped into her, perhaps?

'I'm as sure as I can be,' he said.

'And you feel you have done nothing to earn such a plight?'

'That is the case, yes.'

'You don't surprise me there,' Jenfi Mierlo said. 'Young men rarely do.' She leaned back. 'I fear I have little help to offer – except for the prospect of employment. You're new to the city, clearly, and in need of friends. I could make an introduction or two, if you liked.'

There was a predatory cast to her face. Ros had seen such before, on traders who recognised a bargain and sought to claim it before its true price became known. Clearly his imposture as a victim of a Change-worker, rather than a practitioner himself, was thinner than he had hoped.

'Thank you,' he said. 'I'll keep that thought in mind.'

'You'll do better than that,' she said, rising suddenly from her chair. 'Wait here. I'll be back in a moment.'

He stood, wishing now he had never come. Instead of rescue, he had found himself swept out to deeper water still. One of the many reasons for studying under Master Pukje had been to defer the attention of sharks who, like Jenfi Mierlo, were drawn to his talent. Many times in his childhood he had been exploited, unknowingly and cruelly, and he would not suffer such again.

'You will go to Madam Van Haasteren.'

He glanced around in surprise. The man'kin had spoken.

'I know that name,' he said. 'Magda Van Haasteren, the seer?'

'You will go to her.'

'Why?' He frowned. 'Can she tell me where Adi is?'

The man'kin didn't answer.

At the sound of Jenfi Mierlo's heels clicking in the hallway outside, Ros turned. She was holding a trinket that was part charm, part business card, which she pressed upon him with irresistible insistence.

Desperate to return to the subject he had come to pursue, Ros indicated the man'kin and said, 'Is your friend here always so reticent?'

'Mawson? He hasn't spoken in a hundred years. If he ever does, the roof will probably fall in.'

She burst into another coughing fit, and Ros took the opportunity to leave her presence. The man'kin's advice had taken on a new significance in the context of its usual silence, and he wanted to avoid another sales pitch. The trinket he kept, though. It was harmless. Apart from the clothes he wore, it was also his sole material possession.

Night had fallen. Ros had almost lost count of how many he had spent in the city now. Eight, he decided. He wouldn't spend this one chasing phantoms. He would take the man'kin at its word and pursue the mystery to its conclusion.

Even from the outside, Magda Van Haasteren's stall reeked of smoke and the murkier applications of power. The Change was neither good nor bad; like air, though, it could be befouled. He hesitated before knocking on the door, irrationally convinced that nothing good would come of it. His senses were muddled. Adi could have been standing right next to him and he wouldn't have known.

To its conclusion, he reminded himself, knocking firmly upon the portal.

'Finally made up your mind, did you?' came the croaky voice from within. 'Come in before you change it again, and shut the door fast behind you.'

Ros kept his first impressions from showing as best he could. The place was crowded, dirty and worn, and the seer herself fared little better in his assessment. But for the aura of potency swirling around her like a cape – thick and dark, as reptilian as a snake – he would have walked out in an instant.

'You're chasing someone,' she said, heavy-lidded eyes sweeping down and then up his frame. 'What's the matter? Has your face frightened her away?'

That same face betrayed him while he considered how best to answer. Blushing furiously, except for the white of his scars, he could only think of the wild-bearded man mocking him in the dosshouse. It was true that there was nothing to be done about his appearance. He could only try to put his fears behind him and trust that Adi would see beyond the mask to what lay beneath.

'Neither of us is going to win any beauty pageants,' he said, not about to have that fear reinforced by a creature like this.

'Indeed we're not.' She waved imperiously. 'You're crooking my neck, making me look up at you. Sit, sit, and tell me about your elusive girlfriend.'

'What do you need to know?'

'How much can you tell me?' Her eyes slitted fractionally. 'No, really – how much?'

Ros gave the matter the attention it deserved. How much did he know about Adi now? It had been five years since he had last seen her. And even then, had he known her well? They had been kids, really, in exceptional straits. It had been easy to let the stories dictate how the rest of their lives were supposed to go. Should he be so surprised that their poorly laid plans had gone awry?

'I thought so,' the seer said as the silence dragged on. 'Yet there was something about her, something that transcends knowledge, requiring no words or explanations. Wasn't there?'

'Yes,' he said, the answer tugged out of him almost against his will. 'I thought – I thought it would be easy. All we had to do was grow up and become – become whoever we needed to be. And then we could be together. Why hasn't it worked like that? I know it was wrong to think she'd drop everything for me, but I've come back for her as I promised, and now she—'

He stopped, unable to speak past the lump that had grown in his throat.

'Perhaps she's testing you,' the seer said. The candle that burned on the table at her side filled the deep lines of her face with shadow. 'Not just you, but the legacy of your first meeting. Has the spark you originally felt survived the passage of time? Sometimes it may not, and they fare badly who try to draw on a power that isn't there. You know that much; you've felt the Void at your feet; you know what awaits us all, in the end. The death of love is no different, and the fear of it drives people to strange exploits.

'You feel you must prove yourself,' she went on, 'yet in that very attempt you trap yourself anew. Why is the burden of proof solely upon you? It's like being an apprentice with a master who never speaks. You can only guess at the lesson and bear the punishment when you get it wrong. And what about her? Is she not also required to do as you do, to demonstrate her faithfulness and determination as well?'

'Yes,' he said, springing to his feet and circling the tiny room. 'I'm not just tested – I'm trapped!'

'And what are you going to do about it?'

'I'm doing it, aren't I?'

'Don't round on me, boy. If I solve this puzzle for you, doesn't that make me more worthy of your girlfriend's hand than you?'

'Well, damn it, what?'

The seer smiled. 'Tell me what it's worth to know.'

He sagged, emptying of anger as suddenly as a water-bladder stabbed with a knife.

'I have nothing of value to give you,' he said in the candle's flickering light.

'That's not true,' the seer told him. 'Not true at all, Roslin of Geheb.'

He stared at her, wondering how long she had known. The whole time, perhaps. 'What do you want?'

Her smile widened. 'I'm trying to ask you the same question.'

'I want Adi,' he said. 'That's all. I have no family, friends or future without her. That's the truth of it, so—'

'So the choice is easy. Go through the curtain. You'll find the answer you seek on the other side.'

He glanced at the dirty wall-hanging with disquiet. The squat armoured figure, picked out in tatty thread, stared back at him with eyes as cold as a man'kin's. A woman's gasping sobs came from beyond the cubicle's thin walls. The air was thick with grief and power – and warning, too. No ordinary doorway lay beyond the curtain. Yet where else did he have to go? The trail ended here.

Ros stood straighter and found a clarity of thought that had eluded him earlier. Whatever awaited him, he would face it head-on. Golems and witches hadn't bested him in the past, and neither had dragons and machines from the dawn of history. He might lack money or prospects, but what need had he of them? Master Pukje had taught him to be strong and sure on his own. If this were a test of more than his faith in Adi, he would pass that as well.

Filling his chest with smoky air and ignoring the old woman's potent stare he stepped forward, through the curtain, into darkness.

The Thrall

Adi's outstretched hands found a brick wall ahead of her. She stopped walking and felt to either side. The wall was curved, and would form a circle roughly four yards across if it met itself behind her. There was no light at all, and therefore no quick way to check. The air was entirely too close and warm. Claustrophobia struck her like a fist to the gut, and she turned to find a way back to the door through which she had come.

The sound of an indrawn breath brought her up short. She wasn't alone.

'Who's there?'

The sounds of the city vanished the moment Ros walked through the curtain, leaving him wondering if he had been struck deaf. At the sound of a woman's tremulous inquiry, he knew that was not so. He also recognised her voice.

'Adi?'

'What's going on? Where am I?'

'Hold on.' He reached out with his senses and found the wall. Grateful for something concrete to deal with, he chose one brick at random, pressed the palm of his hand against it, and flexed his will.

Adi blinked as pinkish light flared into life. It brightened and whitened as the man who had cast it removed his hand from the source.

'You!' she gasped, recognising his scarred face immediately. It was the man she'd collided with the night the charm had been broken. He was the last person she had expected to see. Magda Van Haasteren had promised her understanding. What did he have to do with this?

Ros was no less surprised. The woman spoke with Adi's voice but looked like the stranger he'd seen in the courtyard by the dosshouse. So much for finding answers.

'How is this possible?'

'You tell me,' she said through tight lips. 'You got me into this.'

'Me? No,' he protested. 'It wasn't either of us. It was—'

Ros looked behind him, and for the first time they realised that the door they had come through was invisible. Worse than that, as a quick patting down and thumping of the wall soon revealed, the door was no longer there at all.

'A Way,' he said, remembering everything he had learned about such space-bending passages from Master Pukje. 'The curtain must have hidden it. And now it's closed.'

'We're trapped?'

'We certainly appear to be.'

Adi looked up, then down. They were caught in a chimney or well that vanished into shadow at either extremity. A heavy metal grille was all that kept them from falling.

Heights *and* tight spaces, she thought grimly to herself. What next? Crabblers? Ghosts?

She caught her fellow prisoner staring at her oddly. He turned quickly away.

'I think,' Ros said, suppressing the impulse to bring his hand up to his face, 'I think I can get us out of here. A Way leaves a dimple behind, even when closed. It's like a flaw in glass, and if I can find it—'

'You're babbling. What's wrong with you?'

'Nothing. Just hold on for a moment—'

'No, you wait.' She clutched his arm and pulled him around. 'How do you know my name? What kind of trick is this?'

'Trick? If anyone's tricking anyone, it's you.'

'Oh, please. You can't possibly expect me to fall for that one.'

He wrenched himself from her grip and backed away. For a moment they just glared at each other. Then his face softened.

'Take off your veil,' he said.

'No.'

'I already know your name, so what difference does it make?'

'What difference *does* it make?'

'I want to see your face.'

'Get back to finding that door,' she said, 'or by the time I'm finished with you you'll have no face at all.'

He winced at that, but this time didn't turn away.

'Adi, look at me properly. I'm not hiding anything from you. You can see my face perfectly well. The scars are new, but the rest is all me. Just me. Don't you recognise anything?'

He moved around the well so the light caught his features better. She edged away, unable to tear her gaze from them.

'I'm Ros.'

'Yes.'

'And you're Adi.'

'Yes.'

With numb fingers, she pulled the veil aside.

He sagged with relief. Behind the Clan Markings, it was her. Tired and paler than he'd ever seen before, but her all the same. Adi the girl had become Adi the woman, and he hadn't known her – just as she hadn't known him. The familiarity they had felt in their minds had betrayed their senses, leading them badly astray.

'But if you're you,' she said, 'then who . . .?'

She recoiled with a hand over her mouth, remembering the flaccid form she'd left wrapped in her sheet at the hostel.

'What is it?'

He reached for her, but she wasn't yet ready to be touched.

With shaking voice she explained about the comatose version of him she'd struggled with the last day and a half. He responded with a short account of his own trials.

'Someone's been toying with us,' she said, revulsion becoming anger, and fast. 'I'll have that someone's hide when you get us free of here. And you—' She poked him hard in the upper arm, right where his nerve was. 'You really thought I'd put you through a dance like that? How could you?'

Ros could find no good answer to her question. He returned to the task of finding the Way in the hope it would cover his confusion. 'I'd been looking for so long. I was getting frustrated.'

'Well, that makes two of us. It's crazy to think we were so close and never knew.'

'Maddening. And it did drive me a little mad. I was helped, remember? We must have been, both of us. I can't believe you mistook that imposter for me.'

Her features darkened. He hadn't seen Adi blush for five years. It was distracting him from the task at hand.

'Well,' she said, glancing away, then back again. 'I guess this is what Magda Van Haasteren meant by sending us here.'

'I guess so.'

She touched his shoulder and was amazed at the muscle she felt there. 'It really is you.'

'Yes.'

'And I guess I'll get used to having you around again.'

'I hope so.'

Her fingers moved up to his cheek. 'Will you tell me what happened to you?'

The Way was entirely forgotten now. 'I'll tell you everything,' he said, cupping her hand in his and stepping closer.

It happened so fast there was nothing either could do. To Ros it seemed as though a ring of blue flame blossomed beneath their feet and rushed upwards past them with the speed of a dragon at full stretch. To Adi's eyes, it was a fiery dust devil, spinning with furious energy, born at the invisible bottom of the chimney and whipped up around them, tangling their hair and clothes as it swept up to the heights above.

That it was difficult, afterwards, to place their impressions in accord, was the least of their problems.

The force of the thing's passage blew them to opposite sides of the well-like space. Ros's ears blocked, as they had sometimes when Master Pukje ascended with unexpected swiftness. Adi felt a rush of vertigo and relied on the wall at her back to keep her balance. Above them, the apparition writhed and spun, growing smaller with distance until it vanished entirely. The silence it left in its wake was almost supernatural in its intensity.

For a second, neither spoke. Something had changed, something difficult to define but impossible to deny. It was clear that the flame or dust devil hadn't been a random happenstance. There had been purpose behind it.

The clanking of metal broke the silence. The grille beneath them jerked downward an inch. Adi gasped and clutched the wall even more tightly than before. Ros looked around with wide eyes. What new trial was this?

A second racket came, as of rusty gears turning. The grille dropped again, then froze at a canted angle. It was clear now that it was turning, rotating – and that if it continued the two of them would be tipped to their deaths in the depths of the well.

A third time it turned, further than before. Adi dropped to her knees and put her fingers through the rusted metal slats. Could she hold on as it went? What exactly would that achieve? Better to fall quickly, perhaps, than to remain suspended in terror until the strength in her arms gave out.

Despair rose in her. It was impossible to conceive that just moments ago she had been happy.

Hadn't she?

Ros loomed over her, scarred and strange. He who had seemed so familiar now looked alien and wild. His hair stood out about his head. The air prickled, making her feel as though another apparition was about to burst around them.

Instead it was the world itself that tore. She screamed as the grille seemed to lurch beneath her and she was suddenly weightless, falling.

◆ ◆ ◆

With an explosion of brick dust and mortar, the Way opened in a place far from Magda Van Haasteren's stinking hole. Out of it burst Ros, then Adi, tugged by his arm on her wrist. Filthy, shocked, and grateful to be alive, they staggered away from the gaping rent in the wall behind them. The boom of their arrival echoed and re-echoed through the halls of the city, and this portentous announcement did not go unnoticed.

Ros blinked his eyes clear and took in his surroundings. It was dark, but not so dark they couldn't see. They appeared to have emerged in one of the city's industrial quarters, near a tannery by the smell of it. Numerous vehicles rumbled along a major thoroughfare not one block away.

He craned his head back to inspect the rising cloud of dust silhouetted against the living lights in the ceiling. The Way had closed the moment they'd passed through it, but the after-effects were still spreading.

'We should move,' he said, 'in case anything follows.'

Adi coughed and spat. She had staggered off to find her own bearings, slowly recovering from the suddenness of their escape but still feeling a nag of worry. If anything, the nag was growing stronger, not weaker. She felt she had forgotten something important. The more she reached for it, the further it pulled away.

'It took what it wanted,' she said, understanding that much with certainty. 'That's why we were going to be dumped. It didn't need us any more.'

He nodded and put both hands to his temples. The exertion of opening the way had left him dazed. He would recover, but until then his thoughts moved like slugs. 'So much for what lay behind the damned curtain. Do you think she knew this was going to happen?'

'How couldn't she? It was a set-up, and we walked right into it.' Adi was tired, more tired than she had ever been. 'We're idiots.'

He had no humour in him, but attempted a joke anyway. 'A perfect match.'

She stared at him as though he had said something utterly incomprehensible.

'Are you all right?' he asked, alarmed by a sudden, new intensity to her.

'Quite the opposite, I think.' She shook her head and looked away. 'Ros, it's gone.'

'What's gone?'

'The spark. I don't feel it. When I think of you . . .' Her eyes returned to his. 'I feel . . . nothing.'

He took a step backward, rocked as though from a physical blow. Her words pained him, stung even through the dense fog in his mind, but reaching into himself he found exactly the same yawning absence. What had been so strong and clear just moments before was now missing entirely. It had evaporated.

'That thing,' she said with dismay on her face. 'It took it.'

Ros shook his head, reaching through coldness like a drowning man at a rope.

'Let's not jump to conclusions,' he said.

'What other conclusion could there be?'

'I don't know. But we can't just give up.'

'Do you think we can fix this?'

Tears painted dark streaks through the white dust in her face.

He had no answer for her.

'I'll see if I can flag someone down,' she said, heading at haste for the thoroughfare. 'If we're quick, if we come to her in time, maybe we can get it back.'

The cab was cramped but fast. Fuelled by a mixture of alcohol and the Change, the growl of its engine only added to the pounding in Ros's head. The pain paled in comparison, however, to the feeling that his heart seemed to have died in his chest.

They endured the journey in silence. Although they were crammed together on the back seat, they felt as distant from each other as they had at any point during the previous five years. Adi's thoughts returned constantly to that moment when hope had turned to horror. How could neither of them have seen it coming?

She was conscious, also, of the cab driver glancing at them in the mirror. It was well within reason that he should be curious about the dust-covered pair who had hailed him with such urgency, but it was more than that. Only midway through the journey did she realise she had forgotten to replace her veil. The driver had clearly noted her Clan markings and, if not already certain as to the identity of his passengers, was at least speculating wildly.

The only way to stop him talking was to keep him close by.

'Wait here,' she said when they pulled up outside Magda Van Haasteren's dive. 'We'll need you afterwards.'

The value of the coin she gave him was out of all proportion with the request. He understood immediately. 'Of course, miss,' he said. 'I'll not go anywhere.'

They left the cab and warily approached the portal through which they had both entered earlier that night. The magnitude of the charm that had enveloped them boggled Ros's mind. Not only had their paths crossed, but they had also come to this very place practically at the same time. How was it possible they had not noticed, that Magda Van Haasteren had talked to both of them simultaneously, *that he had not seen her*? He was angry at himself for letting the broader illusions distract him while a deeper treachery unfolded. That was a lesson he would not forget in a hurry.

You feel it with your whole body and in all your thoughts, Adi was thinking as she stared at the door. *It's like a little bit of lightning, and it too can start a fire.*

Ros too was remembering what the seer had told him about the spark. *They fare badly who try to draw on a power that isn't there.*

The hovel was empty, but only recently so. That Magda Van Haasteren had fled in a hurry was left in no doubt by the cheroot still smoking in an overflowing ashtray, and the many possessions she had left behind. Even in the absence of candlelight they could make out the curtain still hanging on the wall before them.

Ros tore it down and threw it aside. A featureless wall stared back at them.

'She heard us coming,' Adi said.

Ros nodded. 'We'll never find her. She could be anywhere.'

'So where to now?'

Separately, they reviewed the path that had brought them here. It couldn't have been entirely illusion, unless the entire city had fallen victim to it. Furthermore, man'kin weren't easily influenced . . .

Ros pulled the business card from his pocket and held it up for Adi to see.

Facing each other in the study two couples sat, one old, one new – if they were a couple at all – and on the floor between them rested the bust of the man'kin, Mawson.

'You say he spoke?' asked Jenfi Mierlo. 'To both of you?'

'Without question,' Adi replied. 'He told us the same thing: to go to Magda Van Haasteren.'

'You will go to Madam Van Haasteren,' the bust obediently repeated, like a parrot.

'You see?'

Jenfi Mierlo gaped first at Adi, then at Mawson. Then she started coughing, and Ros thought she would never stop.

'The trouble is,' said Samson, when his wife's fit had subsided, 'that Mawson didn't in fact tell you to go anywhere. He simply said where you were going.'

'I hardly see the difference,' Adi retorted. 'We wouldn't have gone if he hadn't brought it up.'

'And therein lies the problem with man'kin. They don't experience time the same way we do. They see it all at once, so as far as he's concerned: you will go, you have gone, and you are already there – all at once. The notion of intentionality is quite foreign to him. Sometimes, dear, I think it'd be better if they never spoke at all.'

'Yes, yes,' his wife said, tipping her birdlike frame to the right and then straightening again, 'but we're missing the point. Mawson isn't the culprit. It's that wretched Van Haasteren woman again.'

'Again?' Ros asked.

The elder couple exchanged a look. It was clear that neither wanted to be the one to explain.

'If we'd known who you were—'

'If you'd told us about Mawson—'

They cut each other off. Jenfi waved for her husband to continue.

'I mean to say,' he said, 'that you fit her requirements perfectly. The pair of you, not as individuals. She of course knew your history. She had years to study you and to prepare the trap. First she lured you, Ros, to the city, thus ensuring that Adi would also come. Once you were both here, she redoubled her efforts. She took your feelings for each other and turned them around – and did so quite expertly, I must say. You were hopelessly entangled. There was no chance of seeing your way out of it.'

'What he's trying to say,' said Jenfi, 'is that she played on your worst fears: that you wouldn't be recognised or respected for who you were. And of course you played along with those fears. Albeit unwittingly: you *were* both hiding; you both *had* changed. All Van Haasteren had to do was set the ball rolling. You did the rest.'

'But why?' asked Adi.

'Why would she want to do something like this?' Ros echoed. 'To us?'

'You mentioned the spark,' said Samson, taking his wife's hand in his. 'That was what she wanted, as you have deduced, and everything she did was designed to magnify its existence. You enjoyed it in your youth, and you might have reawakened it naturally, simply by being reunited – but the fact that you didn't even recognise each other the first time you crossed paths suggests otherwise. Your spark therefore had to be nurtured – by anxiety, by doubt – and by hope too, for without that the spark never catches.'

'She primed you for that meeting behind the curtain,' Jenfi concluded. 'For the moment in which you truly recognised each other. That was what she wanted. Not just a spark, but first-class ignition.'

Ros and Adi remembered that moment well. What power

their spark had had! Now it was harnessed by another, the value it might have had to them was irrelevant.

'We would have warned you off,' Jenfi repeated, 'if only you'd told us.'

'How could we have known?' Adi rose suddenly to her feet. 'You make it sound like it's our fault. But it's not.'

'No one's saying that. Are you?' Ros asked the Mierlos.

Adi didn't wait for an answer. With fast angry paces, she walked from the room.

'Wait here, Ros.' Jenfi Mierlo hurried after her.

'There's something else,' said Samson Mierlo in a grave voice, leaning forward to look Ros in the eye. 'There's something else you both need to know.'

They received much the same addendum in much the same words, Ros in the study and Adi at the front of the Mierlo mansion, where Jenfi had caught her before she climbed into the cab.

'Magda Van Haasteren doesn't work alone,' the Mierlos told them. 'She's in partnership with something else, a creature that's named in the bestiaries but barely described. No one knows what form such creatures take or where they come from. No one knows where she found this one or why she tamed it. All we know is what it does.

'Van Haasteren is the procurer in the arrangement. She finds the lovers and lures them into her trap, pair by pair as you were lured. At the heart of the trap lies the creature, which thrives on the offerings she brings. They are a meal to it, you see. It has no hunger for flesh and blood, for it isn't a material creature. Like eats like. This being has no physical presence, and has a hunger to match.

'It eats the spark. That's all. And that's how we know what it is. Stone Mages have examined a rash of deaths in recent years – all pairs, all mysterious. Their bodies showed death by falling, but there were other signs, hints of a more sinister rupture before death came to them. We followed the investigation, for it touched on our own interests; we noted its conclusion. The Stone Mages can't convict Magda Van Haasteren of anything, for she herself has done nothing wrong. The lovers came to her of their own free will; her pet does the rest; and she is canny enough to leave no evidence. Since predators are not disallowed in the city – for if they were, the markets would be forced to close forever – all we can do is warn people away, and hope they'll listen.

'But lovers rarely do. They're caught in their own world. That's the great tragedy of it all – that the situation wouldn't be possible without desire and dreams, those things that normally make us flourish. The dark side of the spark, if you will.

'The bait in the trap was set by you yourselves.'

'Not all stories have the happy ending we desire,' Samson said, putting an avuncular hand on Ros's shoulder, 'but that doesn't make them bad stories.'

Jenfi told Adi: 'It's not entirely hopeless. The Mages can tell when a Way opens up outside the city, so they'll know if Van Haasteren is still here, somewhere.'

Neither Ros nor Adi was soothed.

'You said it has a name – the thing that ate our spark?'

Jenfi and Samson Mierlo told them, knowing the value of naming an enemy even when the fight has been lost.

'It's a trystophage,' said Samson.

'It's an amavore,' said Jenfi.

Both said, 'Its common name is the Thrall.'

◆ ◆ ◆

'What now?' Ros asked as they took their leave of the Mierlos, no happier but at least better informed.

'I don't know.' Adi's exhaustion was total. 'Your things are back at the hostel, if you still want them.'

He wasn't sure, but said nonetheless: 'Perhaps I can help you get rid of that doppelganger, while I'm there.'

To the Lost Dolphin they went, where they found the hostel in a state of restrained panic. The doppelganger had dissolved in a shower of fiery arcs an hour ago, startling the maid and setting fire to the bed. The fire had been extinguished before serious damage resulted, but the place remained in an uproar. To this was now added the revelation that Lady Hakamu might be none other than Aditi Sabatino, judging by her Clan markings – for Adi had forgotten once again to replace her veil – and if that were the case, then the long-haired, scarred stranger could only be her legendary betrothed, Roslin of Geheb.

The whispers as they surveyed the damaged room were impossible to ignore. Adi knew she wouldn't be able to bribe the entire staff, as she hoped she had silenced the cab driver when they finally let him go.

'Just give me one night,' she begged the manager and the staff. 'That's all I ask. Then I'll release you. Tell the world then, if you must.'

'There's nothing to tell, anyway,' said Ros, misunderstanding the situation completely.

'If you do it for us,' Adi added more persuasively, 'you will become part of the story. You'll have given us sanctuary when we most needed it.'

The hostel's manager, sensing an opportunity for free publicity, took the matter into his hands. He swore the staff would be discrete, on penalty of his own job. Threats were issued to all in his presence and solemn oaths undertaken. Furthermore, he said, the hostel's other guests would be moved elsewhere – the smell of smoke had given them the jitters anyway – and new arrivals would be carefully vetted before gaining access to the building.

'Thank you,' said Adi. Ros echoed the sentiment wholeheartedly.

And so the room was cleared.

They checked their belongings without talking. It didn't seem to Ros that words were possible between them now. The Thrall had taken them too. There was just emotion, raw and red, too painful to pick at.

Among Adi's scattered effects, none of which appeared to have been burned, she found the broken charm. The wave of grief she felt then was so powerful that she lost all strength in her legs. She let herself fall into a chair and cradled the charm in her hands. What good had following it brought her? All those dreams, all those hopes, shattered like the workings of the charm itself.

Ros walked past her, and the crystal flared bright red.

They both stared at it in surprise. Had it fixed itself somehow? Had it too been afflicted by Van Haasteren's web of deceit?

More likely, they both realised, it had been working all along. When Ros had brushed past Adi by the dosshouse, he had gone from being in front of her to behind her. If she'd turned and pointed the charm his way, it would have glowed as normal. But she didn't. Instead she saw the doppelganger and thought she'd reached the end of her quest. She stopped looking.

The pain on Adi's face was awful to behold. Ros assumed his looked much the same.

'I guess I should leave,' he said, hefting the pack he'd thought lost forever.

'Don't be ridiculous. I'm not sending you back to that horrible place.'

The suite was far more comfortable than the dosshouse, even with the scorch marks on the bed. Ros appreciated the offer.

'I can sleep on the floor.'

'No. You take the bed.'

Fresh linen had been left, but neither of them made a move towards it.

'Are you sure?'

'Positive. You need it more than me, and honestly, I could sleep anywhere.'

'Well, all right.'

Ros replaced the sheets while Adi arranged cushions in a corner, diagonally opposite from the bed. They didn't look at each other as they undressed. They didn't talk, not even to say goodnight. The light was extinguished, and they lay for an eternity, listening to each other breathe.

♦ ♦ ♦

A shaking of the bed woke Ros from a nightmare in which his face and hands were being scarred anew. Adi crouched motionlessly beside him, barely visible in the darkness. Her eyes caught every faint trace of light in the room and sent them, refracted and concentrated, right at him.

'I want to stop her,' she said. 'No one deserves to feel like this.'

'I agree. We'll do it tomorrow. Together.'

'There's no together anymore, Ros. We can't think like that.'

'Then we'll ask for help. Everyone'll know we're here by breakfast anyway, so let's get the whole city looking for her. Use the stories to our advantage for a change.'

Adi didn't confess that she'd already been doing that, when it suited her.

'I want revenge, too,' she said, lying down next to him.

Ros put his arm around her. They stayed that way as sleep claimed them again, and they didn't wake until dawn.

Keepsake

Word spread like fire through tall grass. Where the rumour started wasn't clear. The light-chimneys had barely delivered the distant sun's first rays when its source was obscured behind a wall of friends-of-friends and cousins-in-the-know. Once the news hit the markets, it took on a life of its own.

Roslin of Geheb and Aditi Sabatino – he who vanquished the Golem of Omus and she who walked the Weird – were in Ulum, and in trouble.

Once released, the story accrued strange new details: that a monster walked the city streets, devouring children; that an explosion the previous night heralded an invasion from the depths of the earth; that the pair were impostors whose real selves had been disposed of days earlier. Among the elaborations and fabrications, however, lurked enough of the truth for the message to sink in. That which the famous lovers held most precious in the world had been stolen by a seer.

Every one of the city's innocent seers – if such existed – closed shop for fear of reprisals against them personally or the profession as a whole. Some declared themselves to the authorities in advance of wrongful accusations. A description of the culprit in question circulated, passing from hand to hand and via the more exotic means available to those talented in the Change. Officially, the Stone Mages played no role in the seer-hunt; they could not until the ruling Synod had issued an order to that effect. Unofficially, a growing cadre assembled in the city's Grand Minster in order to lend their weight to the search.

Hastily constructed charms scoured the underworld for clues, while ethereal images and messages wafted along the streets. Regular commerce ground to a halt. Of those with a choice, only the most churlish abstained from the citywide effort. Some grumbled about the jammed thoroughfares or the delays in services, but all pitched in somehow. Reports flooded in of suspicious-looking characters, most bearing no resemblance whatsoever to the missing woman. Boarded-up spaces were exposed to daylight, some for the first time in decades. Panic spread through the city's rodent and insect population as previously safe haunts were overturned. Birds and lizards headed for roosts out of reach of human hands.

The day wore on. Crowds gathered in wait of news, hopeful too for a glimpse of the famous couple. Whispers spread of sightings as leads were followed and dismissed, one after the other. Opportunistic merchants set up stalls and manipulated rumours to direct crowds their way. As night approached, a carnival atmosphere set in, complete with music and impromptu dances. Families and neighbours set up camp on corners, sharing wine, beer and food, and any news that happened to pass through. Not all was merriment and joy, of course, for the reason for the holiday had not been forgotten. Fights broke out in places, among the poor-tempered and those who found the tension too much. The people of the city were waiting for an outcome, each in their own way. Ulum, as a whole, held its breath.

From behind the curtained windows of their hostel room, Ros listened to the crowds moving through the city. They had barely left the building all day, relying on runners and other means to convey messages back and forth. Only twice, when particularly strong evidence had pointed to a near-certain location, had they gone out in pursuit of a resolution, and even then only by a back entrance, secure from the public eye. The hostel had hunkered down around them, the manager enjoying his role as their protector and confidante. Adi dreaded to think about the size of the bill.

'What if she's gone?'

She looked up from double-checking the stack of information that had already been gathered. 'Do you think it's possible?'

He doubted it. The city had been physically sealed all day, as well as blocked against the Change. If she had made a dash for the outside the very moment her latest lovers had been kidnapped, maybe then she could have made it out in time. The still-smoking cheroot haunted that theory like a ghost; it wouldn't be laid to rest, and made a mockery of the attempt.

'She has to be here somewhere.'

A team of volunteer Stone Mages had gone over every inch of her abandoned stall. The Way Ros and Adi had followed was now firmly shut, and the room clear of any other exit. Van Haasteren must, therefore, have had another escape route secreted nearby. Neighbouring buildings had been searched from top to bottom, without success.

Adi pushed the stack aside. 'What about *why* rather than *where*? That's what I'm stuck on. What's in it for her? She fed the Thrall, but she must've gained something in return.'

'Not wealth, that's for sure,' he said.

'Or fame.'

'Look where they've got us.'

'My point's the same, though. She's a criminal. Her motive has to be more than just cruelty.'

Adi remembered the passion with which the seer had spoken of the spark.

'Maybe her own spark died,' she said, posing an answer to her own question, 'and she doesn't want anyone else to be happy.'

Ros felt the thought coming long before it arrived. Something Adi had said had collided with a detail considered irrelevant, and together they prompted another question.

'What about *how*?'

'The Change,' she said. 'All that.'

'But where did she learn it? Even rogue Change-workers have teachers, and I've never heard of anything like this.'

'Maybe she invented it herself.'

'Not from scratch. That's impossible. She would've burned herself out, most likely, or at least attracted serious attention before now.' He tapped his chin. 'No, there had to be someone else. Someone who helped her at least part of the way.'

The thought was still coming. He gave it time while she watched him, wondering what was going on inside his head.

Suddenly he was heading for the door and scooping her up along the way. Come on,' he said. 'I know exactly how to find her.'

'But we've already searched here,' said Adi when the convoy they were leading pulled up at the seer's hovel. 'Over and over.'

'Not well enough,' he said, fairly bounding from the cab and approaching the entrance. Armoured Mages recognised him barely in time and waved him through a split-instant after he had passed.

Adi dragged herself after him, reluctant to return to that awful hole no matter how excited Ros appeared to be about it. He had kept the secret to himself the whole trip, saying he wanted to be sure. She told him not to worry about getting her hopes up, since they were as low as they could possibly go, but he had stayed silent, fairly vibrating with energy.

Before she could reach the door he emerged again, holding something heavy and shapeless in his arms.

'Take one end,' he said. 'Turn it over.'

Together they unfurled the curtain through which they had walked to their spark's doom. The threadbare Stone Mage stared up at the unnatural stars. By their light his indifference looked entirely calculated.

'Lay it down, right here.'

Adi did so and took a wary step backwards.

'Watch,' Ros said.

This was the first time she had witnessed his new skills with the Change. His movements were economical and assured. There was no urgent fumbling, as there had been in his youth or when in the grip of the Thrall. Here he was cool and confident, utterly in command.

The world flexed around them.

Adi and the small crowd that had gathered watched to see what would happen next.

Ros stepped lightly onto the carpet and dropped out of sight into Magda Van Haasteren's hidden Way.

Immediately he stumbled, made clumsy by an awkward tangle of geometries. He had wanted his revelation to be dramatic. He had wanted Adi to be surprised. Too late he realised that they should have fixed the curtain vertically, as it had been originally placed, so he could simply walk through instead of dropping out of the wall on the other end of it.

He was the one caught off-balance. His right foot came down awkwardly, twisting his ankle. Pain shot up his calf and the leg gave way beneath him. He tumbled forward and landed heavily on his side.

'Get ready to catch your girlfriend,' growled a familiar voice.

Ros rolled onto his back with his hands upraised as Adi hurtled through the Way after him. Lighter and more sure on her feet, she merely staggered two steps and came to a halt, standing still before him with both soles firmly planted.

Behind her, the Way snapped shut with a whip-crack, silencing a growing clamour from the far side.

Ros gathered his strength to punch a hole back through.

'Do it,' said the seer, 'and I'll kill all three of us.'

Magda Van Haasteren was a shapeless mass sitting in the centre of the rough-hewn chamber, hunched over a candlestick holder as though for warmth. The candle was lit, casting a flickering yellow light across her walnut features. Adi helped Ros to his feet, watching the seer closely and taking the measure of the place in which she had sought refuge. It was far below the city's deepest extent, that much Adi was sure of, with no physical entrances or exits, windows or exhausts. The air was clammy, hot and foul, and apart from the candle the only light came from tiny glowstones embedded in the ceiling like jewels. Water dripped in a far corner, and trickled elsewhere, leaving gleaming paths and stalactites in its wake.

The seer's hidey-hole wasn't a comfortable space by any human standards. The more Adi saw, the less certain she became that it was intended for human habitation at all. A series of makeshift shelves lined the chamber's walls, and on those shelves were things that hurt the eye to look at.

'Do that too,' said the seer at some plot of Ros's that Adi

couldn't sense, 'and I'll lock you down here forever. With me.'

Ros sagged backwards, favouring his right leg.

'Are we trapped?' Adi asked him, sotto voce.

'No. I'm sure I can get us out.'

'How sure?'

'As sure as he can be, girl,' the seer said with a cackle at their expense. 'You're asking the impossible and he's failing to deliver it. Or he's showing off and you're not being a very good audience. I forget which.'

Adi's fury rose. 'We should leave you to rot.'

'I'm rotten enough as is.' The seer put the candlestick to one side and stood up with a grunt, her shape hardly changing. 'As are we all, on the inside. See that one there?' One twisted finger stabbed at the nearest shelf. 'That's all that remains of your spark.'

Ros stared at the thing she indicated, aware of Adi's hand painfully gripping his arm. It, like the others filling the shelves, was black and twisted, seeming both thorned and half-melted at the same time. Some grass seeds had the same look, seen up close, but this held no vitality or beneficence. It was entirely malefic.

'What did you do to it?'

'I did nothing – and what was done would have been done anyway. You would've killed your spark without the Thrall's intervention.'

'Never,' said Adi, sure that the aching void in her heart had once held something of great permanence.

The seer hobbled to the shelf and picked up the hideous object. 'The surety of youth is a brilliant thing. It takes a brighter fire still to burn it out. You'll see soon enough that I did you a favour. I've seared your soul against the wound of disappointment; the deeper scars of loss and regret you'll never know. You should thank me rather than rail against me.'

'You would've killed us,' said Ros, 'like the others.'

'Yes, but don't you see that would have been a blessing too?' The seer clutched the thing in her hands, not heeding how its wicked points cut her, or at least not minding. 'Where there is life, there is hope – and hope makes us do terrible, terrible things.'

'You're done now,' said Adi, repulsed by the mixture of self-pity and triumph displayed before her. 'Ulum has had enough of your "blessings".'

The seer uttered a sound that might have been a laugh. Blood dripped in heavy splashes to her feet. 'So you plan to kill me. I thought you came to take back what you have lost. What if I told you that I could return it to you? Would you let me go, if I did?'

Ros knew she was lying. She had to be, for such a claim was preposterous. The spark had been eaten. All that remained was the waste, the excreta, of a being that thrived on the dreams of others.

Yet he was tempted. To recover what had been taken – to reclaim the future he had spent five years planning . . .

'And then what?' said Adi. 'We don't have much in common, Ros and I. That's why our story was so popular. We were the odd couple, the mismatch made good. Look at how we tested each other when you gave us the chance. Look at the wedge we drove between ourselves. You didn't create that wedge; it was already there. You just wielded what we would've wielded against each other, in time.'

The seer's lips curled. 'You're not so dense after all. Congratulations.'

'That's what you'd have us believe, anyway.' Adi had let go of Ros and was moving slowly to her left, widening the gap between them. 'You spared us the lie of the spark and an agonised life when it's gone. You tell yourself it's a good thing because you wish someone had done it to you. You don't have the courage to end your own pain, so you end the pain of others instead. You create it, and then you end it. You're your own little industry, aren't you?'

'Stay back.'

The seer's eyes danced between the two of them. She was beginning to feel hemmed in: Ros could see that much. He wanted to warn Adi to be careful, to be wary of pushing her too hard, but he was unwilling to interrupt the tide of words. True or not, Adi's insights were having a profound effect on the seer.

'Stay back, I said!'

'Who did this to you?' Adi pressed, feeling her fortunes turning at last. 'Who did *you* lose?'

The seer snarled. With surprising strength, she hurled the wicked thing at Adi's head. Adi raised her hands to ward it off, but the barbs dug deep. She fell backwards with a cry.

Ros was already reaching for the Change when the seer turned to him. They were surrounded by stone – stone wedded hard to the bedrock by virtue of its depth. He was surrounded by power. All he had to do was channel it.

So too the seer, and she had blood and territory on her side. Their wills locked in strange and deadly shapes in her secret hideaway. Light flared through all colours of the rainbow. Flashes of heat seared their skins. The floor beneath them buckled, and showers of dust and rock rained on them. The black shapes lining the walls exploded like ghastly black rockets, filling the air with soot.

Ros knew within seconds that he had the measure of her. It wasn't in his mind to end it quickly, though. He needed to know the source of her knowledge. He had to be sure his guess was right.

And thus it turned out to be, for behind her wild improvisations and baroque peccadilloes he did recognise a philosophy, a method of teaching that was different from his own but at the same time familiar to him, as it would have been to any Change-worker raised in the Interior. A Stone Mage had taken her part of the road towards mastery – a Stone Mage much like the one depicted on the curtain.

The battle of wills had achieved its purpose. Ros bore down as Master Pukje had taught him, forcing his will upon her so that she could hurt no one else. His intention was not to kill her, but to bind her long enough for the authorities to take her captive. His desire for revenge only went that far.

Movement to one side caught both their attentions. Adi was up and moving, groggily but purposefully. Somehow, despite all the commotion, the candle was still burning. With one bleeding hand she reached for it.

Ros reeled back at a wild attack from the seer. Driven by surprise and panic, she rushed for Adi. From whence the sudden surge came, Ros didn't know. It was all he could do to slow the vicious outpour and prevent Adi from being riven in two.

For herself, Adi was aware of a terrible conflict waging over her, buffeting her from side to side, but she couldn't let it get in the way of what she had to do. She had guessed the source of the seer's tortured motivations. There was a hurt in

Magda Van Haasteren's past that matched Adi's own, and she maintained it still, perversely nurturing it just as she nurtured the Thrall. The two, therefore, the pain and the Thrall, had to be connected by more than just metaphor. If one wasn't literally the other, then perhaps they shared the same origin.

The Thrall had rushed at Ros and Adi like an ascending bubble of flame, sweeping their spark off with it. Adi didn't understand what kind of creature it was, but she did understand the nature of human desires and needs. When Magda Van Haasteren had sensed that Ros and Adi had escaped, she had taken just one thing from her stinking hovel. That one thing was the candle, and she had been cradling it when Ros and Adi had found her.

Adi's right hand was slick with her own blood. Thumb and forefinger hissed when she closed them tight about the flame. It squirmed and writhed, as slippery as a slug, and it burned her as badly as her dead spark's barbs. Pain lanced up her arm and assailed her body and mind. She fought it with fury and maintained her grip. It felt good to reverse the flow of ill fortune. The Thrall would die just as all of Adi's childish hopes were now dead and gone forever.

The Thrall howled as the fire of its existence was slowly extinguished. Adi felt a lifetime of guilt and entrapment burn through her, and knew she had guessed correctly. The source of the seer's despair and power were one and the same. Had he betrayed the young woman he had been teaching? Had he used her love and thought to throw it away? Either way, the seer had taken her revenge on the man who had wronged her, forcing him to kill in order to live on as a captive, and to feed by taking that which he had taken from her.

The storm intensified in direct proportion to the fading

of the flame. When the latter died, so did the other. All resistance collapsed, and Ros and Adi fell to the ground, stunned by the sudden silence, spent.

Ros could barely crawl. The glowstones shone fitfully and the air remained thick with ash. He could hear Adi breathing – or did he simply imagine that he could? – and by painful effort was able to follow the sound to where she lay huddled on her side, cradling the dead spark tenderly with all of her body. He touched her hair, and she rolled over to face him, leaving the awful thing behind.

'Is she dead?' Adi asked.

'I think so. By her own hand.'

She winced, but there was triumph in her eyes, too. 'We managed it, then.'

'We did. Together.'

They lay side by side for a long moment, holding hands tightly, unsure exactly what this meant for them.

'I suppose we should go soon,' he said, thinking with no great joy of the crowds awaiting them.

'I'm taking it with us,' she said with iron in her voice.

He understood, and lacked the strength to argue.

◆ ◆ ◆

The closed cab that whisked Ros and Adi from the scene was the talk of the city's night owls, for its import was ambivalent, perhaps even ominous. While it was good news the pair had survived, the fate of the treacherous seer and the great romance itself was not known. A new kind of anxiety gripped the darkened streets. Was seeing justice done better than seeing damage undone, or vice versa? If one couldn't have both, who could possibly choose between them?

The Mierlos guided them into the mansion, trusting in the cloak of night and a torturously complicated route to keep prying eyes at bay. Adi was shaking, and Ros felt as though every bone in his body might spontaneously shatter. A physician was on-hand to tend their ailments, both physical and otherwise. Adi's wounds were bathed and bandaged; Ros's twisted ankle was bound. Both were given clean clothes and all the food they could stomach. No one asked about the ebon crystal that rested on Mawson's former plinth in the study. That it was to be guarded and not touched was the only instruction issued, by both of the Mierlos' guests.

Shortly before midnight a small gathering convened in the study. There a senior Stone Mage presented his conclusions on the matter of the Thrall and its patron, Magda Van Haasteren. Her body had been recovered from the underground redoubt. An autopsy had confirmed Ros's intuitive diagnosis: her heart had literally burst from the application of her own will. Neither Ros nor Adi were to blame for her death, although if they had been they would surely have been exonerated.

Few doubted Adi's interpretation of the creature's origins, and several candidates were put forward to account for the man the Thrall had been. No one accused Adi of killing the Thrall too quickly, but it was apparent that the lack of an opportunity to test the hypothesis seemed a shame to some. Perhaps all such creatures had undergone the tragic birth and endured the grotesque symbiotic life as this one. Until another appeared, there was little way to tell.

A representative of the city's administration officially apologised for the damage done by one of its residents, and expressed a sincere hope the incident would not affect relations between Ulum and the trading Clans, who were, after all, the lifeblood of the Interior. Adi assured him that it would not, and went on to profess her profound gratitude to the people of the city for lending their aid when need had been greatest.

'On that matter,' Jenfi Mierlo began, but her husband nudged her silent.

There followed several other declarations, clarifications, and interrogations, all of which began to take on a slightly surreal nature until, finally, the hosts declared the convention over and ushered the officials to the door.

'You're welcome to rest here the night,' said the mistress of the house when its halls were quiet once more, 'but there's something we want to tell you first.'

'Your spark was powerful, yes,' said Samson Mierlo, pacing awkwardly about the sealed study. His tone was the same as it had been the day he had informed Adi that Ros was lost in the Void Beneath. He indicated the twisted black thing: 'There's nothing to be done for it now, though. You have to move on.'

'What are you suggesting?' Adi asked, her face taut and pinched. Inside, despite the ministrations of all those who had tried to help, she felt the same.

'I'm suggesting we are not so different, Jenfi and I. That is, we *are* quite different from each other, but that's what makes us the same as you two. We can serve as an example, if you need one.'

'You must feel that all is lost,' Jenfi said, turning violet with the effort of restraining her relentless croup. 'But it isn't. If a spark were all it took for love to survive – not just survive; thrive and grow – Samson and I would have parted years before now. Not one couple in the history of the world has ever been perfectly matched, and not one spark has lasted the length of a marriage. Sparks come and go – that's the secret your twisted friend neglected to learn.'

'You're rather fortunate, after a fashion,' said Samson.

Ros stared at him as he had stared at Magda Van Haasteren, who had suggested the same awful thing.

'This is the worst it will ever be,' Jenfi explained. 'You've seen what happens when expectations aren't met. Hopes dashed, dreams unfulfilled – and that was before the spark was taken.' She waved a hand expressively. 'How much better to move forward with eyes unclouded in search of a new spark, one you brought into being yourselves rather than one that owned you.'

'Because you have all the raw materials,' said Samson. 'You have a history – as anyone can tell you – and now you have shared something else too. Several equally important things. A common enemy and unity of purpose; grief – and a keepsake to remind you of everything that happened here. Sparks have been born from significantly less than that, in my experience.'

'But what if that's not what we want?' Adi interjected. 'What if everything we now have in common,' – she couldn't keep the bitterness from her voice – 'the pain and the suffering, the memories, the exhaustion – what if that becomes self-perpetuating? What if we just want to leave it behind and go back into hiding again?'

Jenfi Mierlo folded her hands in her lap. Ros recognised the fiduciary gleam that returned to her eyes.

'I'm afraid,' she said, 'that isn't an option just yet.'

Dawn crept down Ulum's chimneys and cast the beginning of another day in a muted golden light. It had been a long night for all in the city, and an especially dark night for some. An atmosphere of apprehension had settled in like fog, making restless even the most stoic of dreamers. Rumours continued to fly, if more sluggishly than previously without fact to back them up. Roslin of Geheb and Aditi Sabatino had not been seen for hours. Some said they were gone, and would never visit the city again. Had all of Ulum's help been for nothing? Would the markets ever re-open?

That morning's crowds were simply waiting for answers. Wild-beard was among them, with a mazed look and a leer for any who caught his eye, along with the cab driver who had whisked Ros and Adi to safety after escaping the trap, and the maid who had watched doppelganger-Ros decrepitate. They knew as little as anyone else. Those who did know were, for the moment, not talking.

Ros dressed with a calm he would have though impossible just hours before. Adi helped him fold the fabric; the style had risen to prominence during his long apprenticeship. The terror of the everyday was for the moment deferred, thanks in no small part to her good example. The world of the Thrall and the seer – *his* world – had been no less challenging for her, and she had excelled in it.

They had spent the night at the Mierlos', who had, without obvious dissemblance, explained that only one guestroom was available. Although they had chafed at the intimacy at first, later they been glad for the opportunity to talk through everything they had been told – for a telling-to is what it had amounted to. And later still, with the advice of their benefactors still clear in their minds, they had stopped talking altogether, feeling as though they had no choice in the matter, but not in an inordinately negative sense. The truth of it was that it had been a relief to let go of the expectation that they *should* choose. The head couldn't stand in for the heart when it came to such matters. The moment decided, if anything did, and in that moment all had been well, and something of a release for both of them.

When the folding and tying was done, they held each other tightly and cried. There was nothing shameful or wretched in it. The time for that had passed. New challenges awaited them, deserving their attention. They could still grieve, but at the same time they could also move on.

Ros looked uncomfortable in his finery. Adi wished he would relax into it, but supposed he would in time. He had been so powerful, so potent, in Van Haasteren's subterranean cave, and she was prepared now to give him the benefit of the doubt. For herself, she had chosen something absurdly impractical from her wardrobe, recovered from the Lost Dolphin before souvenir collectors could claim it. She was aware that a large part of her took comfort from the familiar routine of dressing and the novelty of preparing someone else's dress, and although it wasn't a habit she wanted to encourage, for now she would embrace the task.

'True stories don't have endings,' said he in a contemplative tone. Mawson had broken his silence for the third time to deliver that gnomic fragment, which she supposed gave some insight into his stony motivations.

'Indeed,' she said, quoting in turn Jenfi Mierlo's opinion on the importance of the people around them, not merely as customers who spent more when they were happy: 'And love doesn't thrive in isolation.'

Hand in hand, they went to pay their respects to the city.

Jump to . . .

another love story
'Impossible Music' (p. 129)

more fantasy
'Ungentle Fire' (p. 51)

something completely different
'Go' (p. 39)

Notes on *Team Sharon*

There's an accepted and widely adopted form of masculinity that I just don't get. This story is an attempt, albeit a parodic one, to embrace it.

I'm not saying I don't like men. I'm not even saying I don't belong to a group of male friends who occasionally (well, twice) go on 'mancations' together. Because that would be a lie. I don't, however, generally seek the company of men, exclusively, and I find many of the things that men typically talk about alien to my interests. Sport. Cars. The perceived failures of their spouses. Barbecuing.

These interests are clearly not universally 'male', since I am a man and don't share them. That they are often marketed as universal, though, alienates men like me, and leads me to the company of women, among whom I feel more likely to find conversation that interests me, concerning kids, non-meat products, and the arts, say.

Sometimes I am disappointed, because of course women are no more homogenous than men. Furthermore, I'm much more tolerant of the aforementioned 'alien' topics in the company of women. So perhaps the problem is me.

Clearly, the act of writing this story didn't help in the slightest!

Team Sharon

It was a hot Monday evening, and Stan was bubbling over.

Her unit was the first of six in a cul-de-sac two blocks away. A short walk, during which he concentrated on projecting the appearance that he was just *Taking the Air* and *Going Nowhere In Particular*. He followed her jogging route automatically. She ran past his house every morning before work at 7.15 and went to the gym three nights a week: Monday, Wednesday and Friday. She was gorgeous, and completely unaware of the effect she had on Stan.

If he got any hotter he'd explode like an unpricked egg in a microwave. At the entrance to the cul-de-sac, he stopped to survey the scene. Opposite her unit lay the sort of miniature park local councils sometimes added as compensation for closing off a handy shortcut. There was a children's playground and plenty of bushes. From the park one could gain a perfect view of the windows of her home. Stan knew this; he had tried during the day when she was out. He had also noted what time she came home from the gym by waiting for her car around the corner. She was due in ten minutes.

This was it. He couldn't tell if he was excited or terrified. He didn't know whether to follow The Plan or keep walking past the street. If he went home now, he could pretend he'd never got this far. If he *did* do it . . . well, that was the clincher.

He would have crossed a line into uncharted territory. What if he never came back?

But he hadn't had a girlfriend for so long he was starting to forget how it felt to be intimate. He needed to connect, no matter how remotely, to someone *real*. He had been sweating inside, alone, for too long. If this was what it took to make him feel something new – to give him a sort of excitement that didn't originate within him and wasn't under his complete control – then maybe he had to do it.

Maybe.

Yes.

He took a step forward into her street, then another. He kept his eyes down on the pavement – *Don't Mind Me; I'm Just Stretching My Legs* – but tried at the same time to watch the neighbouring houses and parked cars. No one watering their lawn? No one seeing off a friend? No one at all, he hoped.

The park was black and inviting. He slipped into its shadows like an under-sized fish thrown back into the sea. Bushes rustled at him; the grass felt soft beneath his feet. He spied the cover he had chosen – a large, thick bush – out of the corner of his eye and headed for it indirectly, not looking anywhere but at his feet in case someone saw him and read his guilt, as surely they would. His face was burning. His fists were clenched. But he had everything planned. She would be home soon and everything would be perfect. Just perf—

With a muffled thud he bumped into something in the darkness. He put out his arms automatically, and hands grabbed back at him. For one terrifying instant, all he knew was a blur of limbs and lost balance – then he was helping a middle-aged man upright and stuttering inanely.

'What the hell do you think you're doing?' the man asked, dusting himself down. 'You walked right into me!'

'I . . . I wasn't watching—'

'That's bloody obvious!'

'I mean, it's dark and I didn't see you. I didn't think anyone was in here.' Stan backed away, wondering if he should make a run for it – then realised the man had been squatting in the same place he himself hoped to occupy.

'Oh, I *see*,' said the man, who by then had recovered enough to be approaching a realisation of his own. The disgruntled look vanished, replaced by one of indulgence. 'You're new.'

'What?' Stan could manage little more than an addled look and vague sounds.

'It's okay,' said the man, patting Stan on the shoulder. His face was round and his head looked like someone had dusted it with desiccated coconut. He looked about the same age as Stan's father had been when he died. His voice dropped in volume: 'I'm sorry I startled you. You weren't to know I was there.'

'You okay, Reg?' hissed a voice from the shadows, and Stan jumped. A dark figure stepped out from behind a tree, the red eye of a cigarette glinting malevolently in one fist.

'No worries, Tony,' said the old man called Reg. 'Just a mistake.'

The figure coalesced into a lean European man dressed in a singlet and shorts. Tony's face was black with stubble, Stan noted, his eyes adjusting to the near darkness in the park and latching onto comprehensible details as signs he hadn't gone completely mad.

'Mistake, huh?' Tony's voice was low and guttural, hostile in tone. 'Why isn't he moving on, then?'

'I think he wants to stay.' Reg's eyes darted between them.

'Uh.'

'Am I right, young man?'

Stan was momentarily torn. 'I . . . I don't know what you mean.'

'Well, let me spell it out.' The old man glanced at his watch. 'You're alone. You're nervous. You're here at the right time and the right place. And you're *still* here, despite being accosted by two strange men in the bushes. All you need is the hardware. If you had that, I'd be one hundred per cent certain of your intentions.'

Stan's hand obeyed its own will and produced from his pocket the pair of plastic opera glasses he'd bought for five dollars at Cheap as Chips that afternoon.

'Ah.' Reg nodded and glanced at Tony, whose face unexpectedly broke into a white-toothed grin. Tony produced from his shorts a complicated piece of equipment the size of a small dog, the eyepieces of which he thrust into Stan's face. Stan caught a green-tinged glimpse of Reg's midriff glowing within.

'The Scope-O-Tronic Night-Sight 4000X,' pronounced the old man.

'X*G*,' Tony corrected.

'Me, I prefer something a little more stylish.' Reg reached into a pocket and showed Stan a collapsible brass cylinder with glass lenses at either end.

'Shhhhh!' came a call from nearby. 'Someone's coming!'

Tony vanished behind his tree. Reg dragged Stan into the bush. Footsteps crunched toward them, accompanied by faint regular panting. Stan held his breath and huddled down behind the leaves with Reg silent at his side. Bare seconds later, a man walking a Doberman on a leash passed through the park. His eyes glinted in the streetlight, but he didn't seem to notice anything out of the ordinary. He didn't stop, anyway. Stan watched his departing back with breath still held, feeling like a common criminal.

The man disappeared from view. Tony stepped out from behind his tree. His cigarette butt flicked in the general direction of the departing figure. 'Loser.'

Stan rose shakily to his feet.

'You don't look so flash, son,' said Reg. 'Drink?'

The old man pressed a small flask into Stan's hand. Stan tipped it up automatically and downed a mouthful of gin. Only then did he remember to breathe.

'This is insane.'

'Actually,' Reg said, 'it's probably the sanest thing you've ever done. You've taken a step forward, lad. You've taken charge of your life. If you hadn't done this, where do you think you'd be in a month's time? Like that turd-scooper we just saw, pretending to walk a dog? Driving around with your stereo booming? Panty-snatching? We all need to let off a little steam every now and again, or else the boiler blows. We know where you're coming from. Do *we* look crazy?'

'Fuck no,' said Tony, emphasising the words with the bright end of another fag.

Before Stan could reply, a car turned into the street.

'Will you keep it *down* back there?' hissed the same voice that had warned of the dog-walker. A silhouette of a man's head appeared briefly in the window of a parked car, then vanished back into the shadows.

Reg waved and tugged Stan down.

'You can stay here with me,' the old man whispered, 'but

only for tonight. This is my spot, you see. You'll have to find another of your own.'

'But—'

Stan got no further. Headlights lit up the end of the street, blinding his night-adjusted eyes, then swung aside as a shiny purple hatchback pulled into the drive of the front unit across the street. With one final rev, the engine died and the door opened.

And there she was. A vision in lycra toting a bag over one shoulder and looking for her front door key among what sounded like hundreds.

'Evening, Sharon,' breathed the old man.

'That's her name?' Stan exhaled, eyes fixed on her back. Part of him knew he would've liked her name, no matter what it turned out to be.

'That's just what I call her. I don't check her mail or anything. Only sickos do that.'

The screen door opened with a clatter and Sharon disappeared inside. A moment later, lights came on, visible around the edges of the blinds.

'You do this often?' Stan asked. He had to ask the question.

Reg replied without taking his eye off the brass telescope's eyepiece. 'We all do. Tony has a wife, but she goes to bed early. Rob comes after work. Steve stops by on his evening patrol; he's a security guard. Dave—' A rustle went up as Sharon flipped apart the blinds in the front room of her unit. Through that window Stan could see the central hallway leading to the main bedroom and bathroom – almost as though it had been designed that way. He raised the opera glasses; the view was only slightly better, but he was grateful for any improvement at all. Sharon stood in the window for a second, shaking out her hair. The bedroom door behind her was ajar; through it, he could see half a bed, a side table and a lamp. She turned away from the window, and disappeared into the bathroom.

The two men behind the bush gripped their optical devices and sighed spookily similar sighs.

'She's one in a million, isn't she?'

Stan nodded. 'How long have you been coming here?' he managed.

'A month or so. That's when Sharon moved in. Before then there was Alice in Grover Street. When Alice bought new blinds we had to move on, and we'll do it again if Sharon does likewise, or moves in with her boyfriend. We always find somewhere new to meet. Disperse and regroup. That's life.'

'Sharon has a boyfriend?' Stan was stuck on that point, although the thought of asking her out had never seriously crossed his mind: in fantasies he was a different person, someone *she* would want, not the other way around, not quiet little Stan with his over-sized head and occasional stammer.

'Of course she has.' Reg seemed philosophical. 'Sporty type. Plays football, I think.'

'*Loser*,' hissed Tony from the tree behind them.

'You think everyone's a loser, Tony,' Reg called back, sotto voce.

'They *are* losers.'

'What's she doing in there?' Stan was getting restless, and his opera glasses were fogging up.

Just then, Sharon came back into view wearing nothing but a towel.

Her hair was shining, damp.

'Ah, yes.' Reg's telescope was unwavering.

She walked to the bedroom, rummaged around in a cupboard half out of sight, threw something on the bed, then walked back through the hallway and into the bathroom.

Stan's hands, gripping tight, were cramping on the opera glasses.

'Keep going,' Reg muttered.

Sharon emerged from the bathroom with a brush and sat on the end of the bed, tugging vigorously at the knots in her hair. Her cheeks were flushed.

There was no fan in there, Stan noted. It had to be hot. It just *had* to be. Boiling, in fact. Unbearable.

'Almost there,' Reg agreed.

She stood up, scratched her left buttock, then slipped out of the towel. 'Paydirt!'

Stan felt dizzy. Around him rose a muttering of excitement, uncannily like a dawn chorus, as her viewers were rewarded for their patient unrequited adoration. She walked unself-consciously across the lounge and sat on the couch, where she worried at her toenails and picked at a spot on her stomach. She flipped idly through a magazine, then fanned herself with it while she fiddled with the remote control of her TV. Bored by what she found, she got up to make a phone call. She paced while she talked into the handset.

Stan thought he might faint. He felt Reg's hand clutch his shoulder. 'If you're thinking about jerking off,' the old man whispered, 'forget about it. We leave that sort of stuff to the Rugby Street mob.'

Stan shook his head. Sexual gratification was the last thing on his mind. It didn't even matter whether she was attractive or not. Sharon was simply so new and delightful that he wanted to absorb every moment of her, while he could. He could have stared at her for hours. At her reality.

She hung up the phone a minute or two later, and got up to close the blind. The climactic glimpse of her face brought tears to his eyes.

Then she was gone.

The park erupted. Twenty or thirty men emerged from view to gather in the shadows and talk about what they had seen. In the ensuing mess of wisecracks, back slaps and handshakes, Stan kept carefully to one side, basking in the aftermath of the event. The tension had drained out of him, leaving only a warm glow in his stomach.

Relieved at a night not wasted, one by one the men took their leave, heading back to their homes, partners, friends, pets. Reg knew most of them by name, and introduced Stan to a couple. Barry was a bricklayer; Alan sold insurance. Stan gave them his name in return. It seemed the right thing to do.

Harry knew of a girl on Gormley Road that he had heard was worth checking out. He and Alan arranged to survey the area and report to the group later in the week. 'Variety is the spice of life,' he pronounced cheerily while waving goodbye.

Within moments only the three of them were left. Reg took Stan by the arm and indicated a dark corner of the park, away from his bush.

'There's a nice spot over there, Stan, by the bin. It used to be Sam's, but he's been quiet of late. If you want it, it's yours.'

Then it was Tony's turn. Stan's hand was enfolded in an enthusiastic handclasp and shaken vigorously. 'You're all right, Stan. See you Wednesday.'

The two men looked around and headed off in separate directions.

Stan was left alone in the park, feeling dazed and ... something else.

See you Wednesday . . .?

He headed home with a spring in his step. Yes, he thought. They probably would.

Jump to . . .

another short and quirky story
'The Seventh Letter' (p. 25)

more male bonding
'The Lives of Riley' (p. 43)

something completely different
'Death and the Hobbyist' (p. 303)

Notes on *The N-Body Solution*

This story started as a commission to write something science fictional about armoured suits. I added a love story and matter transmitters because I just can't help myself. I also borrowed the world from a story I wrote over twenty years ago, one that has yet to find a home, despite many attempts. It too is a love story, with a very different ending. I even borrowed the names of the main characters, because maybe I was running out of imagination that day. It wasn't my intention at all to create a Frankenstein's monster of a story ... but when I look at the results, my subconscious muse might have known exactly what it was doing.

There are a lot of ideas in here that had never found finished homes before: the woman who has erased the ability to feel negative emotions is one; 'Firstday' is another, referring to days of the week that are numbered instead of named after ancient gods. Stories come together this way, sometimes, condensed out of a morass of unconnected details by the Editorial Force.

The Loop, though, is entirely new.

I'm a sucker for big, alien artefacts, and this is probably the biggest I've ever created. Not that it's a competition. But when something as small as a suit of armour (with a twist) leads the imagination to universe-spanning scales, you know you're doing something right.

The N-Body Solution

What happens next is irrelevant. All that matters is where it started.

♦ ♦ ♦

Harvester bars are pretty much the same wherever you go, but I hadn't learned that yet. Fresh out of Infall and all out of hope, I was looking for the sleaziest, most pointless, dead-end dive that ever existed. I had nothing to look forward to but getting as plastered as the ancients and spending the rest of my days in a hangover.

There were plenty of bars to choose from. They were busy, too. I clearly wasn't the only one looking to drown my sorrows under a sky devoid of stars.

That made it instantly more boring.

I settled on a place called, unimaginatively, the End of the Line. It was full of humans, sub-humans, post-humans, poly-humans – every category I'd ever heard of, plus some types that probably weren't human at all. The Loop has been around a long time, and if half the things I had heard were true, then it was quite likely I Was Not Alone. In that sense, at least.

I knew I should be depressed: I had reason to be. But the possibility of talking to a real, live alien was not just intriguing, it was something the rest of my scattered self might never experience. It was something I could cling to, something that was mine, and would be mine alone for as long as I could bear it.

The thing about aliens, though, I soon realised, is that they're *alien*. After five conversations in which we utterly failed to find opinions and experiences – and in one case even words – in common, I gave up and took to leaning against the long, corroded bar on my own. Nursing a drink in sullen silence turned out to be a natural part of my social inheritance.

'You're new,' said a voice from the other end of the bar.

'It's that obvious, I suppose,' I said without looking up.

'Not really. We're all floundering. I'm just permanently jacked into the news feed. You're the third today. I recognise your face.'

'There's a news feed?'

'Sure, but not much in the way of actual news. No offence.'

I looked up. Judging by the voice, I'd expected the owner to be a woman. What I saw instead was a bipedal mech suit almost twice as tall as me, all ceramics, alloys and plastics, as streamlined as a stiletto. It occupied the deepest darkest corner of the bar but, even so, it gleamed. Pinpricks of light ricocheted off its faceted eyes, the sharp tips of its digits, its many bevelled edges.

'You human in there?'

'I said, "no offence".'

'None taken. I'm just curious.'

'Well, don't be.'

'There must be *something* biological, or else you wouldn't be in this place, messing with your chemistry.'

'It's certainly not for the company.'

'Hey, you spoke to me, remember?'

The suit shifted with a faint whirr of servos, presenting

its back. There, embossed against the silver, was the logo of the Earth Justice Enforcement Agency, and her surname in black: *Ei*.

'Nice to meet you, soldier,' she said.

Maybe I really was that obvious. Stung, I retreated to contemplate my empty shot glass.

'Don't mind her,' said the bartender, a loathsome toad but at least superficially of my species. 'She's spoiling for a fight with someone her size, and you don't really qualify.'

'Gee, thanks.' I was sarcastic, but that was one thing to be grateful for. In my current form, Enforcer Ei could have squashed me like a bug. 'What's her story? I don't recognise the make of her suit.'

'Something new, I guess. She's been here three months. Came after a mark. Caught him almost immediately, they say. He snuck in through the Infall, and she tracked him down. First the Authorities knew of him was when she handed them his body.'

I'd been debriefed on arrival, but there was still so much to learn. 'The Authorities?'

'Closest thing to a government you'll find in Harvester.'

'Maybe I should take a proper look about the place, see what's what. While I can still walk.'

The bartender gave me half a shot, on the house.

'For the road?'

'There's no road from here, my friend. Just ways to pass the time.'

♦ ♦ ♦

Five suns, any one of which was in the sky at any given time. One planetary nebula, casting a permanent glow across the heavens. Permanent settlements scattered across two rocky worlds, plus stations around the system's only gas giant. The gas giant was home to the shipyards.

That's where I went first, in a manner of speaking.

Tideships, stillships, heavyships . . . every species had its own wild fantasy about getting home the hard way. None of them had worked to date and, even if one did, where would it go? The nebula was almost a light-year across. Just getting a clear picture of the universe outside was difficult. No one had a map, and if they did we weren't on it.

'The colony at loop junction one-sixty-three has many names,' said the orientation drone taking my fellow newbs and me on the virtual tour. '"Cyernus" is the oldest known, but almost certainly not the first. The term comes from the Guta tongue, and approximately translates as "harvester", the epithet employed by the colony's human inhabitants.'

Our point of view swept through the ribs of a ship so big it would take another century just to finish the chassis.

'Harvester is home to seventeen species of biological sentient and three machine intelligences. Evidence of habitation stretches back more than a million years, with only two vacant periods, the longest spanning ten thousand years. Fossil records indicate that life did not evolve here. Presumably the Loop's builders were the first inhabitants.'

That told me a little, but not a lot. All things in Harvester started and ended with the Loop, which remained as mysterious as ever.

'Why this junction?' asked someone from the back of the consensual shuttle. 'Why did it break down here?'

'That is unknown. The malfunction remains unexplained, if indeed it is a malfunction. Some maintain that the Loop was always intended to stop here, and is functioning normally.'

'Perhaps this is the home system of the Builders,' said another shell-shocked newb.

'All roads lead to Rome?' I said. 'But there's only one road, and the Builders are conspicuously absent.'

'Perhaps the event that caused the nebula wiped them out.'

The drone didn't dignify that with a response. No species capable of building a wormcaster network spanning the universe would ever let a simple stellar hiccup knock them out of the picture.

'One-hundred-and-sixty-three is the largest Heegner number,' said a third member of my temporary compatriots. 'That might mean something.'

Also doubtful, I thought. Class number problems and almost integers seemed a long way from the seething polyglot around us. As well as the five suns, two rocky worlds and one gas giant, there were streams of asteroids and dust following fiendishly complex orbits through the system. The largest asteroid had been mined out millennia ago. Wars had once been fought over the richest finds, but things were quiet at the moment, while the Authorities' power held.

For the foreseeable future, then, I was out of a job.

'I think it's beautiful,' said a small, dark-haired woman I had barely glanced at before. 'It's so rich and interesting – compared to the other junctions, I mean.'

I looked at her properly, now. We had passed each other at the Outfall on junction one-sixty-two, and then again at Harvester's Infall. Travellers in the same direction, we had had nothing more in common than that.

Now, we were caught in the same trap, and her eyes were shining with something that might actually have been joy.

'What about the singularity kites of forty-five?' asked another passenger.

'Or the multiplex quintuple system of sixty-one?'

Both good suggestions, I thought, to which I would have added the bottomless pit of thirty-nine, the eternally burning world of eighteen, and the stellar graveyard at even one hundred.

'Sideshows,' she said with a wave of one delicate hand. Her expression was rapturous. 'This is the real deal.'

We had all seen the same things. We'd all come to junction one-sixty-three the same way, junction after junction on our intergalactic grand tour. But somehow this woman had arrived at an entirely different place from the rest of us.

'It's hardwired,' she explained after the tour, at a different Harvester bar, one that stank of yeast and sugar like we were inside a giant brewery. 'I don't believe in being negative, so I make sure I can't, surgically. I'm only capable of feeling positive emotions – and it's wonderful.'

'Yes, but you would say that, wouldn't you?'

She laughed, and invited me back to her place. I was amazed she already had quarters organised and furnished. While I had been moping about, grousing at strangers, she had been getting her life together.

Maybe, I thought, there was something to her positivity jag. It could even be infectious.

Her name was Zuzi. She didn't give me anything more than that. And when I told her what I had done for a living, she didn't ask for details.

'So you're Corps,' she said. 'So what? It's all history now, Alex.'

She used my name like she used the rest of me. And when

she was done, neither of us seemed any happier than we had been before.

♦ ♦ ♦

I wasn't the only Corps recruit on Harvester. Embodiment training was mandatory, and the rest of me wasn't the first to opt for the Loop's one-way trip. It was a fair bet that some version of my higher self would be around to pick me up when I reached the far end, full to the brim with experiences and memories for the rest of me to share. That no one had ever gone all the way around wasn't a disincentive. It was assumed the Loop was so big there simply hadn't been time. No one seriously considered the possibility that one of its links might be broken.

As with most colonies, Corps recruits were called corpses, but here that had both a literal and cautionary edge. Some of us did choose death over being isolated from our higher selves. It wasn't that our much-reduced forms weren't viable. It was thinking, *This is all we will ever be,* that did the damage. There were self-help groups, where we talked through our problems. There were training sessions to maintain our skills. There were even a couple of odd little collectives where mismatched corpses tried to link up and form a new emergent self. I stayed away from the first and last, but forced myself to participate in the second.

Other classes of being occasionally joined the fights. Enforcer Ei was one of them. She was hard to miss. There were other suits and larger bipeds prowling the habitats of Harvester, but none as brooding and dagger-sharp as she was. After that first encounter in the End of the Line, I had seen her in green zones, amphitheatre audiences, work crews, and even just standing around, staring at the view from one of Harvester's many lookouts. If she lived anywhere in particular, I never found out.

The first time she came to the dojo I frequented, I didn't fight her; nor the second time. I simply watched her wipe the floor with the toughest members of the crew, one after the other. I noted her moves and catalogued her weaknesses. She was all former, none of the latter.

'Stone cold killer,' said one of the other recruits in an aside she probably couldn't hear, and if she had, might have taken for a compliment. 'I heard rumours of squads like these before I left home. You cross them, you're dead, no matter how far you run. Remember that guy she killed? Probably thought he'd got clean away, coming out here . . .'

I just kept watching, awaiting my opportunity.

The dojo was kitted out with all sorts of tech, but I preferred to fight as close to barehanded as was feasible. I certainly never fought with a mech suit. Enforcer Ei had seen me sparring and knew my style probably as well as I knew hers, so her immediate response when I approached her was: 'You don't want to fight me.'

'Why challenge you, then?'

'I don't know. Because you want me to kill you?'

'You won't kill me. You're an Enforcer. It wouldn't be legal.'

'Earth is a long way from here, soldier.'

'Use my name.'

'I don't know your name.'

'Yes, you do. It was in the news feed.'

She tilted her shining helm. 'Alex Lombard. What difference does it make?'

'Maybe none. Maybe a lot if the thought of killing me does cross your mind.'

A small crowd gathered as we squared off in the arena. I ignored the odd mocking catcall. None came from my fellow recruits. They understood, but they thought I was mad all the same.

I adopted a wary crouch – one she imitated with a whole lot more unfolding of weapon-stalks, fins and antennae.

'Now you're just showing off,' I said, noting the position of everything vulnerable.

'And you're just wasting time.'

'Me? I'm waiting for y—'

I barely registered the sharp clicks of her actuators pushing with explosive force against the arena floor. The next thing I knew I was on my back, in so much pain I could barely breathe.

I blinked up at the shining figure standing over me.

'Enough?' she said.

'Hell, no. They make us tough in the Corps.' That was the truth. I had little conscious control over my body's more advanced abilities, but already the pain was fading and I was able to get to my feet.

'Again,' I said.

She stepped back. 'You can't be serious.'

'I can't believe we're still talking.'

I ducked low under the natural reach of her left arm and lunged for a particular attenuated sensor that looked like it might bend. I didn't try a kick at her knees. I didn't for a second consider I could knock her off-balance. All I saw was the needle-thin tip of that sensor and – in my mind's eye – my fist reaching for it, closing tight around it, twisting . . .

In reality, I probably got no closer than ten centimetres.

She held me upside-down by one leg so we were almost eye-to-eye. This time there was a little laughter.

'Are you done yet?' she asked.

'If it's a fair fight you're looking for—'

'Just getting bored.'

'So come out of the suit and meet me face-to-face.'

She let go and I hit the floor with all of the habitat's 1.2-gravities.

'I guess that's a no.'

'You guessed right.'

She had already turned away. This time I took a running jump for her back, reaching for the panels behind which her sensors and weapons had retracted. There was sufficient grip there for me, and I was able to get to her shoulders before she spun her centre of gravity and punched me hard in the chest.

I was out cold when I hit the dojo wall, and only came to when she shocked me with the tip of an electrical weapon protruding from her mechanical toe.

'Wake up.'

'I'm awake.'

'You're an idiot.'

'Try to understand,' I said, braving the hammering in my head in order to sit up. The walls, floor and ceiling turned around me. 'I don't have a death wish and I'm not expecting to beat you. It's not about winning or losing. It's about the fight.'

'It's not even a fight,' she said.

'But it's a fight I've never had before, with an opponent I've never fought before. That's the point.'

She straightened, and I knew I'd reached her. 'You think your higher self will be grateful for your memories of being pounded over and over again?'

'Maybe not, if that's all you've got to offer.'

'What else is there?'

'Show me.'

'But you're so slow,' she said, 'so primitive.'

'That's the point of legacy genes. My higher self–'

'I *know* what your higher self thinks. It thinks that by making parts of itself old-style human, it'll stay at least partly human rather than evolve into some freak show. That's why you won't wear a suit. Another version of you back home is doing that and recording that experience. You're the grand tourist, the Looper – but you're still a soldier, or part of one, and you think this is what the rest of you wants. Are you sure you aren't kidding yourself?'

'Maybe,' I said, 'but it beats sitting around in bars.'

She towered over me, unmoving for a good ten seconds.

'All right,' she said. 'Get up.'

I did as I was told. 'My higher self is a "him", not an "it", by the way.'

'You think ordinary pronouns apply anymore?' She killed that line of conversation with one savage chop of her right battle glove. 'Do you know what the craziest thing about you is?'

'What?'

'You haven't given in. You still think you might go home.'

'Why not? Or I might meet myself out here, wherever we are. Either way.'

She hit me so hard I was in rehab for a week.

When I recovered, she started teaching me about suits like hers – their weak points, their blind spots, their limitations. It was all relative, of course. I never had a hope of putting her down, but she got that now, and it became about something other than winning for her too.

As we fought, we talked.

'How did you know I was Corps?' I asked during our first spar after rehab. 'That wasn't in the news feed.'

'A lucky guess,' she said.

'No, tell me. What gave it away?'

'You want me to say it was your confidence, or the way you held yourself – *meronymically*, if that's a thing.'

'I just want you to tell me the truth.'

She shrugged. 'Your biochemistry was off. That's all.'

'You can tell that at a glance?'

'I can tell what you had for breakfast . . . yesterday.'

I laughed. 'Well, that's not fair. I don't get to see anything about you.'

She didn't answer.

We sparred for a while, and then I pressed her again.

'Seriously, do you *ever* take your suit off?'

'That's none of your business, soldier.'

'I'm making it my business.'

She jabbed at me a fraction faster than I could dodge. I rode out the blow and came up grinning.

'So tell me about this place instead. What's the deal with the Outfall? Why hasn't anyone fixed it yet?'

'Do I look like a scientist?'

'I don't know what you look like, Enforcer Ei. I don't even know if you have a first name.'

She didn't respond to that little dig, either. 'The Outfall doesn't work. That's all you need to know.'

'Doesn't work how?'

'People walk into it. They stand around looking embarrassed. Then they walk out again. No one goes anywhere.'

'I presume someone's examined it.'

'I think we can be sure of that.'

I thought of the brightly glowing sky and the crowded habitats, the tens of thousands of years of devolution and fruitless industry and cultural mixing. People arrived every day, but they were far outnumbered by the people who already lived here, had even been born here.

'Yes, but *can* we be sure of that?' I asked. 'I bet you haven't looked at it, and neither have I. What if everyone before us did the same – and everyone before them, too? What if that goes right back to the first people here and no one has double-checked the original diagnosis?'

'Why don't you take the tour and find out for yourself?'

'There's a tour?'

'Will you stop talking like this if there is?'

I considered the consequences of not taking the hint. She was sensitive on the subject. I had spent plenty of time pondering that during my week in rehab.

'I will,' I said, 'if you go with me.'

'On the tour?'

'Yes.'

'Why?'

'Because you're such good company, that's why.'

That came out a little sharper than I'd intended. Her movements lost some of their smooth grace, like I had managed to hit her where it counted, inside the suit. I dodged two blows with ease, and was beginning to wonder if I had seriously offended her when she said, 'All right.'

'All right what?'

'I'll take the tour with you.'

'Well, great.'

'And my first name is Nadia – but if you ever call me that, I'll put you back in rehab for good.'

'Understood. It's a date, then.'

She held out her metal right hand.

I shook it, and had my fingers painfully squeezed in return.

'It's a date,' she said, 'if this is fighting.'

I nodded and she let me go.

The Outfall tour was run by a relatively human-friendly Dashizi, an alien of a species I'd never encountered. Its name was Lna. One pendulous segmented body hung from the intersection of its six stilt-like legs, like a sausage in a cage. Sensory organs were at the bottom end of the sausage, so it had to curl up in a U-shape to look at Enforcer Ei. Ribbons in varying shades of grey adorned its legs, Roman-sandal style.

We waited with Lna in silence for the other members of our tour. Five had booked. Only three showed – Enforcer Ei and me, and a near-human called Thiall, whose overlarge eyes leant him a permanently quizzical expression. Lna expressed his disappointment – but not surprise – at the poor turnout.

'Humans evolved in the shadow of volcanoes,' the alien said. 'You have a predisposition for looking down.'

I was pretty sure he wasn't calling us cowards, or depressives, but his expression was unreadable.

'How long have you lived here, Lna?' I asked.

'Three thousand of your years.'

'And you've been tour guide all that time?'

'Only on Firstdays. There is a roster.'

Enforcer Ei nudged me. I shut up.

'This way.'

Lna guided us into the Outfall complex. It seemed much the same as any other, although it looked a little newer, perhaps, showing fewer signs of wear and tear. This junction hadn't seen as much use as the others.

At its heart rested the massive alien disk that was the key to the Loop's existence, a solid lump of ambiguous matter, so grey it was almost black, over a hundred metres across and five high, with one cylindrical tunnel bored in a spiralling arc from the edge to the centre. Lna walked us around the disk's circumference, pointing out markings left by previous inhabitants of the junction. Some were prayers, others curses. Many were simply names. The disk was covered in those, all painted on. The material was too tough to scratch.

'Commemorating the beings who died here,' was the explanation Lna offered. I saw no reason to disbelieve him.

We returned to the tunnel mouth and filed inside. The top of Enforcer Ei's helm was tall enough to scrape the ceiling, making her stoop. Immediately I felt a weird tugging and shifting as gravitational, electric, and magnetic fields wrapped around me. The mech suit creaked, and I wondered if it would survive the stresses imposed upon it by this odd alien space. But it had to, I concluded, as it had one-hundred-and-sixty-two times before. Thus far, this was an Outfall like any other.

Our footsteps echoed along the tunnel. The only lights came from a torch Lna carried and Enforcer Ei's chest lamps. The forces multiplied until my head was swimming with the effort of thinking straight. I felt as though all the atoms and molecules in my body were being stirred like letters in alphabet soup.

The tunnel ended in a blank wall.

'This is the geometric centre of the disk,' Lna said, tapping a point roughly two metres from the end of the tunnel. 'Here, our journey ends.'

Not just the journey through the disk, he meant, but around the Loop as well.

I approached the wall and examined the tunnel's end by the shifting light. There was more graffiti, centimetres thick by the look of it. What lay beyond it felt disconcertingly solid to my questing hands, a sure sign that something was indeed wrong. This wasn't the way it was supposed to go. Normally one walked into the wormcaster transmitter disk of junction (X) and walked out the receiver of junction (X + 1) without breaking stride. The disks did all the hard work for you.

At least they did when they worked.

'What do the scientists say?' I asked.

Lna folded his legs into pairs. 'Many times have I walked this path,' he said. 'I thought myself a scientist, once. What I considered science is a child's perception of the universe compared to the understanding that built this.'

'But people have *tried*, haven't they?' I felt I was speaking normally, but I could hear the echoes of my voice getting louder. 'They've poked it, prodded it . . .?'

A heavy hand came down on my shoulder. Her metal shell quivered under the complex forces roiling around us.

'Until the builders return,' said Lna, 'or the Outfall fixes itself, we can only wait and wonder.'

'Well, that sucks,' said Thiall, startling us all. The near-human hadn't spoken since giving us his name. 'But it could be worse, I guess. At least it didn't *half*-work.'

'What do you mean?' asked Enforcer Ei.

'Well, it could have dumped us in deep space, or left bits of us behind. At least we're still here and in one piece.'

'Some might count that as a curse,' she said, 'not a blessing.'

With heavy steps, the suit turned and began walking out of the tunnel.

Lna uncrossed his legs and followed. 'This concludes the tour,' the alien said as it ambulated after Enforcer Ei. 'There is a register for visitors, if you would like to record your thoughts . . .'

'Spare me,' I told Thiall. 'I need a drink.'

'To each their own,' he said.

I took that as a rebuff, but without rancour. I already had a drinking buddy, if I could get her down off the ledge.

'No goodnight kiss?' I called after her before she could disappear into a crowd.

She indicated the sky. 'There is no night, let alone a *good* one. No moon, no stars – no nothing.'

'Comets I can give you.' Actually, we had those in abundance.

The complex interplay of forces in the system was always throwing something icy towards one sun or other. 'Probably a rainbow, if you ask nicely.'

'I did what you wanted. I took the tour. Now you want me to be nice as well?'

'Just one round. I'll pay, whatever you fancy.'

Her pace slowed. 'All right. Alcohol works for me.'

'So you *are* human.'

'That's not what I said. Alcohol disrupts Karuliesh biochemistry as well.'

'So you're one of two species.' I had met the Karuliesh; they resembled ambulatory prunes and smelled of vinegar. I hoped the real Nadia Ei was nothing like that. 'The End of the Line?'

'That'll do.'

At the bar in which we'd met, we had several rounds, not just one. The front of her suit opened a fraction to allow her access to its inner workings, into which she trickled the drink. I watched curiously as she did so. The outer layer was just millimetres thick, and there seemed to be many more beneath it. I wondered how long it took her to get undressed.

'Maybe Lna's wrong,' I insisted. 'What if there's another disk, one that works, and all we have to do is find it? Or if we could reprogram the Infall to take us back to junction one-sixty-two?'

'You think people haven't tried?' she said. 'You think you're the only one who's thought this way?'

She was right. I was beginning to sound like Zuzi. But Zuzi's relentless optimism was useless on Harvester. It was directed inward, to making the best of a bad deal. I didn't want that. I wanted the deck shuffled and the cards laid out all over again. Or I wanted some way to turn my shitty hand into a game-winning misére.

'What are you afraid of?' I asked her. 'That I might be making sense?'

'I'm going to say yes in the hope it might shut you the hell up.'

'But isn't getting away from here something we should all be talking about?'

'I don't know. Maybe,' she said, staring down into her drink.

'Wait,' I said. 'This I don't get at all. You come here on a mission, you catch the guy, and now you can't get home. What's not to be pissed about?'

'I didn't say I wasn't pissed.'

'But you said—'

'Maybe means maybe. Don't read too much into it. It's got nothing to do with you.'

I supposed that was true, and forced myself to stop prying.

'Shame you didn't catch the guy earlier,' I said, aiming for companionability. 'That way you'd have the rest of the tour to look forward to.'

'You don't know anything about me, soldier.'

Her tone was hard. My plan had backfired, somehow.

'I know you only call me "soldier" when I'm getting close to something.'

'That isn't it at all.'

The outer layer of her suit abruptly slid shut. She stood up.

'Nadia, wait—'

She didn't blast me into next century. She didn't even look at me. She just kept going.

This time I didn't follow. I drained the rest of my drink, and hers, and headed in the opposite direction.

Enforcer Ei didn't show at the dojo for a week, which was fine with me. I had other sparring partners I'd been neglecting, and was pleased to see that working with her had increased my strength and agility, putting me at the top ranking of my fellow corpses. That was new, and not unpleasant.

The buzz was just beginning to pale when she returned, offering neither explanation nor apology for her absence, and I figured she owed me nothing of the sort. She barely said a word, except to accept or reject challenges, as the mood took her. I wasn't her primary sparring partner any more, although we did fight a few times. It felt awkward, like some vital rhythm was missing, one we'd danced to so effortlessly before.

This went on for a couple of months, circling each other, never quite colliding, except physically in the arena. I hitched up with Zuzi again and met some other people through her. Harvester's population lacked nothing when it came to interesting and unique types. Only gradually did the familiarity start to eat at me in that regard, too. We were all refugees, castaways on an unknown shore. Every story ended the same.

Four months after I arrived at Harvester, the Authorities declared a junction-wide celebration of mourning. At first I thought it was some alien thing – I had, as yet, failed to determine who or what the Authorities actually were – but Zuzi, always more integrated than I was, explained that the celebration was for everyone. Any race, culture or creed could participate. Unlike the scrawls I'd seen all over

Outfall, this wasn't just for the people who'd died here; it was to commemorate the ones we'd left behind, too.

And it was simple enough. Every physically bound entity processed past the tunnel leading out of Infall. At the opening they spoke the name of the person they were mourning. A small tribute could be offered. Anyone who arrived through the Infall during the procession was declared a Hero for the day and feted by all. The ceremony concluded with a pageant and lots of drinking.

Zuzi thought it sounded wonderful, of course, and talked me into participating.

'Whose name will you say?' I asked her over dinner the night before. We were, by that time, sharing an apartment, and sleeping regularly in the same bed.

'I don't think I'll do that part,' she said. 'There is no one I feel sad about.'

'You mean you don't miss anyone?'

'I guess that is what I mean. Grief is a negative emotion, isn't it?'

I stared into her smiling eyes, and saw in them a truth I think I'd known from the beginning.

'You wouldn't miss me if I were gone,' I said. 'You'd be just as happy as you are now, and just as happy again when the next person moved in. It's all the same to you.'

'It's not all the same,' she said. 'There are shades of happiness. The way I am with you is different to how I am with someone else. It must be, of course, or I would get terribly bored.'

She held my hands over the table, and I smiled at her. There was no point pushing it. I knew from experience that she was incapable of having a two-sided argument.

We joined the throng the next day, spruced up like Harvester's finest out to welcome a queen. The mood was a happy one, mixed with an undercurrent of loss. Music was sombre as often as it was danceable. Seeing a familiar silver helm standing high above the crowd, I pulled ahead of Zuzi. I felt more comfortable on my own, with the crowd surging and retreating around me. It reminded me of the day I'd left to join the Loop, of the farewell thrown by my higher self. He had been there in dozens of bodies, and I had felt embraced physically as well as mentally. Little did I know that the only way I would ever feel anything like that again would be in the company of strangers, all of whom carried their own burdens.

I caught up with Nadia Ei on the approach to Infall. If she noticed me, she said nothing, and I didn't force the issue. The silver skin of her armour reflected my face back at me as she approached the entrance. I silently rehearsed what I was going to say when the opportunity came to do what we were all there to do.

She turned, dropped to one knee, and bowed her head.

'Grae Bilwis,' she said.

She straightened, stood, moved on.

Then it was my turn to look down the disk's long, curving tunnel. A dead end – but a functioning one, since already that day two Heroes had arrived. It had none of the graffiti and all of the mystery of Outfall. I found it easy to imagine that the words we said would ricochet down a long tunnel of space-time back to the places and people we'd left behind. Maybe they'd make a difference to someone.

'Alex Lombard,' I said. Although I strained to hear an echo, there was nothing.

♦ ♦ ♦

Grae Bilwis.

The name rang a bell.

In post-mourning celebration mode, Harvester was consumed by fireworks, acrobats and drunks. I wasn't much interested in any of them. Seeing Nadia Ei had put me in a contemplative mood, and I didn't have the energy to shuck it off.

Zuzi would be with her friends, expecting me to join her, I supposed, but not relying on it. There might be other corpses there, unless they were feeling as I was. Just thinking about my higher self brought back the sense of isolation that on joining the Loop had been so novel and thrilling, but here on Harvester bled like an open wound. On other days I might have called my fellow corpses friends and a comfort. That day, the loss we all shared was a wedge between us, driving us into isolation and resentment.

I roamed, staring at the clouds the Authorities had thrown up to block out the suns, the laser-painted stars on their undersides. Sublight shuttles occasionally left Harvester with one destination in mind: the edge of the planetary nebula, where light-echoes faded and the universe reappeared. It wouldn't be hard to book a coldseat on one of those, wait out the millennia in the hope of things changing. It would be a new experience, inasmuch as it was an experience at all . . .

But *Grae Bilwis* nagged at me. Who was this person Nadia Ei mourned, and where had I heard the name before?

I found a quiet pocket in a green zone and logged into Harvester's infocore. I didn't know the precise spelling, and the search engines weren't optimised for human vocalisations. It took me a surprising amount of time to find the record, and in the end I kicked myself for not looking in the news feeds first. That's where I'd stumbled across it the first time, while looking up Enforcer Ei herself.

Grae Bilwis was the man Enforcer Ei had been chasing through the Loop. He had been an officer in the Earth Justice Enforcement Agency, just like her. He'd sneaked into Harvester by means still unknown. She'd caught him, killed him, and handed his body to the Authorities.

And now here she was, publically mourning him. Why?

Something parted the ferny fronds to my right. A shadow fell across me. By the size of it, there was only one person it could have belonged to.

'I've been researching, too,' she said. 'Guess what I found.'

Clearly she'd been following my search via some means available to her. I couldn't read her mood, not from the way the suit was standing. I didn't get up. If she was going to kill me, I had as much chance of stopping her lying down as I did on my feet.

'Tell me about him, first,' I said. 'Was he crooked? Or were you the crooked one, and he was blackmailing you?'

'Are they the best theories you've come up with?'

'Well, I haven't had long to think about it. I only just found out he still matters.'

'He doesn't matter anymore.'

'Of course he does. He's the reason you're here. It's his fault. You're allowed to blame him if it'll help you move on.'

'There's nowhere to move on to.'

'You know what I mean.'

'*You don't know anything.*'

I stopped talking – not just because of the fists, suddenly clenched, that could have turned me to paste in an instant. There was such pain in her voice. For the first time, she sounded how I felt.

'What were you researching?' I asked her.

Her fists unclenched. 'Outfall.'

Now I sat up. 'Tell me what you found.'

'The disk has been under observation for half of Harvester's recorded history. It's been studied by people a whole lot more motivated than tour guides – the machine intelligences, for one, and they've got the patience of saints. What's more, all the data is publically available. It makes for pretty dense reading. I've been wading through it for weeks, trying to find a hole. Most of it I don't understand, but everyone's come to the same conclusion.'

'The disk is stuffed.'

'Not quite. The disk is definitely doing *something* – we felt it when we were in there – but exactly what, no one knows. If we did know, maybe we could fix it. All we can say is that it's not working properly, because we're still here.'

I rubbed my temples. 'Everyone thinks that?'

'Well, apart from the cranks and weirdoes, half of whom think this is a kind of punishment sent by the Builders. The other half claim to actually be the Builders, but why they're caught in their own trap is never adequately explained.'

'And you came to tell me this . . . why?'

'Because you started it. And I thought you'd want to know.'

'No,' I said, sensing a different message behind her words, 'it has to be more than that.'

'It doesn't have to be anything.'

She turned to walk away.

I jumped to my feet and followed her, dodging the elastic leaves that snapped back in her wake.

'Don't run from me, Nadia. You always do that – reach out, then push me away. Is that how it's always been? Is that why you never come out of your suit, because you feel safe in there?'

'Don't try to psychoanalyse me,' she said, feet crunching heavily through the undergrowth. 'I'm not afraid of connecting any more than you're afraid of being alone. Neither of us would be here if we weren't.'

'What does *that* mean?'

She didn't answer.

We hit the edge of the green zone and followed the curved inner wall to the nearest airlock. The truth was, I didn't know why I was following her any more than I knew why she'd come to me, but it seemed important to make the attempt. She was on the verge of something, something critical, and as we passed into the human sector of the habitat it came to me what that might be.

'You're giving up,' I said. 'That's it, isn't it? You're thinking about killing yourself.'

'It wouldn't be hard. And it's not illegal.'

'Whether it's hard or legal isn't the point,' I said, struggling to find words for why the suggestion filled me with such alarm. 'It's just crazy. There's so much here. I mean, look around us. Five suns! Aliens! What else do you want?'

'I used to feel that way. Now I've changed my mind. And I know that's not all *you* want.'

'All right – I'm being simplistic in order to defend my own uncertainties. So sue me. But look at the machine intelligences. They haven't given up, have they? What makes them different to you? If they haven't topped themselves, why should anyone?'

'I've no idea what they think, and neither do you.'

'That doesn't make their conclusion invalid.'

'But they think on different scales. Time moves differently for them.'

'So put yourself in cold storage for a bit. See what's happening in a thousand years. Isn't that better than death?'

'You're not saying anything I haven't said myself.'

'Well, you should listen to yourself. These are pretty persuasive arguments.'

She stopped without warning. 'I told you. I changed my mind.'

I stared at her back for a long moment, trying to drill mentally through her armour and see what lay beneath. We were talking about suicide, but I didn't think I'd reached the heart of what was bothering her. Her suit was in the way.

It was immaculate, as always, but she might as well have been bleeding from every joint.

'You changed your mind when, exactly?' I asked her.

'It's none of your business.'

She didn't call me 'soldier,' but she might as well have.

'This is to do with Grae Bilwis, isn't it?'

She half-turned. 'He was my partner.'

'So he broke the law and betrayed you. That's his fault, not yours. You had to do what you did. He had it coming. Right?'

She hung her head. For all the strength and resilience of her alloy shell, she seemed about to sag to the habitat floor and melt away. She actually went down on one knee, so our heads were almost level.

'You're not listening, Alex. He was my *partner.*'

I shut up, thinking that at last I understood.

That's the funny thing about data. A single piece of information can change everything. Like Archimedes and his lever, you need precisely the right one. Everything else is dross. If I'd known sooner what Grae Bilwis meant to Nadia Ei, I thought, maybe I might have understood her better, maybe even helped her. I certainly understood, now, why leaving Harvester – where he had died – had been an ambiguous prospect for her. But I still didn't entirely understand their story. Had she killed him or had he killed himself? Had he run from her or had they been travelling together? It didn't matter. He was gone, and she now wanted to follow him.

Except it's not dross, all that mass of extra data. It has weight and substance. And so do conclusions based on that mass, not to mention behaviour based on those conclusions . . .

I don't know exactly what went through my mind in that moment. It wasn't a revelation borne out of reasoning or logic. It just came to me in a flash and, for a moment, I didn't believe it. Then I thought of how things could be hidden right out in the open. I thought of what a difference it would make, if it were true. I thought of how hard it would be to tell her, and just for a second I considered not telling her at all.

But the thought was too large to keep to myself. I had to do something with this knowledge. I had to share it.

I put one hand on the side of Nadia's helm – a tiny, soft

thing compared to the hard metal – and the other on her left shoulder flange.

'Come with me,' I said.

She said nothing, made no sound at all. Maybe she had shut off her comms so I wouldn't hear her weeping, or laughing, or screaming. I had no way of knowing what she was doing in there. But she did move. She straightened, and she followed me like a sleepwalker through the habitats.

She broke her silence only when it became obvious where we were going.

'We've been here already,' she said. 'Nothing's changed.'

'I'm sure you're right, but bear with me.'

'No,' she said, pulling back. 'I'm not going back there unless you tell me.'

'Okay. It's a small thing, so it might not immediately seem like much, but I think it makes a huge difference. Think of the machine intelligences.'

'What about them?'

'Well, they're conscious, rational beings, like you, Grae, lots of others. But they're still here. They haven't given up. Why not?'

There were no easy answers to that question, but there *was* one really interesting one.

'You're going to have to spell it out for me,' she said.

'They haven't committed suicide because they're like me.'

'You're blaming their stubbornness on your legacy genes?'

'No. They know it won't make a difference. Think about it, Nadia. We don't really know how the wormcaster works, right? We assume it throws us physically from Infall to Outfall, but that's just a guess based on what we see happening.'

'Someone comes out the Infall who didn't go in,' she said.

'Someone goes in the Outfall and emerges somewhere else.'

'Close. What we actually see from the sending end is someone going into Outfall and not emerging.'

'Splitting hairs, surely?'

'Not at all. The Outfall we have here *seems* to be working fine, but no one goes anywhere. We stay here. So instead of assuming that we've misunderstood the way it works, we assume it's not working at all – when in fact it might be doing most of its job just fine, just not the one critical part that has led to the problem we see here.'

'Which critical part is that?'

Here, I hesitated. 'Did you and Grae take the tour of the disk like we did?'

'No.'   .

'Then . . . I'm sorry. I wanted to tell you that everything will be all right, somewhere, but now I can't.'

'I've never thought it would be. Not since we were stuck here, and he . . .'

She stopped. I could tell the thought had sunk in. Maybe not all of it, and she would probably need time to accept the rest, as I had, but the important part was there. I could tell from the way she turned and hurried with renewed urgency for Outfall.

There was a different tour guide this time, one slightly harder to understand. I managed to convince the uncooperative Uotan that we wanted to go in on our own, and he/she/it acquiesced in the end, simply, I think, to get us out of his/her/its hair. It wasn't as if we could damage anything, after all. The disk had been sitting there for more years than humanity had existed. Not even time had dented it.

We had barely entered the tunnel when Nadia stopped and crouched down in front of me.

'If you're right—'

'Then it makes no difference to us. And if I'm wrong, it makes no difference at all.'

'You think the machines really know about this?'

'I suspect they do.'

'Why haven't they told anyone?'

I thought of Zuzi. She would have greeted the news with the sincere but utterly uniform delight she greeted every occurrence.

'It makes sense they would keep this quiet,' I said. 'After all, they can't possibly prove it. Not until someone finally goes all the way around the Loop, or figures out how to make the Outfall work in both ways. It's a guess, and it might be wrong.'

'But you don't think so.'

'No. That's why I'm here.'

'Both of us have already been inside once. Won't that make a difference?'

'To Outfall, we're just dumb matter.'

'So we can do this as many times as we want?'

'I don't see why not.' I stared into the suit's glittering eyes. 'Does that make you feel better? Liberated, somehow? I know it shouldn't but, still . . . I think it does. To me, anyway.'

She said, 'All right, Alex. I'll go with you, all the way. I wasn't sure until now. I wasn't sure if I liked the idea. But I will, if we go together.'

I smiled. 'So let's go.'

'Wait. Not like this. It could be dangerous.'

She stood up. Something whirred and hissed. A panel

lifted out from the front of her suit, then several panels beneath that one. I thought something had malfunctioned in the complex fields of the Outfall disk. Then it occurred to me the suit wasn't falling apart. It was *opening*.

I stepped back, not fully comprehending until all the layers had peeled and I saw what lay within.

'Grae couldn't bear the thought of it,' she said. Her voice was unchanged. 'The Loop was supposed to bring us together, but the truth of it was we were as close as we were ever going to be. Nothing I said or did could change the way he was feeling. He didn't understand himself until we were stuck together in Harvester, and once it was clear we would be stuck here forever, he chose the easy way out. He saw no reason to hope and, after a while, neither did I.'

My head was swimming, and it wasn't from the forces at work inside the disk.

'When I saw you digging for information on Grae, I thought you were being stubborn again, trying to understand – and you were, but you understood the wrong thing.' She made a sound that might have been a laugh. 'I swear I wasn't looking for you to rescue me.'

I stared, thinking of all the times I had misunderstood what Nadia's suit meant to her.

'This place,' she went on. 'It's like some fucked-up metaphor for life. Sometimes we need to destroy the past so we can move on. Otherwise, we're stuck. If we can't shrug off what came before, we can't leave it behind, can't move on. But life does move on, even if we don't always want it to. Even if what lies ahead might be dangerous, or frightening, or whatever. Are you going to say something?'

I didn't know what to say. Her suit was empty. There was

room for a person, with instruments, life support, and black formfit padding that looked beyond comfortable – but there was no one in the seat.

'Where are you?' I asked, thinking absurd thoughts about ghosts in the machine.

'In the armour,' she said. 'Spread thin.'

'Biological?'

'Of course, otherwise alcohol would have no effect. If you want the gruesome details—'

'No thanks. But you *are* human, right?'

'Yes. Would it make a difference if I wasn't?'

'I think so.' It seemed better not to lie. 'You want me to get in?'

'Are you going to?'

'It's a big step.'

'Don't get all Freudian on me. This doesn't have to change anything. You don't even have to do it, if you don't want to—'

'I know,' I said, understanding at last that this was how Grae Bilwis had come to Harvester, why the Authorities had never heard of him until she had given them his body. 'I think it's a good idea, though. We don't know what lies ahead, right?'

'Right. It would be safer this way.'

I still could have backed out. *We* weren't going anywhere, after all. We would still be stuck with Harvester, and the celebration, and the memories of everyone we had lost. But that was the other side of the equation, and she knew it.

'Just let's make it very clear up front,' she said, 'that I won't take your orders. You're not my *pilot*. Okay?'

I thought of the complex equations needed to describe the motions of Harvester's five stars, and extrapolated them out to cover all the beings there, all the people who had ever followed the Loop, all the people back home – including my higher self, who I fully expected never to see again, in this life, and who I would always miss, no matter what substitutes I found . . .

The easy part would be telling Zuzi I probably didn't need her apartment any more.

I said, 'Okay.'

◆ ◆ ◆

She crouches.

I step inside.

She seals up.

We walk to the end of the tunnel, turn around, and come back.

◆ ◆ ◆

Lna was waiting for us in junction one-sixty-four. Nearly seventy Lnas, to be exact, all pretty much identical apart from the length of time they had spent in Harvester. Most of the population here consists of guides, as a matter of fact. Everybody else who comes through moves on, once they make the break from what they've left behind. That's what the Loop is for, when it works.

We were greeted with delight and excitement, but not surprise. We weren't the first versions of us to come through. That we understood the situation this time put us in an elite crowd, though. Most people fall through accidentally. The scientists who had done so were uniformly sheepish, and not without reason, given the gaff they'd help perpetuate – that staying in Harvester *wasn't the same thing* as not appearing in one-sixty-four.

The erasure mechanism worked fine at the next junction. It was a strange feeling, knowing the present version of myself was going to be destroyed when we moved on to the next. But the issue of identity and which version was 'real' was moot by that point, since we'd already gone through the process so many times and felt authentic enough. It didn't matter where our atoms came from, or how many of us there were, now. The really unnerving thought was whether any of the links ahead had failed in different ways. Just because our data went forth along the wormcaster, that didn't mean there was going to be an Infall to receive it at the next stop. What if the last version to be erased was the last ever to exist?

Not knowing was okay. Ignorance loves company.

And besides, there was still Harvester.

Under the dark night skies of junction one-sixty-four, knowing we weren't going to be there forever, we were the living embodiment of what happened next, and that was all that mattered to us.

Jump to . . .

another long story
'The Spark' (p. 181)

more romance
'Impossible Music' (p. 129)

more teleporters
'The Missing Metatarsals' (p. 165)

Notes on *Death and the Hobbyist*

Imagine being locked in a series of dimly lit rooms with no windows, clocks, phones or internet. Your every move is scripted and scrutinised. You are subjected to regular testing, the purpose of which is to study the inevitable decline in your mental fitness. *Your* purpose is to create, as best you can. Failure to create under these exacting circumstances will count as an outcome but will be personally disappointing. Creating is what you do. If you can't create, are you still . . . you?

This is the scenario I found myself in at the beginning of 2013, when I was locked in a one-week sleep study with three other artists (all strangers) to see what effect this would have on our creativity.

The first couple of days were stimulating: there was so much to learn about our new environment and each other. It was so stimulating, in fact, that there wasn't mental space left over to do anything remotely creative. That opportunity came in the middle of the week, when a story took shape, emerged, and underwent substantial polishing – because what else was there to do? That piece is the last story in this collection, one of the works I'm most proud of, and not just because of the lengths I went to in order to make it real.

The final days of the experiment were horrible. A creatively barren *Groundhog Day*-esque blur, the end of that week in confinement gifted us with heartfelt sympathy for anyone in these conditions who *didn't* choose them and *didn't* know they would ever end. None of us would be the same again, we realised later, but at least we had our lives to go back to.

Not everyone lost can find their way again.

Which isn't to say there aren't other ways to go. This is something I learned in the sleep study, and I hope this story, as a synecdoche of the collection as a whole, captures some of those possibilities.

Change is not always bad. Paths are allowed to be crooked. Even endings can be beautiful.

Death and the Hobbyist

It wasn't enough for my mother Juliet to be crazy. Of course not. She was always going to find a uniquely inconvenient way to drive us mad along with her.

That she was a bit odd escaped no one's notice. After Dad died she steadily worsened. I speak with sincere love, but the list of things my mother wouldn't tolerate only grew longer the older she got. Lenses, fabbers, the Air – everything newer than her she considered potentially lethal. I suppose we all slipped into the habit of treating her concerns with, not disdain exactly, but with the same patience one tolerates the night-terrors of a child. Particularly me, her only daughter. Fabbers won't give you cancer any more than chocolate gives you diabetes. So here, Mum, have a cake I *said* I cooked with my own hands but really dialled up the same as everyone else. She never knew the difference, and we in turn never noticed her succumbing to serious degenerative illness.

The first time it occurred to me that she had a problem, she was still in the old house in Texas and I was working in Zambia. I visited her on Thursdays for dinner. Sometimes I brought my daughter Clair when she was still a baby, but on this occasion I didn't. Within moments of walking in the door, it was clear Juliet wasn't entirely herself.

'I wish you wouldn't use that thing,' she said.

'What thing?'

'That terrible machine. *D-mat.*'

I remember not being terribly surprised. It seemed like a perfect extension of how she felt about things the rest of us took for granted. Given her dislike of fabbers it was amazing she had tolerated the idea of matter transmitters this long.

'It's okay, Mum. They're everywhere now, and cheap to use.'

'But you look so *old*,' she told me. 'Don't you see what it's doing to you?'

No one likes being called old. I didn't understand what I'd done to earn her disfavour. A little stung, I asked her to apologise. But she persisted. It soon became clear that she honestly and sincerely meant it. I *did* look old to her, older than I ought to. Time was mixed up in her head. I tried to reassure her that d-mat wasn't sucking the life out of me, but she wasn't going to listen. Never has there existed a woman more unwilling to change her mind. She insisted that unless I stopped using d-mat entirely, as she had, I was headed for an early grave.

Now, I'm not going to argue the merits of her case, because its logic ... well, there *was* no logic. It was her disease talking, and being someone unwilling to admit to infirmity, d-mat was the only way she could think of to explain what her mind was telling her. Furthermore, anyone who wanted to stay in her good books had better make sure she didn't catch them disobeying.

Much later, she explained the mechanism to me. To get from A to B, every object in the universe took a certain amount of time. Most things, people included, had a natural velocity that was much slower than the speed of light. D-mat enabled people to travel instantaneously, but that debt of time wasn't forgotten. Time doesn't just vanish, she reasoned. It has to go somewhere.

She believed this lost time was added to us while we were in transit. So on every occasion we went through d-mat, in the instant we were between here and there, we aged the time it *should* have taken us. The more we travelled, the older we got.

Look at you, she told me once, you should be a young woman of twenty. But you look forty. Why would you do that to yourself?

I looked forty because I *was* forty. But that made no difference to Juliet. She was stubborn and ill, and people like that have always made for entertaining patients.

Juliet's huge heart was untouched by her illness. She meant well, even when she was wrong, and she was ferociously stubborn. So when she told her family and dearest friends that we weren't to use d-mat anymore, none of us had the mettle to argue. We lied out of kindness and did as we always did. I continued to visit her on Thursday evenings and often on Tuesday mornings too, with baby Clair when she wasn't being too fractious, because I took this as a sign that Juliet was in decline. I wanted grandmother and granddaughter to know each other as best they could in what time remained. Clair shared Juliet's middle name, and was already showing signs of the same pigheadedness.

Juliet was sick but she wasn't stupid. Africa to North America was no day trip. And I wasn't the only one who made such journeys. It angered her when she thought she was being treated like a child, as it would anger anyone. Ultimately, she took the perfectly defensible step – in her eyes – of forbidding anyone from visiting her. From now on, she would visit *them*, to spare them from harm.

I don't think it occurred to her to wonder how she would accomplish this feat. In her heart, and now in her mind too, she still occupied the world before the Water Wars, back when people still drove cars, sailed the oceans in vast liners, and bought tickets in planes that flew above the clouds. D-mat had rendered all that obsolete. Why take time getting somewhere when you could be there in a moment? There were no airlines now, no freeways. She was a crazy old woman who wouldn't look in mirrors and didn't recognise old friends. Sometimes she forgot who Clair was. How was she going to get from one side of the world to the other to visit her granddaughter?

The first time she went missing, drones picked her up two miles out of town, lugging a suitcase full of old clothes as though she intended carrying them all the way to Zambia.

I started visiting even more frequently, but that only made her upset and angry. She ran away three more times, and on the last time she slipped and hurt herself. I was waiting at the house when the peacekeepers brought her in. She had been crying. I could see the tear tracks on her dusty face. But you wouldn't have known it from the way she carried on. She had been kidnapped, she said. She didn't need chaperones, she was perfectly capable of looking after herself, she knew what she was doing.

We were forced to accept that she didn't, and it nearly broke her.

♦ ♦ ♦

A prison, she called the assisted-care community I found for her. It was the best available, but of course she hated it. The confinement, the routine, the constant observation – all of it. One of the terrible things about her illness was how, despite causing her so much calamity, she remained recognisably who she had been. If she had become a different person, it would have been easier to do what we had to do. But we had no choice, no matter how she argued and fought with us. It was like smacking a child who honestly thought she was the centre of the universe. My mother had the same sense of drama, if very different strategies, than my daughter, now almost two.

Predictably, she tried to escape and hurt herself again. Her carers started locking her room at night, but she always found a way to slip out. They tried sedating her. They considered tracking devices, physical restraints, drugs. But I didn't want my mother to be treated like a criminal. All she wanted to do was visit her loved ones. All she wanted to do was keep them safe. She was my mother. Could I punish her for that?

Fearing a breakdown, I started coming every day. There was no point to it – there was nothing I could offer her that the staff didn't already provide, except my own anxieties. I became obsessed with the possibility that Juliet might attempt self-harm rather than accept that this was how the world worked now. I would sit with her at nights until she fell asleep, cradling Clair in my lap. These two remarkable women, at opposite ends of their lives, totally ruled my own life now. I was exhausted. I didn't see how I could help both of them much longer.

As I left the hospital one exhausting night, I was hailed by a groundskeeper I had seen a couple of times, tending the roses. A solid man in overalls with white hair poking out from under the hat he wore to keep the moonlight at bay, he was notable because he looked even older than Juliet. I couldn't tell if he was a volunteer or a patient. Perhaps he was both.

'You're Juliet's girl,' he said. 'Your mother has itchy feet.'

There was a smile in his voice. I was tired and unwilling to joke about my mother's predicament.

'No, no,' he said, raising his gloved hands. There were thorns stuck into the thick leather. 'I just want to help. You need to call Andre. He'll know what to do.'

'Who's Andre?'

'He's a good man. We fought in the Wars.'

He didn't say 'together'. Nobody from that generation did. There were no sides in the Water Wars, just like there were no victors. There were only those who survived, and those who didn't.

He gave me an address written on an actual piece of paper by a shaky hand. 'Your mother needs him.'

He returned to his gardening and I walked on, convinced now that he was an inmate, one with problems perhaps as profound as my mother's. I almost threw out the note he had given me, but was stopped by the effort he had gone to. I had no intention of making the call. I remember thinking I would hand it in to the carers the next day. If he was acting out his illness to strangers in the middle of the night, they needed to be told.

That night Juliet sprained an ankle in the garden, not far from where I had met my would-be benefactor. When I came to settle her, she wouldn't look at me. I couldn't tell what pained her more: the sight of me, or that I could see her in such desperate straits. And they *were* desperate. She was at a breaking point, and so was I. Both of us knew this couldn't go on much longer.

I sent Andre a message when I got home. Where carers had failed, locks had failed, daughter and granddaughter had both failed, I would give a complete stranger the chance to work a miracle.

He called two hours later and explained who he was. I didn't need to tell him my situation; the groundskeeper had warned him I would call. The embarrassment of being talked about behind my back was assuaged by his calm, open manner. He was frank, too, in a way I found refreshing.

'There's crazy and there's crazy,' he said, when I explained my mother's predicament. 'I've been called it often enough. But until I hurt someone, I figure I'm allowed to do anything I want. And if there's some way I can help another in need . . .'

'*Can* you help?'

He didn't answer the question directly.

Andre was a hobbyist, he explained. He loved boats. Where some people dabbled in tiny sloops or yachts, taking gentle joyrides in secluded bays, his interest lay in the big ships that had plied the oceans. The outriggers, the tankers, the icebreakers. The whaling vessels that had driven entire species to the brink of extinction. The destroyers the navy of one nation might have sent to do war with another. Humanity had once ruled the oceans by means of such things. That there was no need for them anymore didn't stop Andre from obsessing about the way things had been.

What did that have to do with me, I wanted to know. I already had one crazy person to look after.

He laughed and explained that hobbyists came in all shapes and sizes. Some shared his aquatic passion. Others dreamed of airships, freight trains, racing cars, drilling rigs. Their passions consumed their lives. They became obsessed. Every waking thought was spent searching out old plans, old routes, old ways that were at risk of disappearing forever.

'My mother's never going to take up a hobby like this, if that's what you're suggesting.'

He laughed again. I heard a great joy in it. He might have been crazy, but he found a way to be happy despite it.

'She doesn't need a hobby,' he said. 'She needs a hobby*ist*. We don't just dream and obsess. We build. And we like to *play*.'

♦ ♦ ♦

I glimpsed it then, the solution to our problem. Juliet might not be able to get on a plane and fly to Zambia, but if she could take a train to the coast, then sail across the ocean, and catch a humvee across the plains . . .

It seemed ridiculous at first, I'll admit. I wasn't going to entrust a sick old woman to a pack of strangers and their handmade contraptions.

But the more Andre talked – the more this strange vision came into view – I began to see how, even if nothing concrete eventuated, even if his wild plans came to nothing, it would give Juliet something to focus on that wasn't her prison or her ageing daughter. There was value in this as a distraction, if nothing else.

So I asked him if he would like to meet her. He agreed and we made a time, a week from then. I didn't ask how he was going to get there. It would be easy to talk myself out of it if he said something too weird.

That day, I told Juliet to expect a visitor. I hoped Andre knew a good impression was required of him, for both our sakes. I shouldn't have doubted him. When he strode into the room, a man Juliet's age wearing white pants, blue jacket, cravat, and a sea captain's cap tucked firmly on his head, skin burned brown by the sun and hair bleached salt-white, I saw my mother's eyes light up with delight, and I smiled so hard I almost cried right then.

I introduced them and, after a few moments, slipped out to leave them to it. I don't think they noticed. He was telling her tall tales and she was laughing as I hadn't heard her laugh for a year. I went back home to Clair, and cried. I felt a great weight lifting from my shoulders. I wasn't released yet, but hope had returned. It didn't matter if Andre's wild schemes ever came to fruition. Juliet had exchanged one brand of crazy for another.

A change is as good as a holiday, she used to say.

The details of their first adventure don't matter now. It was clear from the outset that they weren't going to give up until Juliet visited me in Mfuwe, were I was stationed, and who was I to disavow them of their dreams? It wasn't just a case of Andre giving Juliet something to look forward to. I think they fuelled each other's dreams. No, I'm certain of it. I've met quite a few hobbyists now, and there's no one as desperate and guileless as an obsessive who's finally found an audience.

Juliet and Andre's relationship was platonic. What swept her off her feet wasn't his rugged good looks or his salty tales. What drew him to her weren't her queen-in-captivity circumstances. They spoke every day to hone the details of their plan until, three months later, they were ready to put it into effect. I discharged her from the centre and, with Clair and the carers, waved her off from the steps as she drove away – *drove*! – in a cloud of dust.

It wasn't as though she was vanishing from the face of the Earth. We were in constant communication as she jaunted from car to boat, from boat to jeep, from jeep to blimp. She sent me pictures of the hobbyists she met, of dolphins she saw dancing in the waves, of cliffs rising up as land approached, of the road vanishing under as the miles swept by.

Andre was with her the entire time. I had entrusted him with her, threatened to enact a terrible vengeance if so much as a single grey hair was harmed on her head, and he didn't let me down. He loved her for giving his passion an outlet, just as she loved him for saving her life. And when they touched down in the Mfuwe reserve and she stepped from the balloon, as tanned and joyous as he was, I loved them both, and took them in my arms and cried once more.

So that was how Juliet spent her final years, flitting from place to place in the care of her hobbyist friends. She didn't share their interest in the antique crafts they maintained, but they treated her like royalty all the same. She meant as much to them as they meant to her – more, I think, than I'll ever understand. The bond they shared went beyond friendship or admiration. They lived in a fairytale of patronage and chivalry. They moved through the world, unseen, unnoticed, outside of time.

When Juliet died in her sleep high above the Andes, they carried her home to me on a bier of flowers and sang her to her rest with all those who had loved her. These strange, lonely men and women and their families. My heart swells now to think of them.

My mother's final words, Andre said, were, 'Take me home.' And he did.

That wasn't the end of it. Some of the hobbyists had never been to Zambia before. They took the chance to look around while they were here. I fabbed mattresses and put out beds on every flat surface. People slept inside, on the veranda, in their vehicles, on top of their vehicles. There were people everywhere. I never once felt lonely and Clair had so many new friends to play with she didn't know what to do with herself.

It couldn't last. As the hobbyists left in dribs and drabs, I reread the many messages Juliet had sent from far-flung places of the world, putting names to faces and saying heartfelt thanks and goodbyes. I didn't expect to see any of them again. They were Juliet's friends, not mine. Knowing that my crazy mother had done so much both amazed me and left me feeling slightly alienated from her. Where was the difficult woman I had known? Had I lost her without realising it, long before her death?

Andre was the last to leave. He had a present for me, something Juliet had asked him to convey in safety. It was her diary, which she had kept assiduously through her journeys. We hugged, and he said we were always welcome to sail with him, if ever the inclination took us. One day, I said, knowing it was unlikely. Clair, at three, is too young for adventures: although I'm sure she would disagree. By the time she grows up the hobbyists might be gone. Unless a new generation takes up the challenge of keeping these old machines running, they will rust and sink to the ocean floor.

'Juliet was a child at heart,' Andre said. 'We will always miss her.'

When he was gone, I settled Clair on my lap and read the words my mother had written.

The diary was not a profound read. In it she grizzled about the food on the tankers, which was invariably awful. She took Andre to task for constantly taking detours, or for using modern navigational technology, which she said was bound to lead them to becoming breached on an uncharted reef somewhere. She wondered why there had to be so many long delays without even *trying* to grasp the enormous logistical challenges of ferrying one woman across the globe using technologies superseded fifty years ago. She ranted about how d-mat was the source of all her inconveniences. D-mat, and the Air, and fabbers, and lenses . . .

I smiled to read it. She hadn't changed a bit. And it made me think that her journey had been as much about the spaces between her destinations as the destinations themselves. There was and is something reassuring in that. Her adventure is over, but mine continues, and Clair's has barely begun. Wherever we go, we will have gone *somewhere*. The road doesn't vanish just because we have arrived at the end.

Jump to . . .

another story about disability
'Impossible Music' (p. 129)

another story inspired by real life
'The Second Coming of the Martians' (p. 5)

something completely different
'Team Sharon' (p. 255)

Acknowledgements

My thanks go to Michael Bollen, who never gave up on the idea of this book, to Darren Nash, who wrestled it into shape, and to Julia Beaven, who fixed my many errors.

Thanks also to my agent, Jill Grinberg, and to everyone involved in the creation of these stories, by commissioning them or curating the conditions under which they could be written. This list includes John Joseph Adams, Neil Clarke, Phil Crowley, Jack Dann, Gardner Dozois, Ashley Hay, Alisa Krasnostein, Margo Lanagan, Anthony Mitchell, Eva Sallis, Steve Proposch, Julia Rios, Christopher Sequeira, Cat Sparks, Vicki Sowry, Bryce Stevens, and Jonathan Strahan. My sincere apologies to anyone I've forgotten.

I'd also like to shout out to Shane Bevin who created the original cover artwork.

Props to my colleagues and to my wife, family and friends for their support. If any of their faces appear in these stories, I'm not saying.